For the frontline and essential workers of 2020, risking your safety for the greater good.
Thank you.

THE ASSISTANT'S SECRET

A LOCKE INDUSTRIES NOVEL

EMERALD O'BRIEN

CHAPTER ONE

A SIMPLE TEST

This meeting could change my life. I take small steps within the confines of my mother's tweed pencil skirt, my black heels clicking across the shady concrete sidewalk, not yet bathed by the morning sun.

Click, clack. The theme song for adult businesswomen.

Click. Take notice.

Clack. Take me seriously.

Click. I'm professional.

Click. I'm powerful.

Clack. I'm here.

I balance the Styrofoam tray packed with four cups of coffee away from my mother's black, frilled blouse. I've almost convinced myself it's acceptable her entire wardrobe is one size too big for me. I'll allow myself one new outfit, my *first* brand-new outfit, in celebration if this meeting is about what I think it is.

My heart flutters from my chest up to my throat just thinking about it. A chance to prove I'm an asset to the company, increase my responsibilities, and by proxy, my paycheck. I imagine walking through the halls with purpose. More coworkers knowing my name, giving me warm, respectful hellos as we pass. Being invited to business lunches instead of the one sent out to fetch the lunches.

And above all, having a real shot at paying off the crippling debt holding me back from living the life I've worked so hard for— plus being able to take care of Andy.

Philip, the front door security guard, holds one of the large glass double doors open with a small nod and glance at the coffees. His full head of silver hair sticks up on end with his short cut, and his black business uniform looks smart against the clear glass double doors.

We exchange smiles as he looks back up at me. "Thank you, Philip."

"Try to space them out today," he calls.

"Okay then!" My little laughter echoes in the grand white and gray marble front foyer of Locke Industries, and I know Philip is still smiling as I pass the front desk security on the way to the elevators.

Our friendly morning banter began the first week I started the position as Cathrine Locke's assistant almost three years ago. Cathrine is one of the five board members who own stakes in Locke Industries. The company's CEO is her cousin, the former owner's son, Orrick Locke. He passes through our floor most mornings, smiling and waving general hellos to the office personnel and checking in with the four other board members. I've only been acknowledged by him a handful of times without introduction, and I'm glad. He's charming, intimidating, and I'd have nothing to discuss with him, probably embarrassing myself with small talk.

No, we'll have our proper meeting once I've proven I'm a unique asset to the company. Maybe sooner than I thought.

I use my sharp elbow, jabbing the elevator upward arrow button at just the right angle, and the doors ahead spring open. On the days they open up like that, right away, I'm convinced it's a sign. A sign the company is welcoming me with open arms, encouraging me to feel part of their mission, urging me forward to begin the important security work we do here.

I step in and use my elbow once more to press the seventh floor. We're just below Orrick Locke's penthouse office he shares with his wife and assistant. I lean my hip against the gold railing by the mirrored walls, easing the pressure off my toes for a moment of relief.

Today's the day. I can feel it.

My skirt and blouse are wrinkle- and stain-free. I got up at four this morning to make sure of it. With a short puff of breath, I blow a strand of my long, caramel blonde hair out of my face.

Do I look good enough to represent this company? To go out on lunch and dinner dates with clients in fancy hotel lobbies? To sit in on the revered board meetings?

No. Not until I can afford some new clothes without the guilt that accompanies them. Not until I have the financial security to start living life like we should.

My cell phone vibrates in my purse against my waist, as if on cue. At this hour, it has to be a debt collector. This is when they start their days too.

The doors ding open, and I correct my posture and take a deep breath, inhaling the coffee bean scent.

I can handle this. It's not all about looks. They hired me—*chose me* after my internship. No one works harder than I do here at my level. If they give me a chance to prove myself...

I stride forward, down the long, dark gray hallway a few steps from the elevator to the glass door with a bright silver waiting room beyond.

Fern Bishop, Cathrine's long-time receptionist, squints at me behind her thick black-framed glasses, and buzzes me in. The glass door opens, and I stride in with my head held high. I'm steps away from her desk as my right heel slips across the marble floor, and I jerk the tray out of one hand, trying to regain my footing. Fern's eyes open wide as I reach out, grasping at thin air for stability, teetering to the side, gripping the tray hard and clenching my jaw.

No.

Not today.

I lean forward, planting my right heel back on the ground, and grip the tray with both hands.

"Nice reflexes, Josephine." Fern tips her head to me before cocking it to the side with a slight frown. We turn toward the wall on the far side of the room as the door in the middle of it opens, revealing Cathrine Locke.

Her silver-gray hair, lush with the silky volume she gets from visiting a blow-dry bar every morning, perches on her shoulders. She sucks in her gaunt cheeks, staring at me. "Good morning, Josephine," she says in her light, even tone.

"Good morning, Ms. Locke."

"Well, come on then, and don't forget the coffee." She swivels around on her black pumps, letting the door shut behind her.

Now *that woman* has style.

I exhale and stop at Fern's desk. "Two caramel macchiatos for you." I take them from the foam tray and place them on her desk to the right of the framed photos; one of her three cats, Elinor, Mrs. Morris, and Darcy; one with her and the original owner of the company, Lawrence Locke; and one of her and the cats.

"Thank you," she says without looking up from the paperwork on her desk.

"And two black coffees for Ms. Locke." I clear my throat, lick my lips and walk toward the door, taking each step carefully.

"Good luck, Josephine."

I glance over my shoulder to give Fern a smile, but she's still poring over her paperwork, tugging at one of her permed gray curls hanging loose from her soft bun.

It's just as well. She's not a sentimental woman. Cathrine respects her. Seems to listen to her. If she's wishing me well, that's a good sign.

Unless maybe she thinks I'll need all the luck I can get.

I take another deep breath and reach my shaking hand out, grasping the metal door handle and pushing it open.

Two of the three port wine red walls of her office flank the floor-to-ceiling glass wall that sits just behind her desk. The two chairs across from her, the ones I rarely get to stay long enough to sit in, are upholstered a deep burgundy crushed velvet, and she sits behind her large mahogany desk, the top clear of any papers, staring at me once again with a view of the cityscape behind her.

Even the early morning sun bends at her will, staining the sky just above the horizon a hot red.

I set the tray to her right, beside her phone, and step back, waiting for instruction as I do every morning. The bookcase at my back is covered with leather-bound books, and on the other wall ahead of me, on a lengthy bar cart, sit beautiful glass jars filled with clear liquid, likely vodka, and dark green bottles behind them.

She slides a burgundy leather-bound folder off her desk and hands it to me. "All the information you'll need about the potential client is inside. Read every page before your meeting at eleven-thirty *sharp* this morning in Copperfield County. Two copies of the contract are included. Digital copies have already been sent to the client and his lawyer."

"So, I'll be meeting with the client to sign, then?"

"*If* you can and after your morning filing."

I frown. She's sending me alone to seal the deal? She never does that.

She catches my puzzled look before I can relax my expression, and sighs. "I'm giving you the opportunity to sign this client, Josephine, but I'm not handing you the job. This is a half-million-dollar contract, and while that might be considered small in comparison to most here, it's a simple test." She stares up at me, her eyes scanning mine. "Do you have what it takes to meet with a potential client and get them to sign the contract?"

My chest swells with pride. I do.

"Thank you for the opportunity, Ms. Locke." I have to

say something to make her stop looking at me like I might not have what it takes. "You won't regret this."

Her chest heaves, and she grabs a coffee before turning her head toward the window, squinting into the light.

She's trusting me with a client. I haven't been to business school, but me, with my administrative degree, is enough to give an opportunity to. I can't believe this is actually happening.

I fold my hands in front of me. "Is there anything else I should know?"

"You should know *everything*." She turns back to me with a tight-lipped smile as she taps the cup with her manicured nails. "You've attended over fifty initial client meetings with me. How many clients have I signed?"

"All of them."

Her smile grows. "I've done all I can to prepare you for this moment." She looks away, back to the window again. "The signing bonus will be excluded this time around." My chest deflates as the chance to earn more slips away. "*But*, I'm offering you something more. The opportunity to manage a client—this client. Your position will remain the same, but a salary increase would accompany your additional responsibilities."

It's exactly what I've been hoping for. Dreaming of.

"If you succeed, you'll have the opportunity to earn the signing bonus on the next client."

More than I could have hoped for. "Thank you, Ms. Locke," I say breathlessly.

She swivels around in her chair, her sharp features seeming to soften in the warm glow of the rising sun. "This is a high-stakes business, and I think you're fitting in here just fine as my assistant, but you *could* be more. I see potential in you. Show me what you've got, Josephine."

I nod, beaming brightly, marching across the room to the door. My heels click across the marble waiting room floor, past Fern. She doesn't look up or catch the huge smile plastered on my face, and that's for the best. I save that side of myself, that emotional side, for my personal life. A beaming smile isn't taken seriously around here, nor is the woman who fetches coffee for everyone.

This is my chance to earn my place in the company—to earn enough to pay back the debt from the rehab payments. For Andy to live a financially stable life and Maggie to focus on her sobriety. Maybe some of the resentment I feel toward her will disappear after the debt does.

I stride out the glass doors and down the dark hallway toward my cubicle nearest Cathrine's office. I pass one of the other board members, Mr. Mathison, who takes up one of the other four corner offices of this floor. He doesn't even make eye contact as I smile at him—just brushes past me at a clip toward Cathrine's office. His assistant, Rob, gives me a nod and rushes to catch up with him.

I keep my head down, as I always do, and begin filing the paperwork from the day prior. I make a trip to the staff room for a coffee, and when I return, I check my cell phone. The call from this morning was the collection agency, calling on behalf of the New Gilford Rehabilitation Center—more like harassing on behalf of.

I tuck my phone back in my purse and turn to my paperwork once more, but the burgundy folder at the corner of my desk teases me. My heart rate increases, and my skin hums with anticipation. I unzip it and take a peek at the first page of notes.

Raymond Tackman. Thirty-eight-year-old entrepreneur from Copperfield County.

That's almost an hour away.

Once I finish the filing, I check the clock. Almost ten. Not bad. I'll be early if I leave right now. I gather my things, and as I wait for the elevator, I enter the address into my cell phone's GPS program.

A text appears on the screen from my neighbour across the hallway, Don.

Andrew has been locked out of your apartment. He's with me, but I have to leave soon. Can you come and get him?

Locked out? How?

Have you knocked on the door? I type as the elevator doors open, and I step in, juggling my things while I type. *His mom is home.*

She has to be there. Why wouldn't she... No. Before the image of my sister lying in bed with a needle sticking out of her arm and her eyes all fluttered back burns itself even deeper into my memory, I shake the thought away.

She wouldn't. She's clean now.

But she could. She would.

If she did it before to her poor, sweet son, she'll do it again.

He says she must be in the shower. He texts back. *I hear music in there, but when I knock, there's no answer. I have to leave in ten minutes.*

If she's just blasting music and taking her usual long shower, I can't be late for that.

Someone else needs to help him, but who else can? I planned this whole set up to avoid situations like this. All she has to do is stay clean, work her program, and be present for Andy. I told Maggie I don't have the job flexibility to be on standby for Andy. I thought she understood.

She told me she wanted to be there for him again full-time, and I believed her. I pulled him out of childcare because I wanted to believe she could handle that, at least after how successful her doctors said she was through her rehab treatment. If she's just in the shower, she'll be out soon.

Can you wait? I type back, feeling guilty for even asking, but I have to. I have to leave right now to get to the client's home on time.

The elevator doors ding open in the lobby as I send the text, and Katie stands in front of me in her white-collared shirt and black dress pants, her curly black hair pulled back in a bun.

"Katie," I blurt out, relieved to see a familiar face—my best friend.

Maybe she can help. Maybe she could go to my place and help Andy.

"Everything okay?" she asks as another message appears on my screen.

I'm sorry. I can't wait.

And I can't ask Katie to do this for me. She's never helped Andy before. I can't ask her to leave work. And I don't want her to know how irresponsible Maggie can be. To judge her—us.

"Yeah, fine," I huff and nod, touching her arm as I step

past her. I don't have much time. "Just got some exciting news to share, but I have to go."

"Sure." Her bubbly voice lacks enthusiasm as she turns to watch me stride away. "You okay, Jo?"

"Fine, talk to you later!"

I rush out the door, past Philip without a word, and pick up the pace until I reach my car. My heart thuds in my ears and tears flood my eyes as I get in and start it. "I can do this. I have to do this."

Instead of making a U-turn, I follow the one-way street, turn a few rights to make a complete circle, and take a deep breath once I'm finally heading in the right direction.

Anything worth doing is worth doing right.

When I arrive at the apartment, my hand holding the key to the building shakes, and I can barely get it in the hole. I burst through the doors and run for the elevator, but it'll take too long. I stumble up three flights of stairs to our apartment, rush to Don's door and knock three times. The door flings open, and Andy smiles up at me, wrapping his arms around my leg. Has he been waiting right by the door, eager for someone to collect him from this stranger?

"Thank you," I tell Don, grabbing Andy's hand and pulling him toward the apartment.

"Okay then." Don shuts the door quickly so his Maltese pup can't escape.

How could she do this to him? My muscles tense, and I loosen my grip on his arm before it becomes too firm.

"I couldn't get back in, Joey," his voice shakes, and my legs crumple as the fear in his voice sinks in.

I bend to meet his eye level.

Sweet, innocent Andy, abandoned again.

Nothing like the first time; he wouldn't have been old enough to remember, but I was the one who found her. Especially not like the second—after which I decided to take Andy into my care when Maggie and Andy's dad became homeless.

But scary, nonetheless. He can't rely on his only present parent, and I've made the wrong choice. I've pulled him out of proper care I trust to put him back with the woman who has betrayed us both for most of our lives.

I sweep my fingers from his sweaty forehead up his stiff, gelled hair he proudly styles each morning and force a smile on my face. "That must have been scary, but I'm here now."

He shrugs with a pout and runs his hand over the same spot of hair, smoothing it down. "I'm not a baby."

"I know." I squeeze his bony shoulder as my apartment door swings open.

Maggie steps out into the hall, clutching the towel wrapped around her. Her wet, shoulder-length hair drips as her wide eyes narrow in on her son.

"Andy! There you are. Oh, no. I'm so sorry, Joey." She reaches out for him, but he doesn't move. The tears pooling in his eyes send me over the edge.

"Andy, go on back inside and put a game on, okay?" I whisper.

He nods and rounds his mom without looking at her. Her gaze follows him as I lean in toward her and hiss, "Are you kidding me?"

She opens her mouth to speak, but I cringe, staring at her, and she shuts it again. I don't even want to hear her excuses anymore.

I check my cell phone. Fifteen minutes behind, and when I leave here in a rush, Maggie will be feeling guilty, like a burden, and I can't let that happen again. When she feels like that, she uses, ever since we were teens. It's her pattern, and despite the signs she might have broken it this time, the odds are more likely she'll break us again instead.

"I'm going to be late for that meeting I told you about." I lick my lips as I try to even out, take a breath, and relax my tone. Don't let her feel all the anger. "Let's make sure this doesn't happen again. Make sure the door's locked properly, and he knows he can't leave without either of us."

She nods, her eyes full of hurt, but I can't afford to apologize. She needs to understand how serious this is. My job. Taking care of Andy. I did it all at the same time while she was in rehab, and she can't even handle just watching him.

"I'm so sorry, Joey. I promise it won't happen again."

I nod. I don't believe her one bit, but I can't stand here and talk to her like this. Not right now. I've jeopardized my career enough for her. I won't let Andy down. I never thought she would either. We, of all people, know what it feels like to be abandoned by our parents, and the pain that never goes away.

Don't say it. Save the lecture for later.

I shake my head, buzzing with anger, crossing my arms over my chest as I walk away.

13

She knows how important it is to Andy to have her here, but if she can't take care of him, I can't leave him in harm's way again. Not on my watch, and regardless of the fact she's around, it's still my watch. They both are.

I burst through my building doors and dash toward my car.

I'm *never* late. Why did this have to happen today?

Maybe Mr. Tackman won't be a stickler for time.

Maybe the client won't even notice I'm late.

CHAPTER TWO

THE CLIENT

After exiting the bumper-to-bumper highway leading from New Gilford to Copperfield County, the hard rock song I screamed the words to ends, and I click through the radio stations until the violin from a beautiful classical piece fills my car. It's the same music Cathrine listens to after returning from rough meetings, and it seems like such a refined way to relax. I press my back against my warm chair and take deep breaths, letting the music wash over me before I squint at the time.

Eleven-twenty.

"Nothing to do about it now," I mutter, gripping the steering wheel and peering over at the GPS. "Can't control the time. Only the way I react to it."

"Take the next left," the voice from my GPS says. "Then carry on for one half mile. Your destination is on the left."

I make the left turn onto a secluded road surrounded by fields of dirt and forest farther behind them. The sun dips behind the clouds, and a blanket of gray is cast over the wheat fields I pass.

I know this company. I know the services we offer. I know how to do this. I'll do it just like Cathrine. Clients never say no to her.

WWCLD? What would Cathrine Locke do?

"You have arrived at your destination."

I crane my neck back as I pass a long dirt road and ease my foot on the brake, checking my rearview before backing up on the empty road and turning left onto the next one, if you could call it that.

My wheels kick up dirt, and I drive through the clouds of dust until I reach the tree line. Just beyond, nestled into the top of a hill, a large, white, modern build comes into view. Giant windows line half the walls, providing what must be an amazing view of the trees and surrounding area.

Three vehicles, two black trucks and one red Camaro, sit in front of the three-car garage, and I pull up behind them, over to the side, providing me enough cover to read the rest of the first page of the client profile. I unzip the binder and scan it as I dig through my purse for perfume. Cathrine always smells like exotic flowers, and I purchased a similar perfume to emulate hers.

Raymond Tackman... entrepreneur named one of New Gilford's forty under forty most eligible bachelors...

I spritz the perfume on my neck and wrist as I read, and a little mists onto the page. Considering the demographic of the potential client, that's not a bad thing.

Car collector... made a generous donation to the city's hospital...

Quite the resume.

... security needs include outdoor surveillance cameras with an indoor monitoring system...

I have to get in now. I double-check my reflection in the visor mirror before grabbing the red folder and my little black purse and stepping out of the car. As I turn to the house, a large man with a tattoo covering the left side of his neck and his hands shoved into his baggy jeans pockets stares me down. His legs are spaced farther apart, in a guarded, intimidating stance, and his boots are clean.

What kind of business are they in?

I stride toward him. WWCLD? Head up, shoulders back, and smile.

But he doesn't smile back.

He purses his lips and shakes his head. "Name."

I stop two feet away, and he's a bit taller than me in my heels. His height would make it easy to give him direct eye contact, but his attitude doesn't.

"Josephine Oliver from Locke Industries, here to see Mr. Tackman."

He smirks and tilts his head back slightly, revealing more of his tattoo—a clock with roman numerals around it and two blue birds in the middle.

"Follow me." He takes slow strides to the large white front door with long clear glass panes on each side, opening it for me.

I enter a foyer in the middle of one large room. To the right is a seating area with leather couches and wingback chairs, all black furniture. To the left a study with a sliding metal door open and hallway before it. Everything is modern or industrial, with straight lines, fresh white walls, and a black tiled floor.

The large man walks around me with a swagger to his step. "Wait here."

I tuck the folder to my chest and clutch my purse as he disappears past the study, down the hallway. Emerald green walls line the study, interrupted only by over-flowing bookcases wrapping around the room behind a mahogany desk in the middle that reminds me of Cathrine's.

A scuffling down the hall brings my focus back.

This is it. Land the client.

WWCLD? She doesn't try to convince the client why we're the right security service for them. She lets the company's reputation speak for itself, because our clien-tele comes from word of mouth from the highest profile businesses in New Gilford and the surrounding areas.

The large man appears in the hallway and lifts his chin, turning back around. I follow him down the white hallway into a bright and open white kitchen with no wall on the backside, only a floor-to-ceiling window over-looking a long outdoor pool and the surrounding forest.

He stops before the large white island, stepping aside to reveal a man in a black, button-down shirt, his chiseled features prominent and slightly hidden under a well-maintained beard and mustache. His dark eyes stare at me from beneath his furrowed brow. He stands behind the island with a burger in his hands and fries on a plate in front of him. His thick, dark, crew-cut hair is a bit longer on top and suits his facial hair.

He rests the burger on the plate and runs his tongue

over his bottom lip, the one most visible, toward the corner of his mouth. His dark, smoldering stare stops me behind the large man, and I wait for someone to speak.

"*Josephine Oliver* here to see you, *Mr. Tackman*," the large man says with levity to his tone.

Is he laughing?

"Thanks, Danes." Tackman's gravelly timber is warmer than I imagined his voice to sound.

Danes walks past me, back down the hallway, leaving us alone in the giant kitchen.

WWCLD?

She wouldn't just stand here like this.

"Mr. Tackman," I say in a loud voice, too loud, and walk across the room, extending my hand. "Nice to meet you." I almost call him "sir," but he's closer to a contemporary than an elder, and it didn't feel natural.

He smiles and shakes my hand with a polite but firm grip. Soft hands. Doesn't work with them. "I hoped you'd be here at eleven-thirty, so excuse me, but I had to go ahead with lunch."

"Oh, of course." He drops my hand, and I wrap it back around the folder. "My apologies."

"Did you miss the road in?" He cracks a charming smile.

I break into a genuine smile for the first time and nod.

"I picked the right place, then." He picks up his burger again. "Nice and secluded."

I nod, turning to the window wall, barely able to take my eyes off him, but the landscape captivates me once I do. Coniferous and deciduous trees of different kinds

19

sprawl across the back of the property, creating a false sense of privacy.

Privacy. Right.

I turn back to him, and he's staring at me. "Hungry?"

"Oh, no, I'm fine thank you." So fine, I haven't stopped smiling, but he doesn't seem to mind.

"Well, I went ahead and made you one."

He takes a bite of his burger, and I point to it. "Of those?"

He nods to the modern, white marble table where two settings are placed on opposite heads. A plate with a burger and fries sits at the far end. I follow him, stopping beside the chair until he extends his arm. "Take a seat."

I sit across from him, and he follows, picking out a fry and biting it before setting his plate down and grabbing a napkin. He wipes his hands and stares at me.

"How did you hear about our services, Mr. Tackman?"

It's what Cathrine asks on the colder calls, the ones where she doesn't personally know the client. She sets up the interview from the beginning, evaluating the potential client to see if *they're* the right fit for *us*.

But this time, it's not about if he's the right fit. It's about signing him. My success and freedom from debt depend on it.

"Please," he says, "eat." He picks up another fry and takes a bite.

I do the same, taking a bite of the thick fry. The salt dances on my tongue, and my stomach grumbles. I hope he didn't hear that—he didn't seem to. I guess I was hungrier than I thought. I finish that fry and pick up another, popping it into my mouth, watching as he eats his burger and realizing he never answered my question.

Don't seem too eager or talkative.

I pick up the burger and take a small bite. The bright zing of mustard hits my tongue, followed by garlic dill. Pickle. "Mmm." My favourite.

"You like it?" He raises one eyebrow, and I nod. "I made it myself."

I relax, smile, and take another, bigger bite. If anything, it's not improper—it's like a compliment. Dangerously toeing the line between class and mess, I take another bite. He smiles and watches me.

This is the weirdest client meeting I've ever attended, and the best at the same time if it weren't for the fluttering feeling in my chest when he looks at me and all the pressure weighing heavily on me when I'm not distracted by him. A lump fills my throat as I realize, despite the delicious meal we're sharing and his content disposition, I'm getting nowhere.

I swallow and try again. "You're interested in our outdoor surveillance services and indoor monitoring system."

"I am." He takes a sip from a glass of water without taking his eyes off me or giving me anything more to go off of.

I sip from my water glass and wash the food from my mouth before speaking. "We can provide you with those services, Mr. Tackman, and may I suggest our interior cameras for the entrances as well?"

"You can suggest it." He takes a bite of another fry.

"But I was clear about what I'm interested in. It should be right in that folder of yours."

I nod and stare down at the folder. That, and a lot of other information I didn't get the chance to read.

But the contracts, they are what's important. "I brought the contract here with all the particulars—"

"I wanted to meet with someone from your company because I need a more—personal touch—for my intents and purposes. I need assurances." He wipes his hands with the napkin again and balls it up tight in one fist.

"What kind of assurances?"

"I've heard things about Locke Industries. You have a reputation for confidentiality, the best in the business, but I need to know, who is monitoring my video surveillance besides me?"

"That would be our security sector. They're equipped with the technology to protect you and your assets with the fastest reaction time should an alarm be set off, anything suspicious occur on your property, or any other event that would require our security personnel to contact you and dispatch someone from our security sector straight away."

"Not the police?"

"No, that is not our policy." As I say it, his gaze seems to lighten. "We have a highly trained team in place to respond to any security issue on your property that should arise. We handle the needs of each individual client, and a contract has been drawn up for you, specifically, to serve your unique situation."

"My *situation*?" His pitch rises at the end of the word, and he leans back in his chair.

Have I offended him?

WWCLD?

"It's all in here." I tap the folder. Cathrine never hands it to the client to sign. She makes them come to her. "All the needs you made our contact aware of are listed with a detailed plan for security installation, monitoring, and maintenance." I unzip the folder and rearrange the papers, setting both copies of the contract on the table. "It's all here, and if any amendments need to be made, our legal department can draft them and send them over right now. We can sign digitally."

He pushes his plate away and leans right back against the chair. "Is the surveillance video recorded?"

"You have that option, yes."

"No," he leans in over the table, staring from beneath his brow again, "do *you* record it?"

"Our company keeps our clients' business confidential—"

He shakes his head and stands, stepping away from the chair. "Will *your* company have access to *my* recordings?"

"No." I'll tell him the same thing Cathrine always proudly assures our clients: "We do not keep recordings of the surveillance video. That's up to the owner of the footage to keep or delete. To film or not. The control is always in the clients' hands."

And that's why we're the best. We stay out of people's business, and we keep everyone else out of their business too.

He studies me, and his stare drifts off until he walks my way, slowly, with easy, confident steps, past the contracts, stopping beside me. "And the people watching the security footage. They've all signed confidentiality contracts?" We lock eyes, and his friendly warmth has disappeared. This is business Tackman.

He's paranoid. What is he worried we'll see in his footage of the property?

Keep him calm. Reassure him.

"Yes, of course. It's standard procedure and all in the contract." I rest my fingers on the pages but maintain eye contact, staring up into his dark chocolate brown eyes, getting a whiff of his cologne, woody and... citrus? Focus, Jo. "We sent a copy to your lawyer. Did they have any objections?"

He runs his fingers over his beard and picks up one copy of the contract, still looking at me.

No answer. I'll take that as a no.

He holds it up beside him. "I've read the contract already. I've spoken to my lawyer." He sets the contract down again, rests his fingers on it, and leans in toward me. Oak and vanilla? Delicious spice... "I wanted to meet with someone who could put my worries to bed. I'm wondering if you're that person, Josephine."

He grabs my plate, and I sit back, avoiding his arm as he pulls it away. He grabs his own plate on the way back and sets them on the counter. He leans against it with his back to me and runs his fingers through his thick hair.

Do I get up? Do I stay here?

What does he really want? The best security in New Gilford has just been promised to him right there in writing, but he wanted to speak to someone who could put him at ease.

And Cathrine sent *me?* Asking what Cathrine would do isn't working anymore, and maybe that's why I'm here.

I'm doing this my way, and I'm not playing guessing games or being jerked around, led to believe I could earn something that's not even possible.

I stand, and he turns, watching me. I give my blouse a quick tug along the bottom and rest my hand on the back of the chair. "What are you worried about? What haven't we covered in the contract?"

He taps the island countertop with his knuckles and sighs as his fist falls against it.

He's exasperated. This is important to him, but not as important as it is to me.

"What do you want, Mr. Tackman?" I try to keep my voice calm and even, but can he sense my desperation?

He walks to the window wall and crosses his arms, his dress shirt tight against his muscles. He stares out at the trees. "You'll be my contact?"

I amble toward him slowly, folding my hands in front of me. "Yes, you'll have direct contact with me for the duration of your contract with Locke Industries."

And I'll have my first client and a paycheck to match.

I stop at his side, staring at his strong profile, and he turns to me with a serious expression. Something in his eyes scares me, but I can't look away.

"Can I trust you, Josephine?"

My gaze falls to his light pink bottom lip, the top covered by his well-maintained mustache.

"Yes," I tell him without hesitation, because he can. He can trust me, and he can trust the company. "No one will work harder for you, and no other company will keep you safer."

He narrows his eyes, and a twitch of his lips hints at a smirk, but it's gone in seconds. "Follow me."

As he leaves my side, I hesitate.

Follow him where? Have I gotten through to him? Does he believe me?

I follow at a distance behind him, down the hallway to a door just before his study I hadn't noticed before, with only a slight crack around it distinguishing it from the wall.

He takes a white, plastic card from his pocket and, with his back turned to me, something clicks, and he pushes the door open. I approach him with caution, stopping before him, before I can see anything in the room besides the hint of another white wall.

"You protect people, things, and so do I. Before you go in, you need to remember that."

"Okay." A whisper is all I can manage as he walks into the room.

I follow behind him, my heart pounding and my palms sweaty. As he steps aside, he turns to look at me as I take in the view, my eyes opening wide as I scan the room in shock.

CHAPTER THREE

POWDER AND LEAD

My name echoes from somewhere beside me, out of focus, as I take a step back away from the tightly packed bags of white powder stacked high on the metal table in the middle of the room.

More than I can count.

Guns line the walls, mostly automatic, hung on metal racks.

What kind of people are they? Where has the company sent me? To meet with a drug and arms dealer?

Cocaine was Maggie's drug of choice before she didn't have a choice and took whatever she could get her hands on. I'd find little baggies in our room as teenagers, in her wallet, and even hidden in a plastic bag in the back of the toilet at our aunt and uncles', where we stayed after our parents passed from an overdose together.

It's been years since I've seen the powder, but all the feelings of fear and anger I associated with it come flooding back.

"Hey." Tackman's hand reaches toward me.

I take another step back, out of his grasp.

Drugs took my parents from me. They almost took Maggie countless times—and still could. And they want me to protect someone who's dealing them?

I shake my head, backing out of the room, and he follows me.

I turn, my heels clicking across the black tile echoing in the foyer as I reach for the front door knob, sure someone will grab me from behind—stop me–but I open it and step outside in the fresh, pine air where I can finally breathe as I rush to my car.

A tall, lean, blond man stands in front of my hood with his arms folded over his chest.

"We can do this outside if you prefer." Tackman's gravelly, deep voice calls from behind me, and I swivel around to face him, suddenly recognizing the dangerous edge to it I hadn't heard before—or hadn't wanted to. "I told you, I have things to protect. I need to know if you're the people who can help me protect them."

No. No way. This is illegal.

I glance over my shoulder, sure the tall man is approaching me, but he's still by my car, squinting through the sun peeking out from behind the clouds at us.

Now I'm supposed to say no? I have to be the one to say no, when I'm alone with at least three strange drug and arms-dealing men?

This can't be happening. The blame can't all be on me.

"My company," I stammer, "they won't. We can't—"

Tackman stares at me from beneath his brow. "Cathrine knows."

"She knows... what? About the..." I can't even say it because it can't be true.

But he seems confident about it, calm even, and we've protected people who own guns before. Just not *that many* and not the drugs... or not that I've seen.

Could it be true?

"She knows what I want to protect." He looks over my shoulder and shakes his head at the tall man by my car.

The tall man walks toward me, and I step back, creating a triangle of people, but he keeps his distance, keeps walking, and joins Tackman's side.

"I should have known," Tackman says, not to me, or this man, but himself.

Should have known I couldn't handle this? Is that what Cathrine will say too, if she does, in fact, know about everything?

Yes, she will. And my chances of advancing in the company escape me with the answer. The chances of getting out from under all our debt and of providing a stable home for Andy disappear too, at least for a long time.

Could I lose my job over this if *I* deny him?

"She was late." Tackman leans closer to the man beside him, and the man makes a tsking noise. "She's green."

The tall man nods and stares me down. Are they even going to let me go after what I've seen?

Tackman leans over and mutters something to the tall man under his breath. The tall man goes inside, leaving us alone once again.

Can I leave? Should I? What will I be going back to?

Will the tall man be coming back with a gun or bringing the large man, Danes, out to deal with me?

I take a step back toward my car, and Tackman raises his brow. "You sure?"

Andy won't be disappointed at least. He doesn't even know I had the shot at giving him a better life. Of keeping the roof over our heads and buying him the clothes and toys he deserves. Of saving for his future and taking the financial burden off Maggie for long enough to keep her sober. If we lose the apartment, she could spiral...

If I lose my job, I lose everything. The roof over our head, the food we eat.

Everything.

We'd be back to having nothing again, needing help until I can find another job, but there's no one to help. No one to rely on. I won't find a job that pays this much, and it could take weeks, months, to find a job at all.

Tackman stares at me, but I don't know what to say as all my fears engulf me. The tall man comes back out with the burgundy folder and hands it to Tackman. He holds it out to me, and I know once it's in my hands again, it's over.

They're letting me leave, and it's no relief.

I can't let everything go to waste.

"Mr. Tackman, I apologize for running out." I clear my throat and take a step forward. "I can handle this contract for you. Our company can protect your... belongings."

He stares down at me with a straight face. I'm not getting through to him, but what else can I say to convince him this is right? To convince myself this is right?

If Cathrine agreed, this could be standard procedure. Maybe I've been helping her do this all along.

She always says we keep the client's business safe and stay out of their business at the same time.

Turn a blind eye—is that what we do?

"This'll go one of two ways," Tackman says in his slow, gravelly, sultry voice. "You'll either agree to manage me, take me on as a client, and commit to managing the security of my property by the method and means deemed necessary in this contract, including abiding by the confidentiality agreement, or, you'll leave here and tell your boss it's not happening."

I could lose everything I've worked for in one afternoon or gain everything I've hoped for in less than a minute.

He's making me choose, but it's my decision.

And I'll do what I've always done when it comes down to it.

What I'll always do.

I'll choose Andy, because I love him, and because if I don't, no one will.

I extend my hand, and he shakes it, his expression stoic, before opening the folder and grabbing the pen strapped to the inside.

I'm making a deal with a criminal.

Does that make me a criminal too?

He scratches the pen across the bottom of each of the pages, folds it over, and does the same to the second copy before extending the pen toward me.

I grab the pen, my fingers skimming his, and my hand shakes as it returns to the paper. I've read the terms of all our contracts so many times, I know them by heart. I'll be committed to working with him until or unless I'm no longer working for Locke Industries, and I don't plan on leaving them.

No turning back.

I put pen to paper and scratch out my own rushed signature on the bottom of each page, moving on to the second contract, and I can feel him watching me.

Does he think he's intimidated me into signing? Or shamed me by suggesting I'm too green? Does he think he can gaslight me into something like this?

If he does, he's wrong.

This is for Andy.

I sign the final page and hand Tackman a copy. He hands me back the folder and extends his hand once again. I can barely breathe as I make contact with his cool hand once more. A feeling surges through me, adrenaline pumping. It feels like something big.

A big break or a big mistake?

As I begin to release, he holds my hand a moment longer. "Please don't be late again next week."

"Next week?"

"You'll be joining the installers, as per the contract, next Saturday. You'll be here whenever anyone else from your company is."

I nod once. I come with the package now.

He turns around, walking back inside, leaving the tall man still staring at me in the doorway.

My legs feel weak beneath me as I walk back to my car. I should be thrilled, ecstatic I accomplished the task set out for me, but I want to get out of here, far from these people and whatever trouble they're part of.

I toss the folder and my purse on the passenger's seat, start the car, and turn around. I drive back down the dirt road, past the tree line, out onto the open road once again, leaving a cloud of dust behind me.

CHAPTER FOUR

A TASTE OF SUCCESS

Fern Bishop tosses her coffee cup with her dusty rose lipstick stain in the trash bin before buzzing me through the glass door. I'm clutching the folder with white knuckles, more frightened of losing the contract than I am of the mistake I might have made if Cathrine didn't know about the drugs and guns.

"She's due back any minute from her meeting with the board." Fern nods to the white couch across from her on the opposite wall. "Have a seat."

My nervous energy buzzes through me, but I do as I'm told. I always do what Fern tells me to because, although she's not my boss, she never steers me wrong. When I do as she says, Cathrine's always pleased.

Fern's fingers clack away on the keyboard, her eyes focused on the screen.

Isn't she going to ask me if I got the client? Does she even know what I had to do? Does she know about the drugs and guns? Does Cathrine?

My heart races, and I squeeze the folder in my lap as

the heavy metal of the elevator doors grumbles, parting to reveal Cathrine in her signature black bodycon dress, showing off her beautiful long legs. She's holding another red folder of her own.

Fern buzzes her through the glass doors, and I stand as she approaches. Our eyes only meet for a moment, barely acknowledging me before she turns to Fern.

"Cancel my two-thirty," Cathrine says in a huff, "push back the dinner to eight. I'll be out of the office from three to four-thirty and try to get Mathison on the phone for me. Send him right through when you do, please."

Fern nods to me.

Cathrine's gaze follows, and her eyes open a bit when she notices me again. "Come on, then."

I follow behind her into her office once more. She stops in front of her mahogany desk, slides her folder across it, and leans her hip against it, folding her arms over her chest. "Well?"

"He signed."

I don't miss the slight arch of her brow as she reaches out for my folder, her nails shining by the crystal chandelier light above. I hand it to her; she unzips it and begins to scan the contract. Her thin lips twist into a small smile as she stares up at me once more.

My heart races, but now from excitement. I've seen her smile like that at others, but never me.

I don't trust it.

I stifle my smile, waiting to make sure she's pleased, rather than amused at something.

At my willingness to bring a drug and arms dealer on

board at Locke Industries? Have I made a huge mistake? Was this a different kind of test than I thought?

"Congratulations, Josephine." She sets the folder behind her and turns back to me with a sparkle in her eyes accompanying the remaining smile.

I search her face for a hint of the truth betraying her. That she's not actually happy with me. That I've done something wrong.

"I thought you'd be happy." Her smile disappears. "Maybe you will be once you see this." She picks up a small stack of stapled papers from behind her and hands them to me. "We're doubling your salary, beginning with the next pay period, and the conditions of signing bonuses for next time are all laid out there in your promotion package."

I glance at it, but the words are a blur. I can't focus on anything but my new salary, laid out in bold font.

It's real.

This is really happening.

If my calculations are right, I can pay off the rehab debt in three months.

Three months and I'm out of debt, and then saving that much, minus some for Andy's new clothes, shoes, laptop or iPad, whichever he wants...

"There's the smile I was expecting."

I look up at Cathrine, and she's smiling again.

"Thank you," I hear myself say, but it still feels like a dream.

"You earned it." She stands up straight and walks over to her bar cart.

I earned it. I worked my ass off for years to reach this

point, to make Andy proud—make myself proud. Now Cathrine's proud of me too?

Cathrine turns around with two champagne flutes full of bubbly liquid.

This is really happening.

She hands me one, tilts her glass up, and I raise mine, but before they touch, she pulls hers back and takes a sip. I do the same, the bubbles nipping at my nose as I tilt it back and swallow, taking it all in.

"Mr. Tackman has not been an easy client to sign." She sets her glass on her desk and rests her hand on her hip. "*He* approached *us*... but he was hesitant. How did you do it?"

Is Cathrine really asking me how *I* did something *she couldn't*?

My chest swells with pride, but what do I tell her?

The truth. She needs to know what happened.

It all comes back to me, the bags of cocaine and rows of guns. Was it really that easy for me to forget about them? And if I tell her, could everything I've just been handed be taken away?

Maybe. But if this is wrong, for the company, for me, I don't want it.

"He wanted to be assured we could be trusted—that I could be trusted as the manager of his contract." Cathrine nods, and I continue, lowering my voice. "He wanted me to know what he wanted us to protect."

She tips her head back, elongating her neck, her gaze falling to the floor, then back on me. "I see."

Does she already know, like Tackman said?

"So, he showed me—"

She holds up her hand. "Josephine. What have I always told you?"

"That we secure the client's business and mind our own." She nods. "But he made it clear he had to show me before he signed."

"And that happens from time to time." She rounds her desk. "But if it's not mentioned in the contract, it's not something we discuss with the client unless necessary, and we certainly keep our end of the contract by keeping their business confidential. That goes without saying, doesn't it, Josephine?"

She stops in front of her wingback chair by the bookcase against the wall, raising her brow slightly.

She doesn't want to know? Doesn't need to know? Already knows and doesn't want it discussed?

She'd ask if she wanted to know, and what she doesn't want right now are more questions. If I ask more questions, I could ruin her trust in me, and what little faith I've earned.

"Yes, Ms. Locke."

Her expression lightens, and I've made the right choice.

She sits, resting her hands on the armrests. "Well done, then. Enjoy your glass of champagne. We'll see how you handle this client and, in a month or two, we'll send another your way *if* you can manage this one to our standards. The signing bonus is one percent of their contract —you'll see it in your papers." One percent of a million? Two million? How much is that? Ten thousand—twenty thousand! "Here at Locke Industries, we reward loyalty and dedication. Are they important qualities to you?"

"Yes, they are. I hope I've exemplified them during my time here."

Cathrine crosses her legs and leans against the back of her chair, seemingly at peace. "Are you happy here?"

Getting the internship with this company made me the happiest I'd been in a long time, maybe ever, except for becoming an aunt, and even then, Maggie was in a rocky relationship, at an unhealthy time to be having a child, so I was more worried than happy.

Being hired on to Locke Industries affirmed that everything I'd worked toward was within reach, that I could achieve what I put my mind to, despite my background or setbacks, and made me proud to tell people what I did for work. To have a career with the opportunity for advancement that kept people secure and safe.

"I love it here." I clutch my champagne flute tighter in an effort to hold on to the moment, the feeling of pride.

"Well, you go on now, take the rest of the day off, and next week, there are some people I'd like you to meet. And Josephine, all the files—"

As she says my name, her phone rings. Probably Mathison.

"Thank you, Ms. Locke," I say as she stands. "I'm so grateful."

She stares at me and raises her brow. I nod and turn on my heel, pacing out of the room.

"Josephine," she calls as she rounds her desk, reaching for the phone. "Don't forget your folder."

Her folder is mine now. The client is mine.

I take my folder from her desk as she answers the phone. "Well, hello there," she says in a honeyed tone, and her soft laughter quiets as I close her door behind me.

I notice the mouthful of champagne remaining in my glass and down it in one shot.

This is really happening. I'm really making something of myself, for myself—for Andy.

Three more months, and no debt, less resentment, a full fridge all the time, and a kid with stability.

I stride to Fern's desk, and she stares up at me while typing. "Leave your glass there. I'll look after it."

"Thank you." I set it down and wait for her to speak again. To congratulate me. Give me a smile. Something.

She turns back to the computer screen and clacks away at the keys again.

Tough crowd. That won't get me down. Nothing can. Cathrine told me I earned it—and I did. She even asked me how I did it. The realization washes over me again as I walk back to the glass doors, reliving the moment I just shared with Cathrine, replaying it in my mind as if absorbing it for the first time.

I stop before the door and turn to Fern, still clacking away. I open my mouth, about to ask her to open the doors, and she turns to me, her narrow eyes staring me down. I smile, but she presses the button.

I don't get it. She wished me luck just this morning. I thought she'd be pleased too.

My cell phone vibrates in my purse, and Katie's name appears beside her message. "Hang out tonight?"

I grin and press the button to the elevator before typing back.

Meet at my place. Seven.

This is perfect. The three people I care most about will be there to celebrate with me.

Should I get a cake? Maybe something fancy?

This occasion calls for something special, but my account is in overdraft, and I'm brought back to reality.

Pizza maybe? Andy'll love that.

I send the text and step into the elevator, blushing at my reflection as my phone rings in my hand. Another debt collector. I shove it in my purse and notice a bright yellow mark on my black blouse, like a bumblebee. I step closer to the mirror to inspect it.

A mustard stain from this morning...

I tried to put the events of the morning out of my mind, but I see it in a different light now.

Now I remember what our clients do is none of our business, and whatever Tackman does, good or bad, is not my concern. The company's concern is his security. I cannot control others, only myself.

I pinch the material surrounding the yellow stain, remembering the homemade burger Tackman had made for me. How he stood there waiting, full of confidence, wanting to share a meal with me.

I close my eyes as my mouth salivates, remembering the taste, the way he stared at me from across the table with his secrets stashed, just a room away.

Not my business—but now—I have a craving for burgers.

CHAPTER FIVE

FROM THE BOTTOM

"Will you tell us now?" Katie pleads, setting the video game controller on the couch cushion between her and Andy.

Andy rests his controller in his lap, averting his eyes from the screen for the first time since he finished his meal and turning to me on the recliner, shooting me a little smirk.

He seems to have forgotten about getting locked out this morning or put it out of his mind somehow. I'd gotten good at that when I was younger too. Sometimes, when you see the darkness in people you love, it's easier to shove it down deep than see it in their face all the time. To put it away after you're confronted with their pain when you have no way to stop it for them, it takes the sharp edge away from feeling powerless for a while.

"How did it go?" Katie asks again. Maggie turns over her shoulder from the kitchen table with a somber look on her face, no doubt feeling guilty about making me late.

Katie glances over at her. "She had a meeting with her boss today."

"Yeah." Maggie nods and makes eye contact with me for the first time since I got home. "Do okay?"

"Yeah." I can't help but smile. "Not bad."

"*So?*" Katie stares at me, grinning. "Good news?"

"It's good news." Andy nods to himself. "I've figured out that much, 'cause of the burgers."

I take a deep breath. "I got a raise."

"Woohoo!" Andy's eyes open wide as he hollers.

"Congratulations." Katie's drowned out by my nephew's noises.

I laugh and shake my head. "Shh, we have neighbours!"

He opens his arms wide and rushes over to me, wrapping them around my neck. He squeezes me, and I know it's with all his strength. "Great job, Joey," he whispers.

Tears pool in my eyes, and I clear my throat before pulling away.

Maggie jumps up and gives me a quick hug. "I'm really happy for you."

"Thanks," I mutter without standing. She steps away, but just one step, as if she's expecting more information from me, so I turn to Katie. "Can I play next?"

Andy beams. "For sure! Zombies or Mario Kart?"

"Your pick."

"Hey, before you start, I should go." Katie grabs her jacket and pulls it on over her work uniform.

Maggie turns to her. "So soon?"

"Yeah, John's getting in from Vancouver tomorrow morning, and I've got some stuff to do before then."

Maggie nods to her. "Drive safe. Andy, say goodbye to Katie."

"Bye, Katie," he says, staring at the screen.

"Bye, guys." She walks to the door, and I follow her.

Instead of turning to say goodbye, she takes several steps out into the hallway and tilts her head for me to step out too. I guess she wants to talk, so I close the door behind me.

"You okay?" She gives me a little smile. "I didn't know you were up for a promotion, but an order came in this afternoon for a new installation, and your name was on it. So, it's not just a raise, is it?"

I crane my neck back. "So, you knew, and you wanted to see if I'd tell you?"

She shakes her head, and I frown, instinctively defensive of my decision to keep it to myself, but there's something in her eyes. It's not anger. Concern?

"Is there something I did wrong? Something I don't know?"

She sighs and looks down both ends of the hallway. "There's a lot you don't know about Locke Industries. I see... a lot."

"Okay... what are you trying to say?"

"I wasn't worried about you before, when you were just an assistant, but your name is attached to a high-profile case now. Are you managing it?"

"Yeah, it's my first client."

The door across the hallway opens, and Don walks out with his Maltese pup, nodding to us before continuing down the hallway to the elevator. After he gets on, Katie checks down the hall again and steps close to me. "Be careful," she whispers. "They're involved with some bad people, Jo. Once you get involved in that business, once you see more, you don't get out."

"I don't think it's like that..."

It can't be that bad. They're powerful people, well respected, and well known with a great reputation.

"I watch the live footage of these clients all day. Don't you think I know what I'm talking about? You don't believe me?"

I don't want to believe any of it, especially not what I saw today, but this is what it takes to get ahead. To help Andy.

"Is it really that bad?"

She presses her lips together and shakes her head. "It's not that good, I'll tell you that. Did you hear about the bombing of one of our client's businesses?"

"Yeah, but I don't know anything about it. That's the commercial and business sector."

"Well, not much the clients do sees the light of day, thanks to our company, but sometimes, things like that get out..."

"What do you want me to do?" I ask, and she hushes me. "And why do you still work for them if it's not good?"

"I don't plan on being there forever. As soon as John and I get engaged, I'll look for another job in Vancouver, so we don't have to do the long-distance thing."

"You're going to move away?"

"Yes, and that stays between us."

She's leaving me, and it's been her plan all along... "Of course. You don't even have to say that. We're friends."

I thought we were.

She sighs. "I know. Listen, you might not see it now, but if you're managing clients, you will eventually. I don't want you to get in too deep with them."

That's exactly what it feels like I've done.

"I stand by and watch it—what the clients do, and I can't do anything about it."

"What are we talking about here?"

"Illegal things."

Drugs. Guns.

"Like what?"

"I can't talk about this." She lowers her voice and looks up and down the hall. "I know it seems paranoid, but it's not safe."

"So why did you even tell me?"

"Because you're a good person. You and your sister are good people, and I don't want you mixed up in all of it."

She doesn't know my sister, or that she's an addict, or what she's put her family through, but that's not Katie's fault. It's family business. I can't confide in her about things I don't want Maggie judged for. She needs a clean, fresh start.

"Well, I appreciate your concern, but I'm doing what I need to do for us."

Maybe what I need to be doing is looking for another job…

Her gaze falls to the floor in front of her. "Be careful, okay? Remember, you don't need them."

But right now, I do. They're what's going to help me repay the debt faster than I could anywhere else.

Three months, and then I can re-evaluate.

I say goodbye and try to shake off her warning as I walk back inside, but Andy's smile disappears when he sees me from his perch on the couch, and there's no point in putting on a show for him. He's already seen through me.

"What's wrong?"

"I just…" I wish mom and dad were here. None of this would be happening if they hadn't become addicts. Everything wouldn't rest on my shoulders. "I wish our mom and dad could be here with us right now." I turn to Maggie. "Back before, when they were better."

"I know they're proud of you." Maggie takes a seat in my recliner as I plop down on the couch beside Andy.

I nod, letting the small consolation linger as I consider it.

Would they be?

But if they knew what we've been through since they died. If they saw all the judgments passed on us and how lonely we were, lost without them, how sick Maggie got and how much it affected Andy, maybe they'd understand I'm doing what it takes for us.

"So… how much?" Maggie gives me her signature faintly crooked-tooth smile and runs her hand through her shoulder-length, curly brown hair.

"Double my pay," I say, and her little smile is replaced with a wide-eyed stare. "I know."

"That's amazing." She wraps her cardigan over her chest and stares at Andy until he looks back at her.

"You know what it means, right?"

"I can finally get a lizard?" Andy laughs, and I shake my head, smirking until his laughter fades.

"Could you get the game ready for us? I need to talk to your mom for a sec."

"Okay."

Maggie and I walk into my bedroom. "I'm going to be able to pay off the debt in three months."

"Seriously?" She seems like she's about to choke.

"I promised you I'd make it happen."

"Joey, I don't want you spending all your hard-earned money on me. Let me get a job."

I frown and shake my head as tears pool in her eyes. We've been made to feel like burdens for most of our lives, and I know she still feels it now. "The best thing you could do for me is the best thing you can do for yourself. Stay clean, go to meetings, and be there for Andy. One day at a time."

I still remember the day I got the call she was in the hospital after an overdose. Her ex, Andy's dad, had left her on the street and said she felt like she had nothing left to live for. If someone hadn't called it in, she'd have died, and from where she was in that hospital to now, she's come a long way from the bottom already.

I rub her shoulder as tears spill down her red cheeks. "Hey, it's going to be okay."

"You do too much for me." She sniffles.

There's truth to that, but I don't want to talk about it. I don't want to think about it. I just want to repay the money and move on with our lives in a better place.

"Okay, enough with the mush," she chokes out, wiping her eyes with her fingers. "I'll be out soon, okay?"

I nod and go back to the couch with Andy.

"Are we playing, or are you afraid to get your butt kicked?"

"One game." I pick up the controller Katie used. "Then I have to go to bed. I've got to get to the office early."

He turns on our old favourite, Mario Kart.

As we play the game, Katie's alarming warning wears off and the sweet comfort of Andy's company replaces it.

We have something we've never had now. The security of knowing the money is coming, so long as I do my job right. I'll do it right, and then, after that, I'll see where I'm at. After that has only ever been a dream, and now, it's about to come true.

After Andy wins the game, I go to the kitchen and clean up the takeout mess as he plays another game with his online friends.

Yesterday, I didn't think I'd be able to make the internet bill at the end of the month so he could play his games, and now, I'm dreaming of all the games I'll be able to buy him soon.

I start cleaning up the takeout mess, ball the burger wrappers up, and toss them in the garbage.

The burgers were good, but they didn't satisfy my craving.

CHAPTER SIX

INSTALLATION

As I rush toward the front door in the dark, I stumble over Andy's lizard toy, hitting the bookshelf with my shoulder. A hardcover falls from the shelf. I reach out and grab it before it can smack the floor and wake up Andy, rubbing my shoulder as I slip it back on the shelf in its place.

I'll be fifteen minutes early for work, so I *could* slow down, but I won't. I'm building a reputation of dependability, and it's important for Cathrine to know she can rely on me. I have filing to do before the installation at Tackman's this afternoon.

A week and one day since I signed the contract, and I can't stop thinking about my next paycheck. Even when the bill collectors call, it doesn't ignite the same level of fear in me, because soon, they'll have no reason to call.

"Hey," Maggie whispers.

I turn to her, sitting at the kitchen table in the dark with a mug in her hand.

"I didn't even see you there."

"You want some tea before you go?"

"I don't have time."

"Okay." She squints at me through the dark as I turn to leave. "You're working another Saturday? Is that what you're wearing for after work?"

Right, it's Saturday. The days have all been running together lately.

I turn around in a huff. "Yeah, I have an installation today, and then I'll meet my friends at the bowling alley. Why?"

"I really think you should invest in a new top or two. Maybe a blazer to wear over a dress to go from a day to nighttime look."

"I don't have the money for that," I grumble and turn back to the door again.

I was too rough with that one, feeling the underlying resentment of why I don't have the funds with each word I spoke, but I don't know how to stop being mad at her.

She folds her arms over her chest. "Mom's clothes are too big on you."

"They'll have to do for now." I twist the knob and open the door.

"Joey?"

"What?" I turn around and shake my head once, opening my eyes wide. "I have to go to work. I can't be late."

And I won't be, but I just don't want to be around her right now. I don't have the patience. Too much rests on my shoulders.

"Have some fun tonight, okay?"

I let her think I go out with friends from work on

Saturdays, that I have friends other than Katie, because her guilt would be too much if she knew the truth. If she knew how alone I am. That I don't have money for casual drinks or bowling. That I have less than one hundred dollars in the bank to last until this next paycheck, the big one.

But those are all excuses for the fact I can't make friends. That I've never been invited to happy hour by coworkers. And besides, there are more important things to spend money on—like Andy.

"Yeah, fine, see ya." I rush out the door.

I march out to my car, drive to the local cafe, and pick up two caramel macchiatos and two black coffees before driving to Locke Industries a block away. I pull into my designated spot near the middle of the lot and park. I stay in my car, letting the classical station soothe me like it did on my way to Tackman's.

If I could make more friends at work, more connections, it could help me climb the corporate ladder. It would also help if I didn't have to lie to Maggie and Andy about where I am on Saturday nights.

If she knew I stayed behind at work on the near-empty floor and processed paperwork until our sector was caught up, she'd feel sorry for me. She'd think all I did was work, and it's mostly true, but no reason to pity me. She'd feel guilty if she knew what it took to support us, but I have to shield her from that.

And I never mind working all the time. She wouldn't understand. She hasn't held down the same job for more than a year in her whole life.

I grab the tray of coffees and stride to the front door, my head held high.

Do people know about my raise yet? That I'm managing a client? Maybe I'll get invited to happy hours now, or whatever they're doing tonight.

Philip smiles and opens the door for me.

"Good morning," I say as I pass him.

He stares at my tray and smiles. "You're going to be wired today!"

"Uh huh," I laugh. "Have to get my energy to work on a Saturday somehow!"

"Have a good day!" he calls as I pass the front desk on my way to the elevator.

"Josephine?" someone calls, and I turn around. The man behind the front desk leans over and nods to me. Does he know about my promotion? "Ms. Locke will meet you down here. I'll have Mrs. Bishop's coffees taken to her."

"Oh-kay." I walk to the desk and set Fern's macchiatos on it. "Did she say anything else?"

He shakes his head and turns his attention back to the front door as the elevator doors ding open and Cathrine clips out at a quick pace, her heels tapping against the marble floor. She's in a red body-con dress today, her bouncy silver hair tapping her shoulders with each step.

"Good morning Ms. Locke."

"Josephine." She gives me a quick nod. "We're going to Orrick Locke's home this morning for an installation request." She picks up one of the coffees from my tray and takes a sip as I stare at her.

Orrick Locke. CEO of Locke Industries.

"His *house?*"

"The installation technicians will meet us there."

"Okay," is all I can manage to say as she takes another sip.

Will he be there? Will I finally get properly introduced to him?

Does *he* know about my promotion?

A car pulls up in front of the doors, and I follow her. Philip opens the door for us and nods twice. I smile back and keep up with Cathrine as her driver opens the door to her town car for her. She gets in; he closes it, and I follow him to the street side. I extend my hand to open the door, and he lets me, smiling before turning to his door.

I climb into the sleek, spacious back seat. I love riding in the company car by Cathrine's side, the fresh clean smell, the cold beverages sitting in wait each time. I used to be nervous, riding with her in such close proximity, but she takes her business calls, and I do what our company does best: mind my own business, enjoying the reprieve from being at her beck and call, and enjoying the company of the second-most powerful woman at Locke Industries.

If I work hard enough, I could be like her one day. Not exactly like her. I still want to be me. Rather, where she *is*.

As the driver pulls away from the curb, Cathrine turns to me. "Once we arrive, I'll need you to wait out front for the technicians and tell them I'll be inside to oversee the installation." That's not something she usually does, but I nod, and she leans over, supporting her weight with her arm against the middle seat. I turn in instinctively. "And this is very important. Mr. Locke will be arriving late," she rolls her eyes, "as usual, and once he does, I need you to call me and let me know— the minute he arrives on the property. Do you understand?"

So, I'll be seeing him. "Yes, of course."

"Good." She runs her hand over her dress against her leg. "The installation should be complete by the time he arrives, and I'll be meeting with him before we leave."

"Should I come in after he arrives?"

She shifts her body toward her door, stares out the window, and pulls her cell phone from her purse. "That won't be necessary."

For the duration of the ride, she speaks to a client, and as we pass the entrance to the Amaretto Grove Subdivision—New Gilford's nicest and most secluded neighborhood—I know we're close. She ends her call as we turn onto Cordelia Lane, and we stop at the gate before the huge, modern house beyond, composed of geometric shapes and sharp angles. On the maroon front door hangs a regal, inviting green wreath.

The driver rolls his window down and presses a button on the security system Locke Industries designed. A voice answers, and I can't make out their words through the muffled partition, but the gate opens.

"You'll get out here." Cathrine nods to my door.

Outside the gate? I can't even come into the other side?

The driver opens the door for me, and I step out. I guess Cathrine told them I'd be staying out here.

The town car drives on toward the house or, rather, mansion, and as the gates close behind me, the meaning behind my promotion diminishes. More money, more responsibility, but I'm still not good enough to go inside.

I turn my back to the impressive front lawn beyond the gate and begin my duty of lookout, staring down the long road. Any sign of a vehicle would be great, but the sudden burst of a young boy's laughter echoes behind me, and I turn around. Beyond the gate, a young boy about Andy's age runs away from the front doors toward the expansive lawn.

A young woman who looks a bit younger than me, maybe, follows him out and looks across the lawn, stopping once she sees me.

Great, I'm standing here looking like even more of an outsider than I feel, and she's probably wondering what I'm doing.

"Excuse me, can I help you?" she asks as she approaches, her dark hair falling over her shoulder. She must work for the Lockes.

"Hi. I'm Josephine Oliver. Ms. Locke's assistant. We're here for the security updates, and I'm just waiting for our technicians to arrive."

"Mrs. Locke, as in Iris? She didn't mention you'd be dropping by. I'll have to check with security before I can let you in." She reaches for her pocket and rests her hand over it.

Is she going to call security on me? How embarrassing. I *am* security.

"Oh, sorry, no. Cathrine Locke. I must look pretty awkward just standing out here waiting." I give her a small smile.

The boy catches my attention, running around behind

her. He must be the Locke's child. He looks so happy and carefree. I haven't seen Andy play around like that in ages.

That little boy probably has everything. A secure homelife and parents he can depend on. Why couldn't Andy have that? He deserves it. I notice the young woman's still waiting on an explanation.

"Cathrine's inside. She told me to wait out here until they came, but it doesn't feel like I'm doing much of anything."

The young woman turns back toward the house. "Right, Cathrine Locke. So, you don't need me to open the gate? Surely she doesn't want you to wait out there."

You'd think, wouldn't you?

I let out a little laugh followed by a sigh and shake my head. "Thank you, but she really was insistent I stay out here. Is that the Locke's son?" I take a step closer to the gate and point to him.

She turns over her shoulder, and the boy seems to have finally noticed her absence. "It is."

"I have a nephew about his age. What is he, nine?"

"Eight," she says with a nod. "Sorry, I should've introduced myself, I'm Olivia. John's nanny. You said you're...Josephine, right? What's your nephew's name?"

The fullness of my name feels so unnatural when anyone says it. No one used to call me that until I started at Locke Industries. I like that they take me seriously enough to use it, but it makes me feel so distant, and it doesn't sound right coming from their nanny.

"You can just call me Jo. The company likes to keep things formal, but I don't actually like my full name all that much, so just Jo between us? And his name's Andy.

He doesn't get to play outside too often, but he's into video games, big time. How about him?"

John apparently lost interest in whatever Olivia was doing, already back to playing. Olivia chuckles. "Five minutes ago, I practically had to pry his fingers off a controller to get him out here." I laugh and nod as she continues, "I guess it's just that age, but I'm glad to know I'm not the only one dealing with a video game-obsessed preteen. And you can call me Liv." Her smile is warm, disarming even, especially in these surroundings.

The light hum of an engine sounds behind me, and I turn, spotting a black van with the Locke Industries logo on it. It rolls to a stop before the gate beside me. "One second," I tell Olivia, hoping she'll stay to keep me company after they leave.

The driver's side window rolls down, and a technician in a black baseball hat with the same logo sticks his head out.

"Ms. Locke asked me to send you right in, where she'll be overseeing the installation," I tell him.

He raises a brow, perhaps not realizing he'd be working with one of the board members directly, and with a stoic expression, he gives a quick nod before pulling away from the window. He inches up to the keypad security system and presses a button.

The gates open straight away. Are we being watched, or was Cathrine waiting impatiently?

The van rolls through, and the gates close again, parting Olivia and me once more on opposite sides.

Olivia smirks as I turn back around. "I didn't think it

was possible to have any more security installed here. This place is practically a fortress as it is."

"I guess they're beefing it up for some reason I'm not privy to." I sway my weight from heel to heel, my toes squished down to the points of my shoes, aching to be released from their sweaty prison. The only good thing about being outside is the company. "How long have you been the Locke's nanny?"

"I just started last week, actually. He's a sweet kid, and the Locke's seem...nice." She pauses. I wonder what their homelife is like, and what she meant to say instead of nice. "How long have you worked for the other Ms. Locke? Is she any relation to Orrick and Iris, or is that just a strange coincidence?"

"Almost two years now with Cathrine, but I've been with the company for three. Didn't you know Cathrine Locke was Orrick Locke's dad's cousin?" I guess she doesn't know much about the company.

"I thought she had to be his mom or something. It looks like she's quite a bit older than him." She presses her hand to her lips. "Shit, that was probably rude to say. Are they close, Cathrine and Orrick?"

Liv's honesty is refreshing, and she doesn't make me feel like I need to put on a proper act for her. "I can honestly say I'm not close enough to know... But from what I can tell, you wouldn't know they were even related if they didn't share a last name, never mind owning a company together, or at least being a board member. You know what I mean?"

"Totally. Between the two of us, I think the same thing about Orrick and Iris sometimes...this whole place seems like a business. Like they're business partners more than anything. It's sad, you know? Maybe the Lockes in general just aren't great about showing their relationships."

I guess it runs in the family.

"Or their emotions much at all," I add as a lighter hum of an engine makes me turn around again.

A black Tesla rolls toward us. Is it him? "Is that Mr. Locke?"

"Yep," Olivia says, shouting over my shoulder away from me. "John, your dad's home!"

The Tesla stops before the gate, and the tinted window buzzes down.

This is it. I'm meeting him one on one.

I smooth my hands over my blouse and skirt, wishing I could have scrounged the money together to buy something I could be proud to wear. Something more to Locke Industries standards. If he knows about my promotion, will he expect more, and be disappointed in the way I'm representing the company?

I fold my hands in front of me in an effort to hide as much of what I'm wearing as I can. Orrick Locke appears confused as we make eye contact, as if he could drive right past me, so I take a small, shaky step toward the car.

He glances over at Olivia, and I feel like I'm too late. Did I miss my chance to speak to him?

"Good morning, Olivia."

"Good morning, Mr. Locke."

He casts a glance back at me. "Is this a friend of yours?"

My heart sinks in my chest, and I fight to keep my chin held high.

"Good morning, Mr. Locke." My voice shakes as I seize the opportunity, clearing my throat. "I'm Josephine Oliver, Ms. Locke's assistant. She's here with the technicians for your new security updates and installations."

I search for recognition in his eyes, but he just nods.

"Forgive me, Miss Oliver, you caught me off guard. It's a pleasure to see you, as always. Is Cathrine already here?"

Does he really remember me? Does it really matter? I have my chance to make a mark now.

"Yes, sir." I savour the moment, pausing to take in the full attention of the CEO of Locke Industries. "She arrived just a bit ago, and the technicians are inside, already at work. She had me out here waiting for your arrival." I press my lips and hands together tight. Stop there, Jo. Don't ramble on.

He looks toward the house, a hint of worry in his eye, but when he turns his attention back to me, he's cool as ever. "Excellent. Well, thank you for giving me that update. Would you like to come inside now that I'm home? You're more than welcome to. You shouldn't have to stand outside all alone, even though Olivia provides delightful company." There's a hint of a smile on his face. He really is charming. Is his smile for Olivia or me?

Again, doesn't matter. He's inviting me in. This is all I've ever wished for.

And I have to say no.

I smooth my hands over the front of my skirt and tuck my hair behind my ear, releasing a small, comforting sensation as I delay my rejection. "Thank you for the invitation, Mr. Locke, but I was given direct orders to wait outside." I glance from Orrick to the house.

This could be my only chance, but if Cathrine sees me in there, she'll be upset. Maybe, since Orrick says it's okay, she wouldn't be able to be mad. Maybe I could be of good use in there.

I turn back to Orrick, and his gaze is still on me, all his attention, on me. Goosebumps spread across my arms, and the odd sensation of dread fills me.

Take a risk and go inside Casa Locke or live to be invited another day?

"Thank you, again," I nod, "and have a wonderful day, sir."

At least I kept it short and sweet that time.

He raises a skeptical brow. "Suit yourself. If you change your mind, just buzz, and Warren will let you through." He points to the keypad near the gate. "And don't worry about getting into trouble. I'll take care of Cathrine."

Take care of Cathrine. So powerful and reassuring.

I regret saying no immediately as he drives on, pulling through the gate. At seeing his dad's car, John heads in Olivia's direction, throwing a hand in the air to wave. A shadow of Orrick's hand waves back at his son through the tinted back windshield.

Olivia's smiling at me, and I can't hide my own. She's been watching our whole exchange. "Did I just make a huge fool of myself?"

"It's really hard to tell with Orrick." She shrugs one shoulder. "He's always that cool and calm. It's unnerving, isn't it? No one should be allowed to be that handsome and charming. There has to be something wrong with him."

I press my fingers to my lips in an effort to hide my giddy grin and nod. "This might sound pathetic, but aside from the doorman to Locke Industries and the one friend I have at work, no one there has ever been that nice to me."

"Isn't Orrick usually that nice?"

"That's the first time we've met, actually. I was so nervous to meet him—" I stop as she stares intently, realizing I'm confessing this to a stranger, and try to regain my composure. "I just hope that went okay."

"Wait, what?" Olivia lets out a shocked laugh. "That was the literal first time you've met your...boss? How is that possible?"

"I've seen him in the halls. He walks by most mornings and greets everyone, but I've barely ever made eye contact with him, never mind talk to him. The company is... very professional, and while people have working relationships, it tends to stay within our sectors. I've always wanted to meet him. I guess I got my wish today."

Olivia seems to study me. "Well, if my opinion's worth anything, I think it went well. From what I've seen, Orrick leads the conversation; as long as you manage to keep up, you'll have his respect. I'd say you did that."

She has nothing to gain with me from her flattery and kindness. If she's being genuine, it'll make me feel so much better about that first impression I'd be agonizing over later. Maybe it wasn't so bad having an audience.

I grab one of the rungs of the metal gate and ease some of the weight off my heels, still beaming through the pain.

John makes his way toward us, stopping at the gate

and staring at me. He has sweet, round features that will likely sharpen like his father's as he grows older.

"Liv," he says, "can we go back inside now? I want to tell Dad that I finally beat that new level."

"Sure." She pats his head. "I should get back inside. It was so nice to meet you. I hope we'll cross paths again." She steps back but stops. "Oh, and...good luck working for The Lockes. It sounds like we both may need it."

"Thanks for keeping me company." A sadness coats my tone. "I've worked at Locke Industries for three years, and this is the first time I've been to their home. I'm really not sure if I'll see you again, but if I don't, if my opinion's worth anything, I think John's lucky to have someone nice like you looking after him. It takes a village. I hope they see the value you bring to their family."

Olivia gives me a slight smile before walking back up toward the house, catching up with John.

I wish I was going with them, into the house, feeling part of it all.

Orrick wanted me to go in, but Cathrine didn't. This is her fault.

Cathrine.

Oh, no.

Dread washes over me as I remember why she had me here in the first place. I was supposed to call when Orrick arrived.

I scramble for my phone from my purse and hover my finger over her name.

If Orrick's already in there, I'll look so stupid, and how could he not be inside already? I'm so late.

I tap her name and press the phone to my ear as it

trills several times before sending me to her full voicemail service.

I can't go in, could I? No, not at the risk of making her more upset. I screwed something so simple up.

Pacing the fence, I see the black town car before I even hear it.

All I can do is apologize, and what's the worst that can happen? Orrick came in, and someone else let her know he was there? No one let her know, and he walked up to her without warning? It's not even that bad.

The gate opens, and the car pulls through, stopping in front of me. I open the door, and my cheeks are hot as I slide inside beside Cathrine.

Such a rookie mistake.

"Ms. Locke, I apologize for not alerting you when Mr. Locke arrived."

"Not now," she says, her timbre sharp as a whip.

Humiliation rolls over me, followed by the familiar heavy tingle of dread. I'll have to wait to discuss this with her. She's punishing me by keeping me in suspense.

As we roll forward, the black van drives behind us. Maybe they got everything finished, then. Maybe she's not even that upset.

After the short drive back to work, the driver pulls up to the curb, and an eerie silence fills the back of the car.

"I can't believe it." Cathrine whispers, shaking her head, and raises her voice. "I don't have to tell you how disappointed I am in you, do I?"

"No, Ms. Locke."

"I brought you and had you stay at the gate because I thought I could trust you."

The disappointment weighs on me like dirt on a grave, the one I've dug for myself. I swallow back tears and muster up the courage to speak. "I'm sorry—"

"You want to show me you're sorry? You build back my trust by taking care of your client. You *never* let anything like that happen again. You want to be treated like a respected businesswoman? Show me you can think like one, behave like one. No one respects *a fool*, Josephine."

The words burn through me as she exits the car, and I scramble to follow her. Philip opens the door for her, and she walks through without acknowledging him, pressing her phone to her ear.

"I'm back... No," she says, and suddenly, I feel like I'm following too close behind her. That she doesn't even realize I've left the car yet. "If she can't handle this, how could she possibly handle a client installation? Or anything, for that matter." She strides by the deskman as he nods to her, but she ignores him. "I was wrong, Fern, and you know how rare the occasion is I'll admit that."

I stop at the desk as the conversation turns to something else.

The installation. I need to be there in an hour.

CHAPTER SEVEN

BROKEN GLASS

Clouds roll across the dark gray sky over Copperfield as I make the turn down the dirt road, past the tree line, merging onto Tackman's driveway. Both black trucks and the Camaro are here once more, and I park behind them.

Tackman. Danes. The tall guy.

An Escalade sits parked on the other side of the driveway, and a black van with the Locke Industries logo on the side is parked in front of the garage.

The technicians are early. I'm early. Perfect. One less thing to worry about.

Danes stands by the white front door, and I nod to the technicians, holding up a finger as I pass them. "Hi guys. Just a moment."

"Sure thing," one of the men says. "Ready when you are."

"Good afternoon." I stop several feet in front of Danes. "We're here for the security installation."

His face seems softer today, less threatening. "You guys can go ahead and start."

"I need to know where Mr. Tackman would like the monitors set up inside."

He frowns. "It doesn't say in the contract?"

"No, we leave that up to the homeowner to decide. We can set up them up wherever he wants." I know the one place he *won't* want them.

"Do you need to know *now*?" He purses his lips and stares me down.

"No. They'll install the security cameras first—"

"Then you can wait. He'll be out to see you."

Waiting outside again. It's been my place my whole life. Why would I expect it to change because of a promotion? The important thing is the money. I'm here making the money we need.

"Fine." I wave to technicians and call, "You can begin the installation, and then give me a call when you're ready to set up the monitors, please."

The man who spoke before nods to me. I think he's on most of Cathrine's clients' installations and service calls, but I've never formally met him. They open the back doors of the van, ready to unload their equipment. "Josephine Oliver." I extend my hand, and the man shakes it with a smile.

"Casey. Nice to officially meet you."

"You too. How long should this take?"

"One hour," he says. "Not a minute more."

"Great, thank you, Casey."

I turn back to Danes as he walks toward me, and I take a step back.

He smiles and shakes his head. "I'll be with them." He points to the men.

I guess *he's* the manager of this installation. Maybe it's better this way. I could just sit in my car until Tackman wants to see me.

"Mr. Danes, this is Casey, our lead technician."

Casey shakes his hand as the front door opens and someone shouts something from inside. Danes swivels around, his sharp reflexes faster than I'd have guessed for his size.

"Cami, wait."

Is that Tackman's voice? It's hoarse, and as I turn, a woman strides toward me. Her long, dark hair flies in the breeze she's created behind her. I step out of her way as she rushes to the black Escalade. Tackman rushes out the door in jeans and a leather jacket over a crisp white t-shirt.

He turns to me, and his harsh expression twists into confusion or surprise, as if he wasn't expecting to see me. Or more like wasn't expecting me to see whatever this is.

He passes me and calls to her again, "Stop."

Both technicians stare, and Danes sighs. When he catches me staring, he squints at me. "Best you wait inside now."

I follow him to the house as I hear the woman, Cami, shouting something about *he has no right*, or *it's not his place*, and Tackman's unable to get a word in.

Danes opens the door for me, and I walk inside, expecting him to follow, but he only leans in. "Carver," he shouts. "Security lady's here. I'll be outside. Wait with her."

69

Which more likely means watch the security lady.

When did I become "lady"?

"Yeah, fine!" Someone shouts from down the hallway, and Danes shuts the front door behind him.

I turn around and peer out one of the long glass windows beside the door, squinting to make out Tackman and Cami's figures near the Escalade. She's dressed in jeans and a tight tank top, with heels much higher than mine. I can't make out what they're saying, but she's jabbing her finger in his direction, and he keeps shaking his head.

Danes follows the technicians around the other side of the house. I guess they'll begin in the back to give them privacy.

Who is Cami? His girlfriend?

"You're back."

I jump, clutching the fabric of my blouse at my chest, and turn around.

The tall, lean man from yesterday stands right behind me, staring at me. No, past me, outside.

Carver.

"He know you're here?"

"I'm waiting to see where he wants the monitors, and he may have some questions for me."

I don't know why else he'd insist I be here if one of his men is already watching over the technicians.

Carver purses his big lips and nods, running his hands through his long, golden blond hair. "He'll probably want them in his study." He turns to the emerald green room behind the metal sliding door. "Actually, maybe the—

70

never mind. He'll tell you once he comes back. You want to follow me?"

I follow him, past the study, down the hallway, past the room filled with guns and drugs as my stomach tenses, toward the kitchen.

I won't have to be back here again for a long time, if ever, and the thought settles my twisted stomach.

Just focus. Please the client; please Cathrine.

Carver grabs the broom leaning against the kitchen island and sweeps at clear, broken shards of glass on the white tile, the bristles dragging through a clear liquid.

"You can have a seat or whatever." He clutches the broom with both hands. "But be careful of the glass. There's a broken one over there too." He uses the broom to point to the table. Shattered glass with pink lipstick on a large piece of it lays scattered around the leg closest to the head of the table.

Cami was wearing pink lipstick, wasn't she?

So, they fought, and it got heated. That much seems clear.

The technicians appear around the back with Danes close behind. They set their ladder up against the wall, pointing to the roof. Carver takes one look at them before he continues to sweep at the glass, making a big mess of the liquid.

It smells strong and reminds me of Cathrine's office on Fridays.

Vodka martinis.

I clear my throat and break the awkward silence. "You should pick the glass up and *then* mop the rest."

He cocks his head to the side and raises his pierced

brow as he turns to me. "You want me to tell you how to do your job?"

"No," I huff. "I didn't know you were the custodian, though."

He smirks and scowls at me, and I can't tell if he's amused or offended.

"You don't need to know anything, *Ma'am*." He shakes his head and continues to sweep. "Just chill out and wait."

Believe me, I'm trying. I want to get this done as soon as possible.

Once I'm finished with this, I can try to get another client, and the bonus could cover the debt even sooner than planned.

"You're not going to sit?"

My feet are killing me, but I'm too antsy. "I don't want to step on glass."

He purses his lips. "Fair enough."

"Could I use the washroom, please?"

He sighs and rests the broom handle against the island counter again. "Come on."

I follow him through the hallway once again, through the foyer, into the seating room, and down another long hallway with a narrow floor-to-ceiling window at the end. "That door there," he points. "Then come right back."

The washroom has a beautiful, simple layout, and it's as big as my bedroom. All white tiles, sink, counter, and towels. I bet this washroom never even gets used. I finish my business, and as I walk out into the hallway, Danes stands on the other side of the long window, watching one of the technicians set up another ladder.

There won't be a piece of property Tackman won't be able to see if they do their job right.

Danes notices me, and I turn away, back down the hallway and through the seating room to the foyer. I sneak a glance out the window by the door again, and I can't see anyone, but the Escalade's still out there. Tinted windows. Maybe they're inside.

I walk past the study again. A thud comes from the other side of the wall, and I stop. I take a few steps back and scan the study. It's empty. Is Tackman back inside?

I peer down the hallway, and Carver's back is turned to me. His whistle echoes in the kitchen and carries down the long hallway as he sweeps up the glass. I step into the study and scan all the books. Encyclopedias on one shelf. Leather-bound books without writing on the spines on another.

A thud comes from the other side of the room.

Close to the desk.

I walk around it, Carver's faint whistle still carrying down the hallway, and listen near the bookshelf. Is it one of those trap ones?

Another thud comes from somewhere close. Somewhere below me?

It's from the basement. Maybe a laundry room?

"What are you doing in here?"

I turn on my heel as Carver lingers in the doorway. "I thought I heard something."

He frowns and rolls his eyes. "Like what?"

"I don't know."

"Uh huh, okay, let's go." He waves for me to follow him

to the kitchen, taking out his phone and typing something on it before shoving it in his pocket.

A thud comes from below us again, and he stops before the kitchen, turning to me, his eyes wide with shock. "Go outside, now." He pulls out his cell phone and pushes me along with him toward the front door as he presses it to his ear. "Danes, get in here now," he says behind me.

A pounding from the direction of the seating room startles me, and I stumble, reaching out for the front doorknob, checking over my shoulder.

A man with pale skin in a wrinkled, dirty t-shirt with black and white tattoos covering his arms, skirts out of the hallway toward the foyer and stops, staring at Carver. Carver pulls a gun out from behind him, aiming it at the man.

I scream, yanking the door open. I need to get out.

Danes stands on the other side, scowling at me. "Get inside," he shouts and pushes past me, slamming the door shut behind him.

I turn around and back up against the window by the door. The man in the dirty shirt remains frozen with his hands in the air, red scratches and rashes on both his wrists.

"Take him back down," Carver says, keeping the gun aimed at the man.

Danes approaches him and as he blocks the line of sight from the gun, the man tries to run. Danes takes a few steps, reaches out, and grabs the back of his shirt. The man almost trips, but Danes grabs his arm, yanking it behind his back and tugging his hand up toward his neck.

The man cries out in pain as Danes guides him back down the hallway. Carver walks across the foyer with his gun, following them.

What the hell is this? I try to move, but I can barely turn to the door. I twist the knob.

"Hey," Carver shouts from behind me.

I freeze, shaking, scared his gun is now aimed at the back of me.

"I have to check on the technicians." My voice shakes, and I press my lips together as tears pool in my eyes.

Please let me go.

"We sent them off on a break until Tackman's ready for them," Carver says.

No. I'm alone?

The work van is gone. The black Escalade is gone too.

"I have to get something from my car." I open the door.

He grabs my wrist and pulls me back in.

I stumble on my heels as he shouts, "You have to get back inside, *now*."

Anxiety erupts within me.

It's now or never.

I jab my sharp elbow against his chest and pull my hand out of his while he gasps in shock. I make it to the door again, but he grabs both my arms and hauls me into the house, right off my feet.

My stomach and vision swirl as the door slams behind us.

CHAPTER EIGHT

QUIET

"Put me down," I shriek, kicking to gain traction, hit him, connect with the ground—anything to stop it.

He stumbles back to the middle of the foyer, and I kick my heels right off as his grip loosens.

What's he going to do to me?

"Stop," another voice commands, calm and even, from the hallway.

Tackman.

Carver sets me down, and I stumble with my bare feet against the cold tile, catching my footing, gasping for breath. Carver reaches out for me, and I swat him away, turning to Tackman standing in the hallway as Danes shuffles up from the other hallway across from us.

I'm stuck in the middle, trapped between them with tears in my eyes.

What's happening? Who was that man in the dirty shirt?

I feel powerless, embarrassed, my heels strewn across

the foyer and tears spilling down my hot cheeks. They all just stare at me.

"He grabbed me," I huff and push my hair from my face, wiping my cheeks as I stare at Tackman.

He remains stoic and turns to Carver. I take a step away from Carver, keeping my eye on him too.

"She saw some things she shouldn't have." His voice is defeated, and he stares at the ground in front of him.

Tackman's chest heaves, and he bites his lip, shaking his head. The three of them stare at me, and I open my mouth to speak, but I don't know what to say. My hands tremble, and I wipe at my cheek once more before grabbing my heels and putting them back on to regain some sense of composure.

"What did you see?" Tackman asks once I'm in my shoes.

I can't lie and say I didn't see anything. If I try to run, I'll never get out of here, and that's all I want.

I clear my throat and tug my blouse down, back in place. "Some man came running in," I point to the hallway, "and then he told me to go outside," I point to Carver, "and I tried to, and then he yanked me back in here."

Tackman turns to Carver, and he nods, running his fingers through his blond hair once again. Tackman runs his hand over his beard and stares at Danes.

"It's taken care of," Danes mumbles.

Tackman looks back to me. "I'm sorry you had to see that."

But I can't hear the regret in his voice. Is he sorry I was

subjected to it, or that I saw something I shouldn't have seen, and now they have to deal with me?

"Whatever's going on here is none of my business," I blurt out.

"I didn't know what was happening," Carver tells Tackman. "I didn't want her involved, but—"

"We'll talk after," Tackman tells Carver, still calm, and turns to Danes. "We're good?"

Danes nods.

I turn to Carver. "*We're* not." My body buzzes with anger, raging against the calm in the room. Against the way I feel like a victim. Why am I embarrassed? How've they made me feel that way? "If you ever touch me again," I shout, "*that* will be my business." I clench my jaw and give him a stern look before turning back to Tackman. "And speaking of business," I bring some control back to my tone as best I can, "I'd like to conclude ours for the day. Where would you like your monitors set up?"

"How about we worry about that when your guys get back?" he says. "Follow me."

He glares at Carver until he steps out of the way, before walking back down the hallway toward the kitchen. I follow him with my legs shaking beneath me as we walk through the clean kitchen to the back wall where a hidden, sliding glass door sits open. He walks through it, and I follow with footsteps behind me into the gray of the afternoon.

"You can wait at the door, Danes." Tackman doesn't turn around, and as I step outside onto the solid concrete patio, the footsteps behind me stop.

Tackman passes the sleek, white patio furniture and

stops before the long, rectangular pool. Birds chirp around us, easing the tension but adding a false sense of peace. I don't know when I caught my breath, or when my tears stopped falling, but anger still lingers with the confusion swirling inside of me.

Tackman folds his arms over his chest. "I'd like to assume the confidentiality agreement we signed covers what you saw," he turns to me, his sharp, dark eyes fixed on mine, "but I never make assumptions."

He wants my assurance, and I'll give it to him. Whatever it takes to get out of here.

"It covers it." I fold my arms over my chest.

He shoves his hands in his coat pockets and tilts his chin up as if considering the sincerity of my voice.

I don't want to push it, so I stand still and maintain eye contact. His confident stare intimidates me, but he's not hard to look at, and he seems like my best shot at reason out of the three men, with the most power.

"The men in the basement were involved in a business deal gone bad."

Men? More than one?

I hold up my hand. "That is none of my business. Your security is our top priority—"

"They will not be harmed," he continues, and I wonder if he heard what I said at all. "I'm keeping them both safe until their business associate sets things straight."

Keeping them safe. That's not what I saw in there. Is that what he expects me to believe?

"Mr. Tackman, I'm here to oversee the security installation and manage your contract. I don't need to know your specific business to do my job with the utmost care and confidence."

"Understand they will not be harmed. They are not in danger. I am keeping them safe, and your security will help me accomplish that until their associate gets back, and then they'll be released."

I shake my head and hug myself tighter. "Why are you telling me all this when I told you it's none of my business?"

"This isn't about what you need to do your job properly," he raises his voice. "It's about what I need." He jabs his finger at his chest. "I need to know I can trust you, and I don't think you'll keep quiet unless you understand the situation."

He really wants me to believe him, but does it even matter? Once I leave, I'm telling Cathrine everything, and I'm calling the police. He can't just hold people hostage here. His men can't just grab me.

"Both men will remain safe, and it isn't for you to worry about."

I clench my jaw and nod. Whatever gets me out of here. "Yes, I understand."

He scratches the scruff of his chin. It's less maintained than yesterday. A little longer.

"Josephine Oliver." My name on his lips, said slowly like that, sounds like silk magic. "Thirty-three. Lives in New Gilford. Parents passed away when you were young." What is he doing? "One sibling. Maggie Oliver. One nephew, Andrew Oliver." I ball my hands into fists. He's threatening me. "Aunt and Uncle raised you. You went to college after high school. Worked and attended night school for administrative professionals. Changed career paths when you were thirty. Began working at Locke Industries. You live at 115 Haverstock Street with your sister and nephew. You take care of them."

"Was that supposed to scare me?" I sneer. "You know where I live; you know the basic facts about my life that anyone with a Google search engine and social media could find. What was the point of all that?"

He purses his lips and tilts his head to the side. "I know more than you think, and we have more in common than you know." He turns and sits on one of the long cabana chairs by the pool, interlocking his fingers and cracking his knuckles as he stares down at them. "I've been a care-taker too."

"What does that have to do with anything?" The cold air brings the shivers back, and I press my lips together to fend off the cold.

"I know you're having financial troubles. That's putting it too nicely and doing you a disservice not to acknowledge what you're really up against. You're drowning in debt because of your sister's rehab bill."

I turn away, staring at the trees as the wind blows through the leaves, rustling them softly.

"I'd give anything to have my brother back and well again. Anything. I think you would too, for your sister. I'm going to give you the money for her debts *if* you abide by the confidentiality agreement. Keep my secret, keep your job, and keep your sister well."

Just that easy? No. I don't want his charity. He can't buy my silence.

If Maggie knew where the money was from, what I

had to do to get it, she'd call me a hypocrite, and she'd hate herself for it. It's wrong.

"I don't want your money." My teeth chatter together.

He stands up in front of me, but I keep still. "No?" he asks, taking off his coat.

"No." I squeeze myself tighter. "I'll abide by the contract, but I don't want your money."

I want out of here.

He walks around me and hangs his jacket over my shoulder. I cock my head to the side, ready to shrug it right back off onto the ground, but it smells of oak and citrus cologne, and staves off the chill enough to stop me from shaking as he walks around to face me again.

I turn to look away, and he leans in closer. "You're a nice girl. You saw something bad. You've got problems. Let me fix them."

"I don't take handouts."

He steps toward me and leans in closer. "It's not a handout," he whispers. "I'm buying your silence. This is just between us. No one will know—not Cathrine, and not your sister."

"I'm already being paid to keep your information confidential. I don't need a bribe," I whisper, turning away from him.

He takes a step back, studies me, and walks to the open sliding door. He leans over to Danes and says something before walking back through the kitchen, down the hallway. Danes comes outside, and I steel myself, not letting him see my fear as he approaches.

"You're done for the day." Danes waves his hand away from me. "You can go. Have your phone with you at all times. If a security call comes through to your company, or anything *suspicious* happens, we want you here *before* the security personnel from your company. If you don't answer your phone, we'll consider the contract null and void."

I nod and walk past him.

"I—" he says, and I turn to face him. "I wanted to say sorry for before. Carver didn't mean to hurt you."

"He didn't," I spit.

But he did. Not much, but enough that I'm still rattled.

"I really am sorry." His face is crestfallen as his gaze slips away from me.

I walk away as his apology lingers in the air, and he follows me to my car until I slam the door behind me, sitting in my driver's seat, shaking as I absorb the afternoon's events.

I have to get back to the office and tell Cathrine. She needs to know what we've been involved in, and she'll know how to handle it.

CHAPTER NINE

SEE NO EVIL

I drove back to New Gilford on autopilot, straight to the office, and as I walked across the lobby, my legs still shook.

Everything happened so fast in that house. I couldn't see straight; I couldn't think straight—and the gun.

Was that the scariest part?

Or the fact they're keeping people trapped there?

Or was it being grabbed from behind and trapped there too?

Dane's apology made it seem like Carver had no other choice, but he could have let me go.

Even if they didn't trust me not to say anything... but I guess they couldn't. I guess he saw no other way to make sure their terrible secret was kept safe.

When people find out about this—what they're hiding in that house.

"Hey, Jo!" Rob, board member Mathison's assistant, calls to me across the lobby, jarring me out of my thoughts, and I haven't even pressed the elevator arrow yet.

I press the button and glance over my shoulder. Two young women from the accounting department follow him. "You working today too?" Rob asks.

I nod as the two women stay back a bit and whisper to each other.

"Coming out to The Twisted Olive when you're finished?"

One of the most popular bars in New Gilford, the place traditionally hosted happy hour for Locke Industries associates.

I shake my head as I distinguish a few of the words from one of the women. "...doesn't even know...wasn't invited."

"She's weird," the other says a little louder and shoots me a fake smile.

"I heard you got your own contract." Rob ignores them. "Congrats."

"Word travels fast." But these elevator doors don't. Not for me today.

"Sure does." He smiles and turns to one of the women. "What time will you be finished?

"Shouldn't take more than an hour," she says. "We'll meet back here in the lobby."

Rob nods as the elevator doors open and turns back to me. "After you."

I step in, and the other women file in behind me.

"Maybe you'll join us next Friday." Rob grins, and one of the women jabs him with their elbow. He steps to the side, pressing the button to our floor and then the one below for the other women. I remember the resistance as my elbow connected with Carver's chest. "It's our pre-anniversary celebration." He stares at me, and I stare back blankly, remembering how close I was to freedom. To getting outside, into my car, and driving away. "The fiftieth anniversary of Locke Industries. At the Lockes. Next Saturday?"

"Right." I nod. One of the women giggles. I glare at her and turn back to Rob. "Probably won't have time."

"That's too bad." He shoves his hands in his pockets and stares at me in the reflection of the elevator walls. "I'd love to buy you a drink to celebrate your raise."

My cheeks flush, and I bite my lip, turning away to hide my smile, but out of my peripheral, I can see he's smiling too. The doors rumble open, and the women step out, shooting each other looks before disappearing down the hallway without a word.

As the doors close, he takes a step away from me and leans against the gold railing. "I hope you don't give a shit what they say or think."

I turn to him with what's left of my smile. "I've got more important things to deal with than office gossip."

Like the clients we'll need to turn in to the police.

I lick my lips and sigh.

"You work too hard." He corrects his posture, pushing his chest out and shoulders back as the doors rumble open. I lift my brows, surprised he believes in such a thing in a culture of hustle. But he's just trying to get a drink with me. He'll say what he needs to to make it happen, even if it's making me feel bad for being no fun. "If you decide to come next Friday for the pre-celebration, come find me, okay?"

I nod and stride out of the elevator, down the hall a few steps to the glass door. As Fern comes into view, my body buzzes with adrenaline, and the nagging feeling of relief annoys me while there's so much left to deal with. I could have ended up in the basement too, but I didn't. They let me go. I wasn't truly harmed, but I feel like I came close. This false sense of security since I got away leaves a hazy film over my judgment.

Was I ever in danger?

Of course I was.

Was it as bad as it seemed?

Fern buzzes the door open, and I march in. I need to get this over with.

"Is Cathrine in?" I ask, my tone more level than I feel, but as Fern studies me, I decide I'm not hiding my anxiety well. "I need to see her straight away."

She studies her computer screen. "Ah, your client's installation. Is that where you've just come from?"

"Yes."

She nods once and slides out from behind her desk, standing at just over half my height, resting her hands on her hips. "What's the matter?"

I shake my head with an uneasy smile. "I just really need to speak with Ms. Locke."

She makes a tsking noise and stares at the desk with pursed lips.

"Is she in a meeting? I'll just wait here. I really have to speak with her."

"What you really need to do is get ahold of yourself."

My eyes open wide and then squint at her, as if looking harder could assure me I'd just actually heard what she said. "You need to sit down and think about the issue you're bringing to her."

"I have. I thought about it for the hour it took to get here in rush hour traffic."

She rounds the desk and leans against the front of it, much like Cathrine does. "Something's upset you, but I can guarantee, if you take a problem to Cathrine without a solution, you won't like her conclusion. Do you understand?"

She's warning me, like I don't know Cathrine. Like I wasn't just called out this morning for my incompetence, but that's not what this is. This wasn't my fault. She'll see that, even after this morning.

But Fern has a point. I can't expect Cathrine to fix it. A good assistant doesn't take their problems to their boss without possible solutions. Even in this terrible case, I know what needs to be done, and I'll be the one to do it.

"I have a solution." I say with confidence.

I'll talk to the police and tell them everything I know. Everything I saw. We'll disassociate with the client and let it be known we don't deal with criminals who harass us— threaten us—and think they can get away with whatever they want.

Fern makes her tsking sound once more and rounds the desk again, sitting back in her seat and grabbing the phone. "If you're doing something to compromise the contract you just signed, the best solution is to smooth things over yourself." She presses a button and stares at me, raising her brows. "What'll it be?"

She's never steered me wrong before, but this is different. This is something Cathrine needs to know about. If Fern knew what had just happened—happened to me—she'd understand.

"I'd like to see her, please."

Without a word, she presses another button on the phone. "Josephine is here to see you... Yes."

She hangs up and nods to me. I stride to the door and pull it open, eager to unburden myself. No more waiting.

Cathrine's holding the phone and her finger up for me to wait. I nod and stay where I am.

"Thank you," she speaks into the phone. "You too."

She hangs up and waves me over.

"Ms. Locke, I've come from Mr. Tackman's residence, and the concerns I had yesterday have turned into a confirmed issue. More than an issue—"

"I just finished speaking with Mr. Tackman."

My breath catches in my throat as I choke out, "You did?"

"He has some concerns about you. About us."

"He has concerns?" I shake my head. "No. Ms. Locke, I know you always say that our clients' business is their own, but he took it upon himself to show me the drugs and guns in his home."

She holds her hand up and presses her thin lips together. "That's enough."

She's not shocked. Maybe she really did already know about them.

"I saw them there yesterday. A room full of them, and today, I saw a man." Running to escape. Running for his life.

"A man." She frowns and stares at me.

This might be the first time she's surprised.

"Yes, a man they're holding there against his will. There's two of them!"

Her eyes open wider, and she takes a step back, resting her hands on her hips. "Two men?"

"Yes."

It's finally sinking in for her.

"Drugs, guns…" She takes a cigarette out of her little box. She only smokes when she's anxious or stressed. She's finally getting it. "…and two men held hostage in your client's home."

"Yes, and I'm telling you to protect the company. One of them grabbed me. Held me there against my will. I should have told you yesterday, but I was confused."

She clicks the gear to her lighter, a flame igniting, but takes her thumb away, and it disappears. "Someone grabbed you?"

"Yes." Why does she keep echoing me? Is it that unbelievable?

"Why?"

"After one of them pulled a gun on the man they're holding hostage there, I tried to get out, but they wouldn't let me." My chin quivers, and I wrap my arms over my chest, holding myself once more.

"They thought you were going to leave and report what you saw to me or the police." She lights her cigarette, takes a puff, and a little cloud escapes her lips as she tucks the lighter back in the box.

I nod. "I'm not afraid, though. I'm ready to tell you

everything I know, and then we can let the authorities know."

She stands from her chair, behind her desk, and folds her arms over her chest too. "Is that so?"

I frown and take a step forward. Isn't she listening? "It's illegal. What they're doing. Our association with them."

She takes another puff of her cigarette and marvels at her view, the golden light from the sun creating contrasting light and shadow over the cityscape, taking her time with her thoughts.

I'm eager to call this in before the day is done.

"Do you want to work at this company?" Cathrine asks in a calm, emotionless voice.

How is that even a question? "Yes, of course I do."

"Do you know what you're paid to do here?" Her condescending tone is so off-putting, I can't understand if she wants me to answer the question, so I stare, waiting for another cue. "You're paid to assist me. To assist the company. The moment I gave you another responsibility, you forgot that."

"No, Ms. Locke. I haven't forgotten. I'm trying to protect the company."

"We protect our clients. You focus on protecting the clients, mind your own business, and keep everything confidential." She shakes her head and runs her fingers across her forehead with the cigarette wedged between them. "What's so difficult to understand about that?"

"So, we... we're okay with servicing drug dealers and—"

This can't be right.

Cathrine holds up her hand again. "If you continue on like that, I'll dismiss you right now."

Dismiss. That's what she's been doing this whole time, but she means my job, doesn't she?

Fern was right—she doesn't want to hear it. Fern's always right.

"I didn't take you to be so naive, Josephine." Her stare burns through me as my eyes tear up. "You're being paid *so much more* to take care of the client. To keep their security needs as your number one priority. To keep their business confidential. You seem to be struggling with that, despite the multiple agreements you've signed, not to mention the client's contract. The moment things got ugly —and understand, they can get *ugly*—you turned your back on the client and your agreement... and that means we can no longer have you here."

She's firing me?

"No. Please, Ms. Locke."

"You're not cut out for the business world."

I've heard that from my high school guidance counselor, my aunt and uncle, teachers, even my sister, but I proved them all wrong. I'm here, and she doesn't think I belong.

My chance at repaying the debt, supporting my family, all the hard work I've put in to get where I am, and it's slipping away, out of my grasp. I can't. The money, we need the money.

Say something. Anything. "I was confused. I just didn't understand—"

She leans over the table, one hand on her hip. "But *now you do?*" She scoffs and takes another puff of her cigarette before striding to the bar cart and dropping it into one of the champagne flutes.

No. I don't. I don't know what to think or do, except I need this job. I need to repay the debt, or by next month, we'll be out of the apartment, out of food, and in major legal trouble.

Tackman wanted to buy my silence, and I was above it, but it's what my employers have been doing this whole time, and even more so now.

"There are things going on in that house that are wrong." My voice trembles as I remember the fear in the hostage's eye as the gun was aimed at him. "That I don't know how to unsee." I press my hand over my mouth and shake my head as the helpless feeling of being lifted off the ground comes rushing back. "I was scared. I need this job. I want this job. Please."

"That's why I've told you to mind your business." She rounds the desk again and sits back in her seat. "What's happening in that house was none of your concern. The security of that house was, and you've left the client feeling quite the opposite. And now you mean to violate client confidentiality?"

"No, I won't." I can't believe I'm saying it.

I still have a choice, don't I? I can still do the right thing. But what is right?

Debt repayment and taking care of my family or reporting Tackman and his dealings to the authorities and losing my job?

We can't be homeless. I can't lose everything I've worked for.

She pulls her laptop open and slides on a pair of glasses, focusing on the screen. "Your client still wants you on. It's not his decision, but I'll take it into consideration."

That's the impression he left me with. That I was still working for him. At least there's that.

"Thank you."

But if Tackman's so concerned about me divulging his secrets, why would he still want me? I tried to run.

"I've never had this happen." She looks up at me over the computer screen. "In the history of this business, no client has ever called in their concerns about one of our employees, from the security guards, to the technicians, and definitely not a project manager." I open my mouth to speak, to apologize once again, as she continues, "*But*, this is an admittedly unusual circumstance." So, she might have known about the drugs and guns, but not the men held hostage. "*And*, despite the client's concerns, he's willing to proceed with certain reassurances."

A heavy pit forms in my stomach, its weight making me ache in anticipation of what's to come.

"What do I need to do?"

"Before a decision can be made, you'll need to meet with Mr. Locke, in his office, Monday morning. Don't be late."

I nod and turn to leave.

"And you'd better think long and hard about whether you should be here. Whether or not you want to be here, and why we should keep you on. You have those answers ready; you show him the Josephine I thought I knew when I decided to give you this opportunity, and you might get another chance."

"Yes, Ms. Locke." I turn to walk out.

"Oh, and Josephine?" She waits until I turn to face her to continue. "*Never* cross a Locke."

I leave the office and turn around. Fern's not behind her desk. She's on the couch, and she pats the seat beside her.

I don't want to sit. I want to go home, to bed, and curl up in a ball, but I join Fern on the couch on the opposite side. She turns her body in toward me. "You must never do that again," she says in a hushed tone, folding her hands in her lap. "Your client could have had Cathrine as his case manager, but he didn't want her. He wanted someone he thought he could trust. Have you ever lost trust in someone before, Josephine?"

I nod, wide-eyed, in some alternate universe where what just happened to me was my fault, and where this lecture seems appropriate. "Of course."

I've never truly been able to trust anyone in my life, but losing trust in my position, in this company, in Cathrine after I'd gained her respect is a new, brutal kind of betrayal.

She nods too. "Terrible feeling, isn't it? If *just one client* loses trust in us, it poisons the well." I turn to her, and we lock eyes. "I know you feel hurt right now, but this is business, and a hard lesson that's been a long time coming. Keep your emotions separate, keep your focus on the client's security, and mind your business, Josephine.

It'll keep you safe." She stands and walks back to her desk, and I rise from my seat in a daze.

She buzzes the door open for me, and I walk through, right to the elevator.

What have I done?

What do I do?

CHAPTER TEN

RENDEZVOUS

I leave the building shaking and wait until I'm inside my car to call Katie. She tried to warn me. Maybe she can give me some more insight and help me work this out before my meeting with Orrick.

I tap her name and press the phone to my ear as it rings.

"Hello?" Her voice calms me.

I take a deep breath. "Katie. Hi."

"Hey, Jo, what's up?" I hear an echoing in her background.

"I need to talk for a sec. Do you have time?"

"I'm at The Twisted Olive. Just in the bathroom right now." A pause and some muffled voices in the background follows. "Do you want to come and have a drink?"

Since Maggie moved in, I don't drink anymore. I threw out my assortment of alcohol I kept in the apartment. I don't even want her to smell it on me, but Katie doesn't know that.

"I'm having—" a hard time. "What we were talking about last night? Things have gotten... worse."

"Worse? What do you mean? You said everything was fine."

"It's not. It's bad." More voices in her background drown out my voice.

"Hey," she raises her volume, "how about you pick me up and drive me home? I got a ride with Pam, but it would be great if you could be my DD."

Maybe she can hear the desperation in my voice. "Is now okay?"

"Yeah, I'll be waiting out front."

I breathe a sigh of relief. "See you soon." I end the call, toss the phone in my purse, and head out of the lot.

What am I going to say? What do I really want from her?

I want to know what she's seen. She said things were bad, and I believe her now, but I don't believe the company lets these things happen all the time. How could they work with people like Tackman without worrying about the blowback on them? Without worrying that if they got caught in a scandal or illegal activity, how it could affect their other high-profile clients. Destroy their reputation.

Even for self-preservation as a business, this can't go on all the time. Cathrine said this was an unusual situation. Maybe it only happens once in a while—that Locke Industries knows of, because it's true, we mind our own business.

That's what I'm being paid to do. Take care of the client. Mind my business.

And why did Tackman specifically tell her he wanted me to stay on? *He* called *her*, and I'll never know what he said.

I pull up in front of the bar, and Katie's talking to another girl I don't recognize outside the door beside a bouncer. She spots me, waves goodbye to the girl, and jogs over to my car.

"Hey," she says, getting in with a smile. "Thanks."

"No problem."

After she clicks on her seatbelt, I pull away from the curb, and we drive in silence, staring at the last of the pink sky through the windshield as it fades away into the dark blue of early evening. I reach my hand out to turn on the music, but she speaks.

"You can't talk to me about work *like that* over the phone."

"Why? Do you think they're listening?"

"I honestly don't know, but I don't want to find out." She shifts to turn in my direction. "What's going on, Jo?"

"There are things I can't say because of client confidentiality, but I was almost fired today."

"What?"

"I want to know what you know. About the company. About the bad things you were talking about."

"I signed the same confidentiality contracts you have. Maybe more. I can't discuss it either, but I've seen enough to worry something would happen. Are you okay?"

Tears slide down my cheeks as her caring voice allows me to break. I grip the wheel tight, embarrassed she's seeing me cry for the first time, but I can't help it. I choke back my tears and try to swallow down the lump in my throat. "You wouldn't believe the day I've had," I choke out, shaking my head.

"Oh, Jo, what happened?"

I squeeze the steering wheel again, steeling myself as I remember the man running down the hall into the foyer, and Carver taking out his gun. I want to leave. I didn't even think about the threat I was to them. I just wanted out.

What would have happened if Tackman hadn't told him to stop? "I'm still shaken up. I—I told Cathrine everything, and she practically blamed me for what happened. She said I shouldn't have—done what I did." I shake my head and roll down the window, letting the fresh night air soothe my hot cheeks.

Without being able to tell Katie everything, it's pointless to even talk about it at all.

I click my signal to turn onto her street, but she points ahead. "Let's go to a drive-through."

"You're hungry?" I scoff.

"I have a craving for chicken fingers and fries. I always do when I've had a few beers."

I continue straight, and she turns to the window. Is she trying to avoid the conversation? Is she scared she might say too much like I am? Walking on eggshells with her makes me sick.

If I could just tell her everything, even if she just believed me, told me I'm not crazy for how I reacted—how I feel... But I can't put her in danger.

"Katie, can you please tell me, do these bad things you hinted at happen a lot? Are they a regular occurrence with the company?"

She rubs her palms on her dress pants, still staring out the window away from me.

"Are we working for bad people?"

She rubs her temple and stares straight ahead.

"I don't want to play a guessing game. Can you tell me what I should know about Locke Industries?"

"They're powerful and dangerous, but you already knew that."

"You know way more than I do."

"Then listen to what I've been trying to tell you and let them fire you."

"Are you scared of them?" I ask. "Because I was scared today, of losing my job, and of what this company is really into, but I was most scared at the client's home for their installation."

"What happened?"

"You know I can't tell you."

I turn onto a side street, and a glowing neon sign appears in the distance.

She points ahead. "Yellow Dip, okay?"

"Yeah, fine, whatever, but you didn't answer me. Are you scared of them?"

She tugs at one of her tight ringlets in her ponytail and avoids my glances. "Like I told you last night, I want to leave as soon as possible. As soon as John proposes, I'll give my two weeks' notice."

"So, you're not okay with what they do?"

She lets out a heavy huff of incredulous laughter. "I'm not okay with what I do."

"So why do you stay?"

"It's not that simple."

"Leaving?"

She rubs her forehead and rests her head against the back of her seat with a deep sigh. "I see a lot of bad things, but I also stop a lot of bad things from happening."

"To the clients?"

She nods. "When I see something going on, I contact the client and their contact with our company. If they don't respond, or if they do and agree, I dispatch one of our security units to the premises. It's checks and balances. I've seen some bad I've been able to stop. Bad that could have been worse. It's how I'm able to stay there. It's not where I want to be, but as long as I do my job well, I'm taken care of. You know it's just me when John's not here, and since he hasn't proposed, I have no assurances of our future. I have to take care of myself."

I pull into the drive-through and roll my window down while she calls out her order to the screen.

We have more in common than she knows, and she'd know more if I opened up to her about my situation, but I can't risk her sympathy or judgment ruining our friendship.

It ruined all my friendships as a kid when our parents died. Kids either judged them for being addicts, or they didn't know how to be with us anymore. The pity was unbearable. People have a hard time with uncomfortable situations, and I don't want to put Katie in the position where she knows so much about me and is unable to handle it.

Once we're at the next window, she leans over the seat. "Hey, is Billy working tonight?"

"Yeah," the teen girl says and turns around. "Billy!"

"Who's Billy?"

He steps up to the window, and the curiosity on his faces twists into shock.

"Meet us out back," Katie tells him, and he steps back slowly as the girl hands us a brown paper bag. "Thanks!"

The window closes, and Katie points to the back of the lot by a dumpster.

"What's going on?"

"Just park back there."

I drive around the Yellow Dip and park by the dumpster. "Katie, this is so sketchy."

"Why'd you really want to talk?" she asks. "If you can't tell me what's going on, what can I do? I tried to warn you, but you didn't want to hear it."

I didn't. I didn't want to believe the company I believe in could be involved with people like Tackman. I didn't want to believe I'd allow myself to stay involved, but I'm supposed to meet with Locke tomorrow and beg for a job I'm not even sure I believe in anymore.

"I think working in your position could be dangerous," Katie says as we turn to each other. "I don't want you getting tangled up in it. Is it the money? Is that why you want to stay?"

I nod. "And what it could do for my family."

She takes a deep breath and gets out of the car, rounding the back to my side, and waves for me to get out as a man a little younger than us walks across the lot in his uniform. Billy stops a few feet away and folds his arms over his chest.

"Why are you here, Katie?" he asks in a high-pitched voice.

"I want you to meet my friend. She works with me."

He scowls at her. "Why are you here?"

"Because she's thinking about getting out, and I'm bound by contract, but you're not anymore. Tell her what they did to you."

"I can't believe you'd bring a stranger here." He searches the dark lot around us and stares at me. "Why do you wanna leave?"

"Things have happened recently..." I don't know what else to say.

"She just needs to know what she's getting herself into if she stays." I can feel her eyes on my but I can't stop staring at this guy. The dark circles under his eyes and his greasy hair beneath the visor hat he wears higher on his forehead. "She's a good person. She needs to get out before—"

"Before they do to her what they did to me? Uh huh." He shoves his hands in his pockets and turns to me. "Well, I used to work with Katie, and I trust her with my life because we saw the same things together, and she helped me get through some things until I couldn't take it anymore."

"Did you quit?" I ask in a meek voice.

"Oh, I tried." He shakes his head at Katie. "Sometimes I think I should have listened to you and stayed instead of putting in that complaint."

Katie lets out a shaky sigh. "Tell her what happened."

"I gave my two weeks' notice, and because I'd made some complaints about the situations we were dealing with, they gave me this exit interview, which was really a way to bully me back into working there, but it didn't work, so they threatened me. If I left, they'd discredit me, and no one would believe what I said anymore. They knew I smoked pot, and the next day, they planted bags of it in my car, and I got pulled over on the highway."

I look at Katie, and she stares at me with a blank expression.

"You don't believe me? Look up William Peterson. My name's all over the place for a robbery I never did and possession with intent to distribute. All made up."

Katie looks at me with a straight face and folds her arms over her chest, kicking a stone in front of her toward the dumpster. "He got five years in prison."

"And the worst thing was, they were right. No one believed me." He throws his hands up. "And now, this is my life. This will always be my life. Criminal record, probation, and some of my own family members still don't believe I'm innocent."

"Are you sure it was them?"

He cranes his neck back. "If you truly believe it could have been someone else, you might actually still have a shot at getting out unscathed." He turns around and walks back across the lot, calling out, "Don't ever bring anyone to see me again!"

Katie rounds the car and gets back in. My body shakes as I climb into the driver's seat. I don't even think I can drive right now.

"He's telling the truth."

And if it's true, it's confirmed my worst fears.

"They're firing you, and you'll go free. Let them."

Maybe I should… "But there's nowhere I'd get better pay straight away. Especially not after my raise, and I *need* the money." My cheeks grow hot, and I lean toward my open window. All the calls from the debt collectors seem more menacing than they did last week, and imagining an eviction notice hanging from our apartment door makes me sick. "I don't know what to do."

"I risked a lot bringing you out here to see Billy, and it sounds like it was for nothing."

"No, Katie." I turn to her. "I appreciate what you did. I'm so glad you believe me. That you don't think I'm over-reacting."

"It sounds like your mind's made up to stay," she says, her tone defeated. "Maybe your next client won't be like this one. Maybe none of the others will be." She doesn't believe that. Her dejected expression confirms it. "We have to do what we have to do to get by, Jo. Just be careful and watch out for yourself."

The rest of the drive back to her place is silent. I can't think straight, and I can't trust what Billy said, but I don't know why he'd lie.

I don't know why I'm trying to justify working for these people who are sounding more like monsters, but with everything she knows, Katie stays too.

"Do you feel trapped?" I ask.

"In a sense. I've been good, though, and I think they'll let me leave when it's time, and they'd be right to, because I won't say anything to anyone."

"Does John know what you do? What you see?"

"No. I've never talked about it with anyone except the co-workers who see the same things I do."

But she tried to warn me. She stuck her neck out for me.

I reach out and grab her arm, squeeze it, and give a faint smile. "Thank you for being here for me. I appreciate everything you've done, and you're right."

"I am?"

"I'm going to let them fire me. I need this job—or a job —but knowing what I've seen first-hand, I can't find a good enough excuse to go along with any of it, never mind the things I don't have proof of."

She lets out a huff of air, leans over the console, and wraps her arms around me. "That's great."

"Yeah, I wouldn't call getting fired great." I give her a quick squeeze and relax in her arms.

I'll need to get another job straight away. And maybe Maggie can too. Something easy for her. Low stress. Just enough so we can make ends meet for a while, until I can make the kind of salary I had before the raise.

"Drive safe," she whispers, pulling away and opening her door. "And if you need to talk to me again, in person, okay?" I nod. "Be safe, Jo."

As she leaves, jogging up to her building, I feel my only lifeline fade away as I pull away from the curb and head home.

Katie's the only one who has an idea of what I've been through. The only one I speak to who's seen things, who I can talk to, and we can't even really share what we know. But I was right to call her for help. She was like an amplifier to my conscience, helping me hear it clearly, even through my fears.

And what she said about helping people, that's why I picked Locke Industries for my internship. They have power in this city, and they use it to make people feel secure, or that's what I thought.

Maybe I'm not as trapped as I feel, and the debt will have to take longer to pay off. This time next year, we could have a real chance at a better future.

Let them fire me. I let the plan sink in as I ride the elevator up to my apartment and check my cell phone. It's the usual time I come home on Saturdays, pretending I've been having fun at whatever group activity I was doing.

I have to tell Maggie I'm losing my job. My heart sinks as I slide the key into the hole and grip the knob, hanging on the thought of the burden this decision places on both of us.

I can't support a dealer, a man who holds people hostage in his house, or a company who protects a man like that. I can't let what happened to Billy eventually happen to me.

We'll make it work. Make do with what little we can get, like I always have. Maggie's not as strong, but she's better than she's been in a long time, and maybe together, we can finally build a life for our family.

I twist the knob, and as I step into the dark apartment, my sister's silhouette sits at the kitchen table, staring at something in front of her.

"Maggie?" I ask in a hushed tone, and my stomach twists.

Something's wrong.

"I'm sorry, Jo," she whimpers.

I flip on the light, and my breath catches in my throat.

CHAPTER ELEVEN

TRAPPED

A bottle of whiskey sits on the table in front of Maggie, and she's holding an empty glass.

"What are you doing?" I blurt out.

Her lips tremble as she presses them together, and I drop my purse, marching to the table and grabbing the bottle. I carry it to the sink, ready to pour it out, when I notice the lid is tight, fastened on, and the bottle is full.

I sit it on the counter and turn around as she deadpans the table in front of her. "You didn't?"

She shakes her head. "But I want to. I called my sponsor, and they talked me down. They told me once you got home, I needed to let you know what I was trying to do. They told me I need to ask for help."

Help?

I stare at her with eyes wide open, and although she's not looking in my direction, I bet she feels my glare.

What more could I possibly do for her? She's staying with me for free; I'm taking care of her and Andy financially, I haven't asked her to get a job, and I didn't even want her to until now. I went into debt for her rehab stay and treatments, and I've been trying to help her for as long as I can remember—since I was barely a teenager.

All she has to do is stay with Andy and go to meetings.

"Maggie," I huff, then count to three in my head with steady breaths before continuing, "I don't understand."

She covers her mouth with her hands and mutters something I can't make out. I round the table and stand in front of her, waiting. "Pardon?"

"I'm a fuck up!" she shouts, and I turn to their bedroom. The door's shut, but she could still wake him up. "He's at a friend's, okay?" Thank God. "I took him there after my interview, well, after the run to the liquor store."

"And then you came here ready to throw away everything you've worked for?"

"Yep, pretty much, or at least that's as far as *your understanding* will take you." She glances at me with anger in her eyes. "Can't blame you. You've done all you can for me and Andy. I'm a lost cause, Jo. You know it. I know it."

I shake my head and pull out the chair, but lean against it instead of sitting, the heavy hit of her words crashing against me in waves. "You're not. You're a mom. Your son needs you."

"He'd be better off without me."

"Whoa, that's enough!" I hold my hand up to stop her. "That's not true!"

"I know that's what you think, and I have to agree. You've done everything for me—us—and I can't even get it right. When I was gone, Andy had a stable home; you

110

had reliable care for him, and he didn't have to watch me ruin our lives anymore."

I imagine her pulling up to a liquor store with him in the passenger seat, wondering where they are, what they're doing. Maybe he even knew it was wrong. He must have sensed it with her. He's been through this before. At least she had the sense to drop him off at a friend's.

Maybe I can tell her how I really feel.

"Admit it!" She points at me. "You think you could do a better job of raising Andy! With your fancy job and big fat paycheck, apartment in the city..." She has no clue—and I can't tell her, or it'll send her off the deep end. "You should be the one."

"Yeah, maybe I could do a better job, but it's *not* my job! He's my nephew, not my son. There's a difference between providing for a child and raising a child, and you can't leave both up to me. I'm not his mom. You had him, and he's yours, and you need to take some responsibility. He loves you. He needs you. You think he was so much better off while you were in rehab? He asked about you every day. He worried about you at night. He wasn't really happy—I've seen him happy—and he's happiest with you when you're healthy. I love him, but I'm not a good substitute for a mom."

"Pfft, you walk around like you are. Like you know what's best for him. As if I was never there for him. I was!"

"Yeah, and you were there for me too. Sometimes. Andy deserves to be more than a sometime, and I should have had a big sister who looked out for me and took care of me. Not someone I have to watch over and worry sick about."

"Don't you get it? I feel sick from all the shame festering inside me. For all the slack you've had to pick up and for putting you through what we went through with Mom and Dad. For not being the mom Andy deserves," she chokes on his name as she bursts into tears and hides her face in her hands, trying to speak, but it all comes out muddled and wet.

I want to go to her. Comfort her, because I hate seeing her this way, so trapped. I can't get inside her head. I don't know what she's thinking or how she got here, but I've been left to pick up the pieces, and I'm tired of it. I can't even hug my sister because I'm scared if I let her in, it could be the last time.

I wish I could feel numb to her pain and to the worry accompanying her choices, but I feel every bit of it, and it's too much to take, but I have no choice. My body aches as I watch her aching.

"I tried to get a job today," she chokes out. "I know the pressure you're under with my debt, and just—just everything—and I got an interview, and I was so damn excited. The woman said with my history, they couldn't accept me. I didn't know they'd do a background check, and they saw the drug charges against me. The way she looked at me, Jo." She shakes her head and covers her eyes.

I remember the shame from our childhood, and I know exactly what look she's talking about—full of judgment and sometimes pity.

I walk to her side and rest a hand on her shoulder, but she shrugs it off to my dismay and stares up at me with mascara-stained cheeks and pain-filled eyes. "It's how *you* look at me."

The punch of truth to the gut hits hard and fast and I release an instinctive, incredulous breath of defense.

Because I can't be who she sees me as. I've been here for her. I've taken care of her and her son, and this is what she wants? The drugs and alcohol? To tell me I make her feel ashamed?

She storms from the table and through the living room to her room, reaching out for the door. "And don't worry. I'm not going to use. I just can't take *that look anymore!*" She slams the door behind her, and I slump down, falling as my tears do, plunking down on the kitchen floor and covering my mouth to hide my cries.

What more can I do for her? For Andy?

I'm doing the best I can—the best I know how—and nothing helps her. She'll do what she wants no matter what I try, and I wish I could take her place. I wish it were me who went into the bedroom and found our parents. I wish I could take her pain as my own, but it fills me up with suffering, and she still suffers too.

There's no winning with her. The best I can do. All I can do is try to keep her alive when she doesn't want to be here, and it's a losing fight every time.

But I have to try. I have to keep her and Andy safe. They're all I have.

And there's only one way to do that right now.

CHAPTER TWELVE

THE BOSS

I ride the elevator past my floor for the first time, and it clicks into place on the penthouse suite. The heavy door rolls open to reveal an airy layout of what must be the whole floor, separated by glass, somewhat like Cathrine's office, but you can see everything here.

The far-left wall is the exterior to the building, wall-to-ceiling glass. It's a reminder of Tackman's kitchen—the broken glass with the woman's lipstick on it and the strong smell of vodka from the puddle on the floor.

In the penthouse, the air smells of leather and flowers like car air fresheners, but with richer, deeper notes. I step off the elevator and scan the space, immediately feeling the difference between the modern feel of one side, and the dark, leather, and masculine touches of the other—Orrick's office.

I stride down the hallway, my legs trembling beneath me. Each wobbly step I take clicks with my heel, echoing in the huge space.

Click. Turn around.

Clack. I can't.

Click. I need this job.

Clack. I need to run.

Orrick sits behind his large, L-shaped wooden desk in the middle of the room. On the other side, two dark leather chairs.

I'll be sitting in one of them when my fate will be decided for me.

Stay or go. Employed or homeless. Debt-free or continue drowning in it.

My emotions bubble up to the surface as I press forward and catch a better look of Orrick Locke as I get closer. He's dressed in his sharp suit, his fit frame leaning over the desk, broad shoulders intimidating me in a primal way. No other noises or people. We're alone up here.

As I reach his office, he checks the expensive watch on his wrist and presses his lips together as he stands, making eye contact with me. I pull the glass door open, and his expression is unreadable, so I break into a nervous smile.

"Good morning, Josephine. It's lovely to see you again."

Lovely? Really? Maybe I'm not in trouble. Maybe he understands I've done nothing wrong. "Good morning, Mr. Locke."

He knows my name now, and not for the reasons I'd always hoped.

He waves a hand toward himself. "Please come in. Have a seat."

I walk toward the center of the room.

Click. Cathrine seemed so upset.

Clack. Why doesn't he?

Click. Maybe he'll be on my side.

My tight chest opens enough to draw in quick breaths as he smiles at me, moving around to the front of the desk and leaning against it, more like Cathrine. When I sit, I'll be feet from him.

I take a seat, crossing my legs at the ankles, and grab on to the arms of the chair, bracing myself for impact. I turn my body away from him while maintaining eye contact, letting an awkward smile remain on my lips as I fuss with the collar of my blouse. Do my clothes please him? What must he think of me?

"So, Josephine, Cathrine tells me you're having an issue with a client of yours. Would you like to tell me what's going on?" He folds his arms across his chest, waiting.

The barrier it creates between us is welcome, less intimidating.

I fold my hands in my lap and clear my throat, ready to rehearse the speech I created this morning. If I work from the speech, there's less chance to veer off course, away from the opportunity to be heard and clear up any misunderstandings.

"First, I'd like to make it clear that I now understand and respect the company's confidentiality policy. When I first met with the client before he signed the contract for the job, I..." The white room, full of cocaine and guns. "I was brought to a room, made to be aware of the drugs and guns the client was holding, that he presumably wanted protection for. It was unsettling to say the least, but above all, I'd never seen anything like it on the trips I'd take with

Ms. Locke to sign client contracts. If I could get a handle on your expectations of me and the clients we sign, I could understand the boundaries of the company and my position to better uphold them. I didn't know what the company policy was, and I tried to speak with Ms. Locke about my concerns for the purposes of clarity, but it was difficult to tell what was or wasn't acceptable, besides keeping it to myself." I study his unsympathetic facial expression. I'm getting nowhere, and I can't remember the rest of the speech.

"I see." He scratches a finger over his clean-shaven jaw. "I can certainly understand why that would be upsetting to you, and I'm sorry you had to go through that." He inhales sharply, taking a seat in the chair next to me, his body incredibly close to mine. So close, I can smell the heavy aroma of his woodsy cologne, not as strong as Tackman's, but reminiscent.

Tackman's arm, reaching out for me as I stepped away from the white room, flashes before my eyes.

"Josephine, can I be frank with you? You're in the big leagues now. The client Cathrine has given you, the client *I* have trusted you with—" he pokes a finger into his chest against his gray silk tie, "is a big deal. You've been entrusted with his secrets, not just by him, but by Cathrine and me. I like to think we treat our employees fairly here. I like to think we don't ask for too much. How much am I paying you, Josephine, remind me?"

He's steering this conversation in the wrong direction. I don't need to be made aware of what they're doing for me. It's the only thing keeping me here at this point, but his eyes bore into me, and I'm compelled to answer.

"Before my raise, it was forty thousand, sir, but after signing the client, it was doubled, with the potential of signing bonuses for new clients henceforth."

He smirks, his eyes darkening. "Eighty thousand. That doesn't seem like just a *little* salary, now, does it? No, it's a big salary. For a big job. There are plenty of people here making much less than that and dealing with much more." It's true. Katie's one of them. "I understand your hesitations with your client; we've all been there, but I guess I thought you were in this with us for the long haul." He pauses, his eyes traveling around the room.

Thought I was in it for the long haul? I didn't think he even knew who I was... but maybe I was wrong.

Maybe he was caught off guard on Saturday, seeing me at his home, and he didn't recognize me.

Maybe he's had his eye on me this whole time, just like Cathrine, and my cheeks grow hot.

"Cathrine tells me you have goals to move up, like she has, like Mathison, like I have. Do you think any of us got where we are by running away from trouble?" Is that what I did? Run away? I guess I had—tried to anyway, until I was forced back into the house. I can still feel Carver's arms wrapped around me, dragging me back in. "By breaking the client's trust?"

"No, sir," I say straight away. "That wasn't my intention at all."

The crease in his forehead deepens, and his brows draw together in obvious frustration. I lean back in my chair, away from him ever so slightly, and reconsider what he said.

Did they get where they were by running away? No.

But as far as I can tell, it was by nepotism for Orrick and Cathrine. They were hired and given their positions by the founder, their father and cousin respectively, Lawrence Locke.

"Intention or not, Josephine, that's what's happened. My family built this company from the ground up with one goal—to protect our clients and their secrets. In a world where secrets are so hard to protect thanks to technology, we stand in defense of those who need it."

That's why I joined the company, I believed in that, but in protecting people like Tackman? No.

"One thing I don't like to do is play God. I'm not the judge of character, and neither are you. We don't get to look at our clients as *good* or *bad.*" He pauses as if checking to see if I follow, but I can't get over the slap in the face of his statement. That I've somehow unfairly judged the client.

"They are simply people who require a service, and we are the people who can provide that service. Anyone who can pay our fees, giving us the assets to provide for our families, gets our protection. Good, bad, or in between. If we were to get involved, we would lose all credibility, even with the clients who are entirely innocent. Our business would collapse. Everything I've worked for, everything *you've* worked for, would be gone. With the leaking of one tiny secret, the turning away of even one paying client, all of this," he gestures to the room around us and snaps his fingers, "could be gone. That's why we don't judge. We protect. That's it."

I can understand it to an extent, enough to parrot it back to him right now to make him believe it, but is it true? Could the business even judge clients accurately to determine if they were good enough to protect?

If we betrayed one client's trust, he's right, and Fern said as much. The house of cards would topple down. Who could trust us after that?

But couldn't the hard line be the law? Isn't it there for a reason?

Legal and illegal.

Good and bad.

"That is *literally* your only job here." As he echoes Cathrine's sentiments, I shift in my seat. He sees the world in gray. He truly believes in turning a blind eye and protecting all who can afford it, and I'm falling for it, because why? He's wearing an expensive suit, cologne, and watch. Because he owns the building? He doesn't own the people in it.

I feel it in my gut now more than ever. This company has the power to make someone into something, just as they have the power to destroy them like they did Billy.

Katie's right.

Will Orrick make or break me?

The kindness reappears in his eyes as he leans his head to the side. "I could tell you what potential I see in you." He lets the words rest between us, but I soak them in. "I could tell you that Cathrine greatly respects you, and though we don't always see eye to eye, I trust her judgment—in this case." He smirks. "I know she has trouble showing it, but trust me, I've heard the way she talks about you. I can promise you that if you stick it out with us, you could have a lifelong career here, with unlimited possibilities." He scoots forward in the chair a bit, clasping his hands in front of him, and I can almost feel the heat radiating off him. "So, Josephine," I lean forward to hear him, his words weighted and low, "I guess the ball is in your court. What's it going to be?"

He says he wants me to succeed, and he thinks it's possible. Whether I have trouble believing it or not, why else would I be given this opportunity in the first place or be allowed a second chance?

He seems to believe in my potential, and no one else has seen it in me or believed I could be something more.

The opportunities he's offered sit before me, within reach, and I've run away from them instead of grabbing at them as I have all my life.

Could I really look past the clients' business and take care of them, no matter what they did or who they were? Can I do it with Tackman?

But I don't have a choice. Does Locke know I know that?

Does he know I'm trapped, financially, or does he truly wonder if I'll choose to leave the company after what I've seen and been through?

I don't have that luxury anymore. Not after last night with Maggie.

"Mr. Locke, I've been so grateful for my job, and the new opportunity I've been given here. Please let me assure you, I was only trying to look out for the company's best interests when I brought the client's activities into question." I press my lips together, take a deep breath, and tread lightly. "I appreciate my job, and I want my job, Mr. Locke, and you've made your policies very clear to me now. What will it take for me to keep my job and earn my way back into your good graces?"

It's the only thing left to do. For Maggie and Andy.

He stands from the chair with a sigh and makes his way back behind the desk, looking down at the stack of papers in front of him. "From what I understand, Mr. Tackman is upset with the way you handled yourself, and he doubts your ability to maintain professionalism where his business is concerned. If, and this is a *big if*, you think —no, you *know*—you can do this, the only option is for you to convince him of that. I'd like to know that you can own up for your mistakes and win back his trust with an apology. Do or say whatever it takes to make sure he knows you will do your job to the best of your abilities. That's what this is, Josephine—*your job.* I trust that you can make it right, and he wants you to do that, still hopes you can, for some reason, so now you have to prove it to us all. I don't want you to let me down."

"I don't want to let anyone down, sir. I can make sure the client is taken care of by apologizing and re-establishing trust, like I hope to do with myself and your company. Moving forward," I pause, searching his face for the patience I need to ask my question, "may I ask whom I should talk to about matters of concern regarding the welfare of the company?"

"I'd like to remind you of our company policy: *We take care of our clients' business by minding our own.* If you have issues, you should be the one to take care of them however you see fit. At the end of the day, yours is the name on the contract, and it's your judgment you should defer to. And as for re-establishing trust with the client and my company, I have no doubts you can. I see that in you—the fire it takes to do a job like this and do it well. You have it; you just have to trust yourself to use it. Cathrine may have helped you as much as she has the means to, but it's up to you now." He taps his knuckles on the wood of his desk. "Welcome to the big leagues, Josephine."

As I sweep my hair over my shoulder, my stomach churns as my cheeks flush. His flattery and attention juxtaposed against his threats and intimidation confuse every fiber of me.

How can I be so flattered, and yet disgusted with myself?

He sees potential in me. How can I ignore that? How can I reject it when I know what I'm capable of? How can I reject the money to pay off the debt and take care of my family? How can I deny myself the opportunity to be recognized for my loyalty, the same trait that has never been respected or acknowledged by anyone else in my life?

Are my own ideals of loyalty so far from his vision for the company? I'm loyal to a fault, and I need to prove it to keep my job, regardless of the personal conflicts.

I have what they are looking for. I can be what they need. I can earn my position, pay, and power.

"I appreciate the second chance, Mr. Locke. I won't let you down, sir."

"I'm trusting you not to." He stands up and offers his hand to me, his gaze intense. "I'll have you meet with Cathrine now to discuss your next steps."

I reach for his hand, his smooth skin skimming my palm, and he squeezes, his strong grip matching mine.

Am I making a deal with the devil himself or my saviour?

"Thank you. I hope to make you proud."

"Don't hope, Josephine. *Do.*" With that, he drops my hand and steps back to his chair, settling in without giving me another glance.

A coldness settles in with his absence, and I step to the side of the chair and turn, striding out of the office.

I belong here. I'm wanted here.

A means to an end.

And maybe more.

CHAPTER THIRTEEN

SPEAK NO EVIL

F ern buzzes me in through the glass door, and I walk
through, stopping at her desk.

She looks up at me, and the words "poison the well"
come to mind. Does she think I'm a poison only cured by
absence, or will she be pleased I've been given a second
chance?

"Ms. Locke's expecting me."

She raises her brow. "You had your meeting with Mr.
Locke, then?"

I nod.

She gives me a once-over and picks up the phone.
"You survived," she mutters before hitting a button and
pressing it to her ear. "Josephine's here for you. Yes. Fine."
She hangs up and folds her hands together on the desk.
"She'll see you now."

I stride to the door with my head held high.

"Josephine?" Fern calls to me, and I turn over my
shoulder. "Remember what I told you. It's business."

I nod and reach for the knob, twisting it and pushing it

in as I walk into the room. Cathrine's in her wingback chair beside the bookcase with a martini in hand, her toned legs crossed, and her elbow resting on one of the arms. I close the door behind me and walk to the front of her desk.

"Sit," she says.

I obey, rounding the chair, and sit. I rest my hands in my lap, against my mother's black chiffon skirt, more matronly than Cathrine's, staring at her, awaiting the next hoop to jump through.

"I just got off the phone with Orrick." She glances at me out of the corner of her eye. "He let me know he's decided you should have another chance."

"Yes, ma'am."

"But I haven't. Not yet." She takes a sip of her drink and lets it sit in her mouth before swallowing. "You've embarrassed me in front of him, and I just don't think you understand the way your poor decisions have affected your future here."

I straighten my posture. "Mr. Locke said I could have a bright future here."

She lets out a little burst of laughter. "Did he? Well, that's what I thought too, before you made a fool of me." She turns her body toward me, her vodka splashing around in her glass. "Haven't you noticed how much more often my decisions are questioned here? How I'm put under a microscope and judged as the most powerful female board member."

"I hadn't noticed. No."

"Open your eyes, Josephine. If you want to get ahead as a woman, you have to work twice as hard as the men, especially *these* men. You haven't done that. You've made Orrick and the other board members question my judgment with the stunt you pulled."

"Stunt?" I scoff.

She stands, wobbling to her feet at first, but then she balances, staring down at me. "You've forgotten who you're talking to, Josephine. You might have smoothed things over with Orrick, but I'm your direct boss, and your actions are a direct reflection on me. You broke company policy."

I sit, tight-lipped, knowing any explanation will be the wrong one. Especially while she's on her way to being three sheets to the wind.

"Now," she rests her martini glass on her desk and turns back to me, leaning against it, "I could threaten you with legal action for breaching the contract." I open my mouth to ask how, but she's too quick. "I could tell you about all of the information we've learned about you and your...family...over the years." She's using the same tactic as Tackman. Getting to me through my family. A lump forms in my throat, and I clutch my own hands tightly. "I could tell you that we can make sure you aren't able to work, not only in New Gilford, but anywhere ever again. I could tell you about all the documents I have with your signature on them, signing off on *very unsavory things.*"

She's close; I can smell the vodka on her breath, and I fight the cringe coming on as I try to imagine the scenarios in the order she listed them, but all I can think about is Maggie and Andy.

Without me, what would they do? I shudder, a cold

chill ensnaring me as she stares into my eyes like she's reading me. Like she's ready to do something.

I swallow hard at the lump in my throat, but I can't choke it down. Whatever happened between the time I confessed what happened and now, she's been punished for my actions. She's taking it out on me.

It's business, like Fern said, but I'm still digging my nails into my fingers to keep from defending myself against her.

"I don't want to have to do any of that, but if you make the wrong move again, if you violate our company policy in any way, I'm afraid you'll leave me with no choice. Understood?"

"Yes, Ms. Locke."

She pushes herself away from the desk and picks up her martini once more, turning to the window wall. "Make things right. Go."

I leave the office, grab my purse, and rush downstairs to the parking lot. A few minutes later, I merge onto the highway, heading toward Copperfield County, and press my Bluetooth speaker set. "Call Maggie."

If she picks up, it'll be the first time we've said more than a few words to each other since the night she almost relapsed. With each ring, I'm praying she'll pick up.

"Hi," she says in a dry tone.

"Hi. I'm calling to let you know I'll be home late tonight if you want to go ahead and have dinner without me."

"Okay."

I want to ask her how she's doing, if she's okay, but it's too weird after the night before and the whole Sunday we spent not talking. I still feel the burn left from what she said about me—about how I make her feel. Walking on eggshells isn't the answer, but until we're face to face, I don't think we can have a proper conversation.

Still, I worry for her. Every minute I'm away, she could fall into that mindset again. I need to get a better feel for how she's doing, or I won't be able to concentrate.

"Andy okay?"

"Yeah," she sighs, "we're playing Zombies."

"Oh, nice. Okay, well, I'll see you later."

"Okay."

But I don't want to end the conversation this way, feeling bad about how I reacted to the way she shared her feelings with me. "Um, anything I can pick up on my way home or?"

"Nope. We're good."

I take a deep breath and let out my words on exhale. "*Are* you good?"

"Yeah, I'm fine, Joey." Joey. When she calls me that, just like Andy, there's an innocence about her and an affection toward me I can feel in her voice. "I am."

"Okay." I relax my shoulders. "Good. See you later."

I hang up and crack my knuckles as I ride down the highway toward the sun as it dips ever closer to the horizon.

It's the best I can do for Maggie for now. If I had the money to send her back to rehab, I would. She could stay another three months and see if she feels any stronger then. Any more prepared to face the real world and its real challenges so I can stop doing it on behalf of us both.

And now I can focus on the apology.

I turn on the radio, and the classical station plays a beautiful symphony. I try to clear my mind and focus on my gratitude for a second chance. For financial stability.

Orrick's words ring in my mind. The client was upset but hopes I can assure him I'm trustworthy.

I have to prove I'm an asset. That I'm not threatening their security—Tackman's or Locke Industries—in any way. It's like I'm playing dead, and it's not far off from how I feel.

I pull onto the dirt road once more, and a faint glimmer of hope lingers in the dust and dirt kicked up by the tires I leave behind me.

Maybe this will be the last time I have to come here.

Maybe I really can move on and up, like Orrick suggested, and *maybe* things aren't as bad with the rest of the company as Katie and Billy made them seem.

I park behind the red Camaro once again, and as I approach the white front door. It opens, and Carver steps out onto the front path. I slow my step, and he speaks before I reach him.

"I'm sorry for the other day," he mumbles quickly, staring somewhere past me down the driveway before turning around and walking back inside.

Real genuine.

I walk inside and close the door behind me as Carver approaches the study and knocks on the closed metal sliding door.

"She's here," he calls.

"You can do better than that," Tackman calls back, an edge to his tone.

Carver's shoulders droop, and he turns around to face

me once again, running his fingers through his hair. He must do that when he's nervous or feels guilty. "Seriously, I'm sorry for putting my hands on you the other day."

I give him a blank stare. I can't muster up the energy to accept an apology I still don't believe. I have to save my energy for my own apology for something I *really* shouldn't have to apologize for.

"Better," Tackman calls.

Carver shoves his hands in his pockets and waits, as if I'll say something, and when I don't, he ambles down the hallway toward the kitchen.

The sliding door to the study opens, and Tackman stands there in worn jeans and a fitted black t-shirt, the most dressed down I've seen him, and nods to me. "Come in."

I follow him and linger by the door. "Should I close it?"

He waves me off, and I stand in front of his desk as he rounds it, but before he can sit, a ringtone fills the room. He reaches into his pocket, checks the screen, and clicks a button so the noise stops before setting it on the desk and taking his seat. "Please." He gestures to the wooden chair across from him.

I sit, crossing my feet by the ankles and take my purse off my shoulder, tucking it against my side and the chair.

Do it just like Orrick Locke said.

"Mr. Tackman, I apologize for the way I handled our business the other day."

He frowns and seems to consider this for a moment before standing and pacing slowly behind his desk with his arms crossed.

He's not buying it? I have to do a better job of selling it.

"I want to reassure you once again, I'm the right person for this job, and keeping your business confidential is of the utmost—"

His cell phone rings again, and as he peers over at it, his fists squeeze into balls as he stares, letting it ring.

"I'm sorry, did you want me to give you some privacy?"

He grabs the phone and holds down a button until it chimes.

Did he turn it off?

He clutches it while turning around and facing the front window. It's getting dark out, and I squint to make out the tree line on either side of the driveway where he seems to be staring. The monitors can see everything outside with night vision, but I don't even know where he had them installed after I left.

"Are you really sorry?" he asks, his back turned to me.

This is my last chance. If I can't keep the client, I won't be able to keep my job. I lose my job; I lose the apartment; I lose stability for Andy and Maggie.

I lose them—I lose everything.

"I'm very sorry for upsetting you or making you feel like you couldn't trust me. This job is very important to me." My voice shakes, and I try to control it, but it doesn't help. "And I want to do whatever it takes to keep it."

He runs his hand over the stubble of his chin and releases a huff of breath. "You don't have anything to apologize for. We do. I do." He turns to me, staring me straight in the eyes. "I'm sorry Carver grabbed you. He feels terrible about it, even if it doesn't sound like it. He felt trapped, like there was nothing else he could do, and I know it's not an excuse, but I'm sure you've felt like that at one point or another." He knows I do right now. "I'm sorry I had to call Cathrine, but I needed to be reassured of the confidentiality we agreed upon after you left last time... And now, they've told you you had to come and apologize, and you did it, but it's not for me. I won't accept it because you didn't do anything wrong."

"I don't know if I understand."

He shakes his head and walks back behind his desk. "There's a lot you wouldn't understand about my business, but if you take your obligation to my security seriously, we shouldn't have any other problems."

I nod and stand, facing him. "Understood."

I turn to leave, and he steps out from behind the desk once again, stopping a foot away. He doesn't speak, just stares at me.

"Is there something else?"

He rests his fingertips on the desk, leaning against them as he stares down at it. "Why did you come back?"

"I told you. I'll do whatever it takes to keep my job."

"Do you think that might have been why you were given it?"

Cathrine knows how hard I work. That's why she gave me the opportunity. But she knows about my family too—and my debts. She knows how desperate I am. Maybe he's right. He knows more about me than I do about him, and I bet I know more about him than most already, with the guns, drugs, and hostages.

I bet *no one else* knows about that last one, besides Carver and Danes.

"Maybe," I mutter. "I don't know anymore, and it doesn't matter." He raises one eyebrow, and I continue. "I'll do my job to the best of my ability. Is there anything else I can do for you this evening?"

He rubs the stubble on his chin again, considering the question. "That'll be it. Unless there's a security issue, you won't have to come here again."

He says it like he knows it's some sort of consolation. He knows I just want far away from here, and he's granting me some small relief, but he continues to stare, locking me in his gaze. He steps toward me, dragging his fingers across the desk until they fall away, and he's so close, he could reach out and touch me.

"Don't apologize to anyone anymore when you don't mean it." He licks his lips and shakes his head. "It's a waste of breath, and it gives someone the upper hand on you, like you owe them something. Admitting when you're wrong is fine, great even, but otherwise, you're handing over your power."

"Ha," I laugh without meaning to, but when he looks at me, I keep the sad smile on my lips and shake my head.

Power. I have none, and it's easy for him to say. Whatever he says, his goons do. Whatever he wants, he's so rich, he can have. He gets away with drugs and guns and hostages, but all he seems to know about power is that he has it. He doesn't understand that I don't—he couldn't.

"I know you're doing what you need to do for your family, and it doesn't bring me any pleasure to know the situation you're in, but you're not powerless." He takes another step forward, and I smell his cologne again. "No more apologizing," he says in a hushed tone, just above a whisper.

"Easy for you to say." The words are out before I can stop them, but his expression doesn't change. His eyes keep searching mine.

"Is it?" he whispers, "I just apologized to you, didn't I?"

"Yes," I let out a hiss of air with my "s" and avoid his gaze.

"Well, let me say it again: I'm sorry you're in this position, and if I can help it…" He reaches out toward my hand. I keep it still, close to me as his finger grazes my wrist and glides down the rest of my hand, onto my pinky finger, lifting it slightly in one smooth motion. "I won't put you in this position again."

"Hey," Carver calls from the door of the study, and we both turn around, his spell broken. He's holding up a phone. "Call's for you."

"Tell them I'll call them back." Tackman lifts his brow, staring at him, still so close to me, I'm warm by his side.

"It's Cami." Carver leans against the door frame. "And she's called me five times in the past five minutes. I thought you'd want to know."

Cami. From the day before.

Anything I felt moments before washes away with her name as jealousy replaces it, and Tackman runs his hand over his chin. He steps away from me and joins Carver at the door, leaving me cold.

"See her to her car," he says, and Carver nods as he hands him his cell phone.

Tackman looks down at it, turns back to me, and walks away. Just like that. He's letting me go.

Carver leads me to the door, and I stop beside it. "I can see myself out."

"No can do." Carver opens the door.

I follow him out to my car, and he scans the front, stopping at my hood. I pass him and walk between the Camaro and him, around to the driver's side as a cell phone rings. He takes his phone out of his pocket and presses it to his ear, his eyes still on me. "What?" he asks. "Yeah, fine. She's just leaving."

I open my door as he holds up a hand to me. Is he telling me to stop?

"Drive safe," he says in a tone I'd almost call warm, and in reflex, I give him a small smile and nod to be polite.

Goodbye, Carver. For good.

He jogs back to the dark house, closing the door behind him.

Just as I'm about to duck in the car, I realize I've forgotten my purse.

As I scurry up the driveway to the door, a light in the foyer flicks on, and movement on the other side of the narrow window by the door catches my eye. In the bright foyer, Danes and Carver each bend and pick up the sides of a dark blue tarp with something wrapped inside.

On instinct, my body knows—it's not something.

Some*one*.

CHAPTER FOURTEEN

BLOODY HANDS

I take a step back, still in view of the window, with the sense that whatever I'm seeing is wrong.

As they shuffle toward the door, an arm falls out of the blue tarp. A bloody arm, dripping down to a hand covered in blood.

A dead body. They're carrying a dead body.

I cover my mouth and turn back, running to my car, panting as I reach it and stop, but I'm unable to catch a proper breath as my heart pulses in my ears. I duck inside, but I don't have my keys.

They're in my purse. In the study.

I stare at the front door in horror, covering my mouth once more, waiting for it to open. For them to come out and see I'm still here.

The garage light flickers on.

What do I do? I need my purse, my phone, or I can't leave.

I have to go to the door and make some noise. Let them know I'm still here. If I wait too long, they'll think something's up. Why would I just be waiting out here without my keys?

Do I have a spare in the glovebox? I open it, and a bunch of napkins fall out onto the seat as the garage door slides open.

Now. I have to go now.

I step out of the car and walk calmly up the driveway toward the front door in the dark, as one of their black trucks backs out of the garage. Danes sits behind the wheel, does a double-take out his rearview mirror, and stops beside me.

A dead man's right beside me.

As he rolls down the window, my stomach heaves, and I point to the house. "I forgot my purse."

His face twists in confusion.

"My purse is in the house."

He looks over at Carver and nods to him. Carver opens his door, hops out of the truck, and jogs past me. "I'll get it."

"Thanks!" I call out, far too kindly as he disappears into the house.

Danes scratches his chin and rests his arm on the window ledge, staring at me. "Goin' home?"

I nod.

I have to get out of here.

Carver slams the front door behind him, my purse in his hand, and jogs to me.

"Thanks," I say in a muted tone, grabbing it.

He jogs around the hood of the truck and back to the passenger's side as I turn swiftly for my car.

I duck inside and close the door, and they're still

sitting there in the truck in the same spot. Every second I'm here is a second they could catch on to what I saw. Even if they're a bit suspicious, they could trap me here like they did before. I could end up beside the dead man in the truck. The man wearing the dirty t-shirt from the other day.

Besides blood, the man in the tarp had tattoos covering his arms.

It was him. The hostage.

The hostage Tackman promised wouldn't get hurt.

My stomach swirls as I put the car in reverse and back down the dark driveway. I turn over my shoulder to check behind me, but turning back, Danes is already backing the truck up.

I said nothing, and now a man is dead.

A hard lump in my throat forms as I pass the tree line and continue on to the road, and by the time I pull out, my mouth pools with saliva.

I'm going to be sick.

Danes pulls out after me and speeds down the road as I follow slowly behind them, my stomach churning. I roll down the window, slow the car down, and just as I pull over, a lump rises in my throat as I open the car door and brace myself against it while I'm sick.

I gasp for breath, turning back ahead to the road, but their truck keeps going further into the distance. Leaning back against my seat, I grab a napkin from the seat and wipe my mouth and chin, grabbing another and rubbing it over my hands until the slimy feeling is almost gone.

How could I let myself do this?

I gasp for breath again and slam my hand against the wheel.

They guilted me into this. Scared me into it. They *all* did.

I couldn't really call the police, could I? No, because they'll do what they did to Billy if I tell anyone what I know. I need to get out of here. I slam the door closed and drive ahead, rocking in my seat, forward and back against the seat over and over to ease away the pain and guilt building inside me.

What have I done? Why didn't I call for help once I was out of there on Saturday? Why did I have to get Cathrine's approval to do the right thing?

The silence against my own thoughts keeps me rocking until I reach the highway. I have to drown them out. I have to numb this feeling, or else I won't be able to drive. I won't be able to get home.

I turn on the radio, and classical music comes on.

I'm complicit in murder.

I turn the station back to a familiar hard rock channel and crank the volume of a song I recognize as I merge onto the highway. I listen to the lyrics and cry as my thoughts scatter among the sounds of drums, guitar and the voice of a legendary rock singer whose name I can't remember.

What was that man's name? The dead man in the tarp. No one will ever know where he went.

I turn the music up more and sob, driving along the open highway until my head throbs in pain.

As I exit the highway and find my way back home, my eyes sting from my tears, and I feel like I'll never take a real, full breath again. My chest won't allow it, constricted and tight because my body is punishing me. It knows what I've done, and it won't let me forget it.

I stumble from my car to the building and open the door, stepping inside and walking through the front entrance.

I'm going home to my family, but the man in the tarp will never go back to his.

The vibrating of my cell phone brings me back into focus, and I'm standing in the elevator, but I don't remember walking to it, never mind getting in.

I reach into my purse and take it out. A reminder my rent is due soon.

A man lost his life so I could pay my rent.

Tears slide down my cheeks as I walk out of the elevator, down the hall, and into my apartment with the familiar sights of Andy's homework magnetized to the fridge and smells of the herbal tea Maggie never stops drinking.

I can't stop crying over everything, but I'm so thankful to be home where it's safe.

I just want to curl up with Maggie and Andy. I want to wrap my arms around them. I want them to hold me. But if they knew what I didn't do, what happened when my silence was bought, they wouldn't want to hold me anymore.

I toss my purse and keys on the counter, shuffle toward my bedroom, but still, I'm drawn to theirs.

I don't deserve it, but I need it. I need their comfort. I need to feel safe because I don't anymore.

Stifling my cries, I open their door and walk in

through the dark. I kick off my heels and slide into bed on the other side of Andy, sandwiching him between us.

My teeth chatter together as I drape my arm over him, and my fingers graze my sister's bare arm. The touch of her skin and the smell of his hair gel ground me, and I nuzzle up against the cold pillow, a relief for my eyes and cheeks.

Billy is what happens when you don't play by Locke Industries rules.

The man in the tarp is what happens when you don't play by Tackman's.

Will I end up like Billy or in a tarp?

What do I deserve?

Andy's arm wraps around me with his eyes still closed, and the extra warmth soothes me enough to close my eyes, but I see the bloody arm and hand again and the dirty t-shirt sleeve.

I picture Carver and Danes carrying me in their tarp but squeeze my eyes shut so tight, I see explosions of light on the backs of my lids.

In my next breath, I smell Andy's hair gel and feel Maggie's skin, so soft, beneath my fingertips once more.

I'm home. I'm safe. I'm doing this for my family. I'm home now.

CHAPTER FIFTEEN

A FRIEND IN NEED

I drive to work through New Gilford morning traffic on autopilot, and when a horn honks behind me, I jump, coming back to reality in the lane of the work parking lot, stopped in front of my spot.

It's like my mind won't let my body go to work, like it knows I won't fit into the slot—that I'll never fit.

I can't stay at a company that makes me work for killers, but where else do I go? The police?

Locke Industries will bury me in illegal activities, theirs and mine, with the paperwork they have on me. Just like Billy said. Like Cathrine confirmed with threats that weren't even thinly veiled.

The man behind me waves his hand away from me, telling me to go.

Go where?

Not the police. Not Tackman's. Never again.

Back into the brutal arms of the ones who own me to complete my journey to my complicit end.

I turn into the slot, and the man flips me the bird as he speeds past.

I can't tell Maggie what's going on, and there's no one else to turn to, except...

I jump out of my car and stride toward the Locke Industries HQ, aware that I've chosen to enter the burning building instead of running from it, for the value inside.

I haven't asked for help for anything since I was a child, for fear of becoming dependent on people who never follow through, reliant on those who can't be trusted, and pitied for my weakness.

But this is different.

This is Katie.

She's stuck her neck out for me already, trying to warn me, and I didn't listen. She already knows my situation, or almost knows, and I need her for the rest. I need her help to escape. She listened when no one else did.

My heels click against the sidewalk pavement as I approach Philip.

He opens the door for me with a puzzled look. "No coffee? Have we quit caffeine?"

Coffee. Right. I've never missed a morning with it.

"Have to go back for it," I mutter, slipping past him into the building, past the front desk to the elevator.

I press the arrow with my finger for the first time since the first day of my internship. Bright-eyed, bushy-tailed, lamb to the slaughter. The doors open, and I enter, pressing the number two button. Just before they close, Elena steps in, Orrick and Iris's temporary assistant. She nods to me, and I nod back, keeping my eyes on the doors.

The elevator's going to stop at the wrong floor for me. I have no reason to be on the second floor, and if it gets back to Orrick or Cathrine, they'll suspect I'm up to something. Am I being too paranoid?

The doors open on the second floor, and I freeze, glancing at Elena through the mirrored walls from my peripheral. She's staring at me.

"Oh," I mutter, "I must have pressed the wrong button."

She gives me a polite smile and presses the seventh floor for me. She knows my place. It's good I didn't get out.

I release a deflated, "thanks," and go back to staring at the door.

It dings, and I step off as she remains on, as I suspected. The doors close behind me, and I press the button, waiting, hoping no one comes up and wonders where I'm going. It's so out of routine for me, but would anyone else know that? Does anyone care, or are they good little lemmings, following the company motto? Mind your own business.

The doors open, and Rob walks through and nods to me. I nod back and enter the elevator again. He doesn't hesitate, just keeps walking down the hall, and I tap the number two button several times as the doors close again.

There will be people on that floor who see me. What will I say? I should have waited until after work, but I can't. I can't be here and pretend I didn't see a body.

I'm here to see Katie.

She left something in my car the other night when I picked her up from The Twisted Olive.

I was her DD.

The doors ding open to an empty hallway, and I step off, trying to remember which room she works from.

I take each step cautiously as a door opens.

Keep going.

An older man walks out into the hall and frowns at me as I pass.

Will he stop me? Ask why I'm here?

As I turn around, he pops back into one of the many monitoring rooms.

She said near the end of the hallway, but she never gave me a room number.

I'll call her.

I call her phone, but it goes to voicemail. Straight away.

Is she forwarding her calls, or is her phone off? They probably make them turn their phones off for confidentiality.

I reach the last five doors on each side of the hallway. Room thirty-three. I think that's what she said. I knock and the door opens with a small, blonde girl peering out from the glowing blue darkness behind her, squinting into the hallway light.

"I'm looking for Katie," I say naturally. "Which room can I find her in?"

"Room thirty-five. I'm sorry, who are you?"

"I work here." I put enough vigor and confidence in my voice that I practically ask *who are you?* right along with it, just the way most of my colleagues would answer the question.

She slips back into her room, and I continue down the hall and knock on Katie's door.

When she pops her head out, her eyes bulge. "Jo? What are you doing here?"

"We have to talk."

She shakes her head and leans in close. "I told you, not here."

"It can't wait."

"Jo."

"I need your help," I hiss.

She studies my face for a moment before smiling. "Oh," she says loudly, "no problem, I have it here."

She walks into the dark room, and I follow behind her. As the door closes, she turns back to me with wall-to-wall monitors behind her.

"You can't do this!" she hisses. "They've got cameras in the hallways."

"Not in here?"

"I don't think so, unless they have someone monitoring the monitors... and I wouldn't put it past them..."

"It's bad, Katie," I whisper with tears in my eyes, and her stare softens. "I saw a dead body at my client's house." The words send chills across my arms and back, and the queasy feeling I fought so hard against this morning returns.

"What?" she asks, shock in her voice.

"But you, you said you see this all the time. Bad things." I tuck my hair behind my ears, away from my hot face, as my voice shakes. "You've seen this kind of thing before, right?"

She shakes her head. "Not personally, no. Billy saw...something."

"You've never seen a murder?"

147

When she shakes her head, tears spill down my cheeks. "Katie, I don't know what to do. I'm trapped."

She grabs my arms and squeezes them until I give her eye contact. "You have to pull it together. You can't let them see you upset. You can't let them see weakness. They're like natural predators, and they'll prey on it. You can't do what Billy did. You can't run and tell—there's no one *to* tell."

"What do I do?"

Katie shakes her head. "You have to go."

"What?"

She lets me go and leans against her chair. "We can't talk here. Meet me at my apartment tonight after dark."

I nod, wiping the tears from my eyes. "I never meant for this to happen. You tried to warn me."

"Why did you do it, Jo? Why did you want to stay after what I told you? No amount of money's worth this."

I could tell her they never suggested firing me.

That Orrick and Cathrine both seemed keen on keeping me, so there wasn't an easy way out, but that's a lie. I could have stood up for myself in those meetings. Agreed that I'd made a big mistake and admitted I wasn't right for the job.

I could tell her the truth, that I'm being both blackmailed and paid to stay silent.

She's gone out of her way for me, been a true friend, and it's what I owe her. The truth.

"My sister... She's been to rehab, and I paid the bill. I'm in so much debt, Katie, it's crazy, and I need to get out from under it. I can't breathe sometimes thinking about it, and this was my way out."

She stares at me for a moment before shaking her head, not out of pity or anger, but fear. "You have to go."

"But you'll help me?"

She nods. "I think I have a plan."

"You do?" My lungs fill with air and shudder as I release the deep breath.

"There's only one way for you to get out, now, unscathed. My place. Make sure you're not followed."

I nod and reach for the door handle.

"Wait." She digs through her purse and pulls out her iPod, handing it to me. "This is why you came. To get your iPod back. I'll get it tonight."

I nod, grabbing it, and slip out the door.

I need to stay calm, as normal as possible for the day, and then tonight, we can make a plan.

CHAPTER SIXTEEN

THE APARTMENT

I dash from my car, parked by the curb on the street in front of Katie's apartment building, and rush through the front doors. As I reach the elevator, I turn around to make sure no one is behind me, following me, and when I'm satisfied, I climb six flights of stairs to the third floor.

As I walk down the empty hall, the weight of my footsteps echoes through the floor until I stop, reaching Katie's apartment. I knock on the cool metal door and wait, clutching my purse strap over my shoulder.

She has a plan. It's the only thing that's gotten me through the day. We'll work this out together.

My phone vibrates in my purse, and I pull it out.

Maggie sent a message. *Went grocery shopping. Spaghetti for dinner. When will you be home?*

Back late, I type, *eat without me.*

I shove the phone back in my purse and knock on the door again. When I step away, I notice the corner of a white paper under the door.

I bend and grab it, a blank white envelope, as my

phone rings, probably Maggie again. I don't need to be made to feel guilty about not coming home to have a family dinner right now.

I knock on the door again, ready to hand Katie her mail, and my phone vibrates. Another text. I open it, and it's a text from a number I don't recognize.

Security issue. Danes will pick you up out front of your place in fifteen.

Tackman.

He doesn't need to leave his name and is smart not to.

Danes is at my place? Of course, they know everything about me, and it's not a question but a demand.

And the service is part of the contract. How did he get here so fast? Wouldn't it be quicker for me to just leave now?

Is there a real security issue, or do they somehow know what I saw?

If I go, I'm on my own there again, trapped.

If I don't, Cathrine will unleash her threats on me —ruin me.

If it's a legitimate security concern, why haven't they called the guards? I'd get a notification about that. I check the text again. Fifteen minutes. It'll take me that long to get to my place.

I tap Katie's name in my phone, and it rings with no answer. She's not home.

I type her a text, *Where are you? I'm at your place, but I have to go. Call me, please.*

She knows how important this is to me... Did I miss her, or has she not come home yet?

I don't have time. Danes will be waiting at my apartment soon. He could be there now. Going back to Tack-man's could be the worst decision I've made yet.

I type to Katie once again. *If you don't hear from me, I'm going to 111 Concession 3, Copperfield.*

At least if it's the wrong decision, she'll know what happened. Maggie and Andy will need closure, and she'll find a way to give it to them, even if it's not the truth.

I send the text and walk back down the hallway to the stairwell before I realize the white envelope is still in my hand. I push the door open with my back and peek inside the envelope.

So sorry I missed our date, Jo.

It's for me. An explanation.

I stop on the stairwell landing and scan the letter.

The craziest thing happened today.
After I saw you, John called and proposed!
You were right, I just had to be patient.
3 years was a long time to wait, but it finally happened.
Things happen for a reason, and this was my time.
Hope you can understand about the rush. You know how
Excited I am about moving to Vancouver.
Now I can be with my fiancé and grow our life together.
My hope is that you know I'm
Over the moon happy for you in your new position.
Very proud to have known you, Jo. I wish you the best.
Even if you hate me for leaving, I'll understand.

I flip the note over, but there's nothing on the back.

This has to be a joke. I can barely breathe, my chest tight with betrayal as I read the letter once more, tears pooling in my eyes and the words blurring.

But I didn't need to read it again. I read it right the first time.

She thinks she's done all she can do for me, all she cares to do for me, and she's leaving me to deal with the mess on my own. The first person I confide my trouble in, and she's gone.

I rush down the staircase and out of the building to my car. The cold night air nips at my wet cheeks and nose until I get in.

No one will be here for me. The runaway train isn't stopping, so I either fling myself off and accept the consequences, or ride it until it crashes.

I reach my apartment, and the black truck, maybe even the one they put the dead body in the back of, is parked at my curb. I can see Dane's outline from behind the tinted windows, and he rolls it down as I approach.

"You got Tackman's message?" I try to read his stoic expression as I nod. "Let's go."

I round the front of the cab and open the door, staring up at him before climbing in. The smell of new leather fills the space before I can even shut the door, and I can barely breathe.

"Can I open the window?"

"Sure." He shifts into drive. As it buzzes down, cars whiz past us, and he waits for an opening to merge onto the road.

I want to be back in the apartment with Maggie and

Andy, eating spaghetti, and listening to Andy talk about his day. But I have no choice anymore.

"What's this about?"

"Tackman will let you know," he says, taking the opportunity of the gap in cars to drive forward. "What's that about?" He nods to the paper in my hand.

Katie's note.

I shake my head and hold it away from his prying eyes, reading it again.

How could she have moved in the middle of my crisis? How did it happen so fast? It can't be a coincidence it happened the same day I confronted her in her monitoring dock.

Did they see and get rid of her?

No, this is her writing.

Did they make her leave this for me to read, to know I was alone—abandoned by the only person who might've been able to help?

She had a plan.

I read the note once more as the wind from the window tousles my hair around my face.

Did John finally propose? It was all she wanted—her chance to escape, and of course it would be more important to her than mine. I never told her she had to be patient about waiting for the proposal, though, and I don't see how she could say what she did in earnest. Over the moon about my promotion?

I've only known her just shy of three years, and they were together for almost five...

I scan over the note again. Is there a hidden message meant for me? I focus on just the first letters of each line.

S
T
A
Y
3
T
H
E
N
M
O
V
E

Stay for three years, and then move? Three months? That's her plan.

She's telling me to be patient, stay, and then move.

It's like she wasn't listening at all. I don't know if I'll survive the night, never mind three months or three years, and what would I have to see in that time? What would I be made to do? What would I become comfortable doing?

The thought, the cold wind, or both give me chills, and I roll the window back up.

"Good. I was getting cold," Danes grumbles.

We're silent on the highway, but as he exits, he makes a different turn than I usually do.

"Where are we going?"

"Tackman's."

"I don't usually go this way."

"I prefer the backroads. Better scenery."

So, we're not in a rush, whatever this security issue is.

This sounds more like a set up than a security issue, and I wish I could grab the handle and jump out of the truck, but I'd be stuck in the middle of nowhere, looking guilty for no reason if they *don't know* what I saw.

Danes turns on the radio to a hip-hop station, and he hums to the bass line, filling the silence between us once more—and he's tone deaf. I can't take the waiting or listening to this.

"What are you really bringing me there for?" So, my car will be back at my own place and no one will know I was here, except Katie, but she's long gone. If not to Vancouver, definitely out of my life.

"I told you, Tackman will fill you in."

As we drive over hills and along winding back roads in the dark, I wonder what Maggie and Andy will do without me. How will Maggie take the responsibility of raising Andy on her own? How will Andy do, depending on her when he's never been able to before, or not for very long, anyway? Can they create a new pattern, or will the devastation over my disappearance or the discovery of my body send Maggie over the edge one last time?

Tears pool in my eyes as we turn down the familiar dirt road, and the truck headlights flash across the house, briefly revealing a figure—Tackman's? —standing in the window of the study.

Danes parks the truck and gets out, walking around to my side, and I sniffle and collect myself before he opens the door for me. I hop down, clutching my purse, and he shuts it behind me and gestures toward the house. The feeling of his presence behind me as I draw near the front door is unnerving.

No escape. I'm just going through the motions now.

The front door opens, and I walk inside. Danes shuts the door behind me, and Tackman steps out of the shadows of the bright study into the dark foyer, his jaw clenched and his gaze long.

"Mr. Tackman. How can I be of service?"

Can he see right through me? Will he catch that the fear in my eyes is caused by more than what I've been subjected to thus far in this house to his knowledge?

"It's come to my attention that while you were here last night, you saw something you shouldn't have."

I swallow hard before I speak. "Is that what this is about?"

His eyes brighten, but his expression remains unchanged. "Tell me what you saw."

Is this a test? Is there a chance they don't know, and this is about something else completely? If they know for sure, will they have to get rid of me? If I lie, will this all be over anyway?

But the security cameras installed outside, as per the contract, reveal every angle of the outdoor property, including the front door. I approached it, ran away—did I run? —and then approached again. But asking for my purse wasn't a lie. I left it there.

"Josephine?" he says, his voice quick, out of patience.

I'm damned no matter what I do. I was when I let hostages—and then a murder—go unreported.

The best I can do is what I always do—fight to live for my family.

"I saw the body," I say in a perfunctory tone that carries through, "and if that is what you brought me here for, I don't understand."

He bows his head slightly and studies me from beneath his furrowed brow.

"I signed a confidentiality contract, Mr. Tackman, and what I saw was not my business. We were hired to protect you. That's my business."

It's been hammered into me for so long, I can say it without my voice betraying me.

He takes a deep sigh and shakes his head. "I *really wish* you hadn't seen that."

He nods to Danes, and he takes a step toward me as Tackman continues, "And—I wish I could believe you."

CHAPTER SEVENTEEN

ONE DRINK

Danes steps beside me and gestures to the seating room. If I don't go, he'll bring me there like Carver did right where I stand, so I take cautious steps toward the seating room, and they follow behind me.

"You *can* believe me," I say. "I really won't tell anyone."

And I won't. My life and the lives of my family depend on my silence.

"Past the hallway." Danes points to the open entrance of a room ahead.

I enter a billiard room with bookcases lining the walls and a pool table on one side of the room, with a poker table on the other side, closest to another floor-to-ceiling glass wall. We're right beside the kitchen, facing the pool in the backyard, and its shimmering green light reflects against the glass, sending waves of light across the walls of the room.

It's beautiful.

Will this be the last thing I see before I die?

No.

I swivel around and face Danes. Tackman's not there anymore.

"Please," I ask him and hold my hands up, as if they could stop him from attacking me at more than three times my size. "Do you have a family?"

He squints at me. "Yeah."

"I have a sister and a nephew who depend on me. They need me. Please."

He folds his arms over his chest. "Take a seat at the poker table."

I take a step backwards, keeping my eyes on him, until I back up against the chair.

Carver enters the room and walks past me to the table, taking a seat with his back facing the pool, and leans his arm over the edge of the back of the chair, staring at me. With the men flanking me, I take a seat directly across from Carver, my shaky legs and aching toes finding relief out from under me.

I feel his presence behind me first, like an unstoppable force. Out of my peripheral, Tackman walks to the sofa table on the wall beside us with a tray of drinks. Lowball glasses of a neon-tinted liquid filled halfway in each.

He picks up two glasses and hands them each to Danes and Carver before grabbing the other two and extending one to me.

I shake my head.

One last drink before I go? No. It could be drugged. Poisoned.

The alcohol itself is poison, and I haven't had a single drop since Maggie got back from rehab.

"Have a drink with us." Tackman lifts the glasses. I

shake my head again, and he stares at me with an intense gaze. "You don't drink?"

"I haven't in a while."

"Since your sister came back." Tackman nods. "It's a whiskey sour. Do you like whiskey?"

"I used to."

The whiskey bottle in front of Maggie at the kitchen table several nights ago was my favourite brand. I'd never even realized—so trivial—but we have the same taste.

Carver raises his glass to us before taking a sip.

"If you'll please indulge me, share a drink with us." Tackman takes a sip from my glass and extends it back to me, as if to show it wasn't drugged or poisoned. "One drink. You're not driving."

No, but will I be leaving wrapped up in a tarp? Just do what he says; he's in control now.

I take the cold glass, wet with condensation, and set it on the table as he takes a sip of his own drink, rubbing his fingers against his lips after he swallows. "We're going to play a game."

"What kind of game?" I ask.

They all stare at me like I'm the only one who doesn't know. I guess I am.

"It's like truth or dare, except we use cards." Tackman removes a deck of cards from a pocket or drawer beneath the poker table. "You pick black or red. If you guess right, you get to pass, but if you guess wrong, the dealer gets to ask truth or dare. And if you tell the truth, all will be *set right* here tonight."

Tackman takes a seat to my left and Danes, my right.

There has to be a reason he wants to play this. It's an interrogation.

"I'll go first." Tackman grins. "And remember, everybody, no lying." He leans a little closer to me and shuffles the cards, cutting the deck and asking, "Red or black?"

Play the game. Get out alive. Maybe.

"Black."

He nods down at the cards, and I pick out the Queen of Diamonds.

Tackman smiles, his eyes narrowing in their deep pockets, and his fingers caress his beard as he locks eyes with me. "Truth or dare, Josephine?"

I fold my arms over my chest and stare into each of their eyes. "I don't see how this has anything to do with our business."

"Humor me," Tackman says.

"Truth," I snap back.

I'm tired; my nerves are shot, and if he's going to string me along, make me play his games and drink his alcohol, I'd better get it over with so I can go home to bed with Maggie and Andy again, but I won't be able to. I can't let Maggie smell the alcohol.

"What were you just thinking about?" Tackman asks. "Your eyes are so sad."

"My family." Tears fill my eyes, blurring my vision, and I turn my head toward the wall.

"Okay." His warm voice is almost comforting. "Your turn."

I shake my head. "I don't have any questions."

Tackman raises his brow. "You don't?"

I shake my head. "There's nothing I need to know about any of you if it's not about our business dealings."

"You asked me if I have a family." Danes studies his drink, lowering his voice. "You seemed like you really wanted to know."

"Tell her." Tackman nods in my direction.

"I have a beautiful wife and a brand-new baby girl." Pride fills his eyes. "Six weeks old."

"Congratulations," I mutter.

"Your turn, Danes." Tackman points to the deck.

Danes shuffles the deck and cuts it, pursing his lips. He scans his friends and shrugs, stopping at me. "Black or red?"

"Red." I turn over the next card, and it's black.

"Truth or dare?" Danes asks and takes a sip of his drink.

"Truth."

He stares out at the pool and sighs before looking back at me. "Where did you go after you saw what you saw last night?"

"Home," I say quickly. "Straight home."

Tackman licks his lips. "Carver, you have a turn."

Carver shuffles the deck, and as he cuts it, I say, "Red."

He grins up at me and turns a card over. Black. Luck's never been on my side, but this is ridiculous.

"Where were you when we called tonight?" Carver grabs his glass. "When we asked to see you." He presses it against his bottom lip with his lingering grin before taking a sip.

"At my friend's apartment."

"And what were you doing there?" Carver asks.

163

"Ah," Tackman holds up a finger away from the grip of his glass, letting the others do the work. "She answered. Your turn's over.

"If you want me to tell you the truth about something, say it." I immediately regret saying that as Tackman puts his drink on the table.

"You want the truth, but you run from it." He pushes air from his nose and runs his fingers through his thick, dark hair. "Like you did on the video last night. I really wish you hadn't seen that, because then Danes wouldn't have needed to follow you." I turn to Danes, and he averts his eyes, staring somewhere between Carver and Tackman. "You've told us the truth, thus far, and I really appreciate that."

I swallow hard. "I don't have anything to hide. Not from you, anyway."

"Maybe you don't." He grabs the deck from Carver and hands it to me. "Your turn."

I shuffle and split the deck in half, turning to Tackman. "Black or Red?"

"Red."

He turns the card over, and it's black. I guess luck isn't on his side, either.

I can ask him a question. It might be my only one.

"Time's tickin'." Carver drums his fingers against the leather edge of the table.

Tackman's staring at me; I can feel it. I want to catch him off guard for once. Put him on the spot.

I want the power.

I turn to him and cock my head to the side. "Who's Cami?'

"Ooo," Carver says, and Danes chuckles a little until Tackman gives him a cold stare.

"Sorry, boss." Danes makes a straight face, but Carver's still smiling.

Tackman takes a sip of his drink and speaks from behind it. "She's a close friend."

"That's it?" I ask, and he almost spills his drink on his shirt, pulling his glass away and staring me down. I don't break eye contact. "Cami's a close friend?"

"A *very* close friend," he almost growls the word "very." "My turn. Red or Black?"

"Black." I pick the next card.

Black. Finally. I smile until Tackman opens his mouth.

"Have you told anyone what you saw last night?" He stares at me from beneath his brow, and I feel all their eyes on me.

I told Katie. I told her, and now she's gone. I might as well have not told her for all the help she was to me... But if they know she knows, they could come after her too.

"No," I mutter.

Tackman's chest heaves, and he takes a drink. "It's your turn, Josephine. Do you want to ask anyone anything?"

I sit up straight. "Truth or dare?"

"Dare," he whispers with a grin.

"I dare you to trust me," I sneer. "I dare you all to leave me alone."

He pulls at his earlobe and wipes his hand over his well-kept beard. "We're bound, Josephine, by contract. I need to know I can trust you, or this won't work. Truth or dare?"

"Dare," I hiss, and he smiles and stands.

He walks to the sofa table, pulls out a drawer, and grabs a brown paper bag. He sets it on the table in front of me. "I dare you to take it out."

I open the bag, stick my hand in, and feel cold heavy metal as I pull it out.

A gun.

I drop it on the table, and Tackman nods to Carver. He pulls out plastic gloves from his pocket, puts them on, grabs the gun, and slides it back into the bag.

"That's the gun you used to kill that man with." They've set me up.

They don't realize I've already got so much pinned on me, this feels like just another drop in the bucket.

"That'll do." Carver takes the bag out of the room.

"Can I go now?" I ask, the weight of my mistake just sinking in now that Carver's so damn happy to have caught me in something.

Tackman frowns. "You realize what the police will find if they investigate a murder around here, right?"

"My prints on the murder weapon." I snap back. "It's not exactly original. Who says they'll believe it?" I sneer.

"The police?" Tackman asks without flinching. "I've got friends—cop friends—with the Copperfield County department. It won't matter if they believe you or not. They'll have their evidence. They'll have an M.O. too."

I frown and crane my neck back. "How? I don't even know whoever he was."

"If I told you that, it wouldn't be a surprise." Tackman purses his lips and nods to Danes. He gets up and leaves the room.

"You can't prove it," I sputter.

"I don't need to."

The light from the pool ripples across the walls, washing over me like the realization that no matter what I do or how I try, it won't be enough. Nothing will change. If the police are in his pocket, it's true. The gun would be enough to put me away for murder. He probably didn't even need my prints. It was probably just to scare me into submission again.

Tackman sighs, presses his hand against his mouth, and rests his elbow on the table, staring at me.

"Was it me?" His muffled voice comes from behind his hand.

I focus on him again, and when I do, I see just one of the people who have complete control over me. "Was what you?" I whisper with the last of the energy I can muster.

"Did I make the life disappear from your eyes?" He licks his lips and takes a sip from his glass. When I don't answer, he continues, speaking slowly, "When you first came here, I saw a passion for life in you. The way you took in my home—the trees outside. The way you savoured the burger I made for you. The way you snapped at Carver after he grabbed you. The fight's all gone. Did I take it?"

Yeah, you took it, but not all.

Everybody takes a little piece of me, and there's not much left anymore.

I shake my head, tears pooling in my eyes. "It's still there," I whisper, "but I don't know how to... to..."

I don't know how to fight this. How to stop it.

The company.

The debt collectors.

Andy's abandonment.

Maggie's addiction.

My emptiness.

"You," I whisper, wiping the tears from my eyes. "I don't know how to survive what's happened after you... but it was already hard. Next to impossible." I shake my head and turn it away so he can't see it anymore.

"Your sister," he says.

I sniffle. "Among a lot of other things."

"They need you. I heard you tell Danes they need you. But you're giving up?"

I shrug. "Giving in."

"I know I don't know you, as a person, very well," he picks up his glass, "but I never pictured you to be a quitter. A victim? Sure. A judge? Yep. A martyr? Definitely. But not a quitter."

I let out a huff of air. Maybe he's right. Maybe he's not, but none of it matters. Not what anybody thinks about me except my family. "Are you going to kill me?"

He runs his fingers over the felt top of the table. "You sound like you want it over with."

"No." My voice shakes, and I turn to him, but he's staring at the table. "I just want to know if I get to see my sister and nephew again."

"You've worried about that before in your life, before me, haven't you?"

My bottom lip quivers as his fingers trace the lines, placeholders for the cards.

"You worried your sister would O.D. That she'd be

irresponsible with your nephew. That something bad would happen."

I nod, wiping the tears from my hot cheeks.

"Sleepless nights, worrying about her, but there was nothing you could do, or you were already doing everything you could, and it wasn't enough. It's never enough, is it?"

"No," I huff.

He nods to me. As we lock eyes, I see another part of him, another kind of light in his pupils.

"I had a brother." His lips twitch, but his expression remains stoic afterward.

It's all he says before tipping the rest of his drink into his mouth and setting the glass down with a loud thunk on the table.

He lost a brother to drugs.

So, he knows.

And he still deals them?

"Truth or dare?" I ask.

"Truth." He leans in toward me.

"Why do you deal drugs, then?"

He shakes his head. "I don't."

I push myself away from the table and stand. "You don't play by your own rules. Tell the truth, right? I want to go home."

"You're not trapped." His voice is void of emotion, and it offends me somehow, frustrates me more.

"I don't have a car."

He looks up at me and leans against the back of his chair, "You're not trapped," he says with force this time.

"What does that *mean*? If I want to go, I have to walk? *Fine.*"

I spin around, and he stands as I do, so I stop. I'm not scared he'll hurt me. Just that I'll miss whatever he's about to say if I leave. "Am I free to go?"

"You're free to go anywhere you want to go." He runs his fingers over his beard. "You're a little bird in a cage, and the door is open, and you don't even know it."

I turn around and face him, mere feet apart. "You don't understand. How could you? You're a dealer. You've got a gang. You've got power and lots of money. You wouldn't know a thing about being trapped."

"Do you know why you were sent here? By Locke Industries? By Cathrine?"

"As a test."

He shakes his head. "Because you're desperate enough to turn a blind eye to the darker things in life, broken enough to bend at their will."

"They told you that?"

He shakes his head again. "It's written all over you. I saw it from the moment we met. You want to advance in your position, but you need money more. You need to pay off your debts and take care of your family. Take care of your sister." His gaze falls to somewhere just before me and a far-off stare replaces it. His fists clench, and he turns to me once again, taking a step toward me. "Do you ever wonder who you'd be if you weren't focusing on everyone else's problems and had to look at your own? You know what your company didn't realize or see or care about? Your morality. They should have seen this coming. I should have trusted my gut."

"What do you mean?"

He grabs my glass from the table and takes a sip. "Judging others isn't going to help you. Getting to know them will."

I squint at him. "What?"

He shakes his head in an instant and calls, "Danes!"

"Please," I whisper.

He takes another step toward me, staring deep into my eyes. "Everything you need, you already have."

He looks past me. "Take her home." He looks back at me and stares, but without the same intention. Whatever moment happened between us is over.

I turn around and follow Danes out of the room, past the hallway and to the foyer.

I glance over my shoulder, expecting Tackman to be there—hoping he is—but he didn't follow.

Is Danes really going to take me back home?

Danes pulls the keys from his pocket and walks to my door, opening it for me. I climb inside, and he closes it lightly behind me before rounding the truck and hopping into his own seat.

He slips the key in the ignition, but his hands slide off it as he faces the garage. I squint through the darkness, trying to see what he sees.

"Tackman needs your help." I give him a side-eye glance. "He needs you to do your job well. Your company picked you because you'd do what they said. Follow orders. He picked you because he needed someone he could trust."

"Haven't I proven that? That I won't say anything to

anyone? You followed me! If I didn't report—" I lick my lips and shake my head.

"Tackman doesn't trust easily." He turns the key in the ignition. "But he must've seen something in you to let it all go this far."

To let me live after how I've reacted and what I've seen.

That's all anyone's letting me do—letting me live—but I'm not living. I haven't in a long time, and I won't be told how to by the man with my life in his hands. By the men who want to control me and the woman who uses me like a pawn in her game to take over the board.

Maybe the fight's left me, but I don't have much left to lose either. End up like Billy or end up dead, and if I don't do that, I work for the worst kind of people and do their dirty work for them.

Keep their secrets.

I have their secrets.

Everything I need, I already have.

They've been the ones threatening me, but I have something they need. Trust.

They trust in me to a certain extent because I'm desperate. Predictable. Even Katie thinks I'll stick it out for a while.

I won't let the company or Tackman use me up.

I'll use their secrets instead until I have my freedom.

They have my signatures on bad papers. My prints on a murder weapon.

But I'm a woman with a lot less to lose in their eyes, and if I can get proof that what they've done is worse, it could be enough to buy back my freedom.

CHAPTER EIGHTEEN

WAKE UP

After ironing another of my mother's skirts to wear before the sun hints at rising, I carry the ironing board back down the hall to the closet as Maggie comes out of her room, her curly hair in a wild, messy bun.

I've been giving her space since she told me she was upset with how I look at her. But the debt collectors keep calling; Andy still asks if she'll be back if she goes anywhere and acts out afterwards. I'm afraid of what she's been doing during the times she goes out.

If I look at her, she'll still see the worry and disappointment in my eyes, and I don't want to hurt her— making her more susceptible to relapse. No signs of using yet, but she's sneaky—one of the best.

She yawns and passes me. "You're up earlier than usual."

"No, it's the same time," I say, just to be contrary, even though she's right. "You were up late last night. What were you doing?"

She'd gone to her room while Andy and I played video games together, and I could hear her talking to someone.

She smiles and rubs her eyes, leaning against the door frame to the bathroom.

"What?" I ask. "You look like the cat who ate the canary."

Something our mom used to say.

She smiles wider, revealing her cute, crooked teeth, and shakes her head. "It's nothing."

I sigh. "Fine."

As I open the closet door, she lingers with the same goofy grin on her face. I put the ironing board away, close the closet, and go to pass her.

"I met someone," she whispers, pressing her lips together after, barely concealing her grin.

"Met someone?"

When did she have time to meet someone? Between taking care of Andy, her meetings, and other errands, she barely has time to clean around here. And that's fine. She doesn't have to clean, but she should be focused on herself and her son. Not somebody else.

"Are you supposed to do that?" I ask. "Like, isn't it a rule once you're recovering, you shouldn't see anybody for like a year or something?" It's only been a few months.

Her smile disappears, and she turns around, walks into the washroom and slams the door behind her.

Well, that's what she gets for expecting I'd be pleased to hear about her new love interest. If she met him at a meeting, this could be so unhealthy. She's not ready for a relationship yet. She almost relapsed the other day.

I rush to gather my things and make sure I leave before she gets out of the washroom.

Don leaves his apartment with his pup at the same time, and I nod and smile. He nods to me, and we walk to the elevator and share the ride down. "Have a nice day," he says to me as the doors open.

"You too." I walk out, and although this couldn't be a good day, I'm filled with purpose again.

With a mission.

Build the loyalty and relationships with the company and Tackman, gain leverage to use in exchange for my freedom, and get another job lined up so we still have enough to live.

Tackman gave me the idea, and with everything he said, if I were as naive as when I started, I'd think he was trying to look out for me. I want that to be true, and I hate that I want it. He's attractive, and when he looks at me, when he's paying attention to only me, it feels good, even if he's not a good person. It was the same with Orrick… but not the same. I've never wanted to kiss Orrick Locke.

I shake the thought from my mind.

Tackman wants to keep his secrets safe, and just like the company, he believes I will.

Now that I know they've all been involved in bad business dealings with dangerous people and have protected them at all costs, I have a chance to look over the files and see if I can make any past connections to scandals involving Locke Industries clients, specifically Cathrine's. She has the power to set me free, and Orrick Locke would be too difficult to get to. I need something so bad on her, she'd do anything to keep it to herself.

To get to Tackman and get that gun back, I need a plan to get me back there.

Something about security.

As I get off the elevator, I walk past the glass doors, and Fern waves me in, opening the door for me.

"Good morning. Your caramel macchiatos." I pull hers from the tray. "And Cathrine's."

She studies me and takes the coffee. "She just got in, and she's got to leave for a meeting soon."

I nod and grab the remaining two coffees, bringing them to her office and knocking on the door.

"Come in," she calls.

I set the coffees on her desk, and she stares up at me from behind her computer screen. I have to gain her trust again. Get back in her good graces.

"Let me give you some advice. If anything else happens, you will be gone, so do your work here, and make sure the client is taken care of. That's all there is to it."

I nod. "And I'd like to apologize for any stress I've caused you and for disappointing you."

"Hmm," she hums before swallowing her mouthful of coffee. "Well, I appreciate a person who can acknowledge their faults and apologize."

"I'll handle this contract and make you proud."

"You've changed your tune." She sets her cup on the desk. "Your talk with Orrick must have been life-changing." She grins. "Or maybe it was mine."

I walk back out to my desk and pull up Cathrine's database of client contracts and files. The particulars are password-protected, but their initial order is there with their names and addresses. I need to search these and see what comes up in connection to the clients, but first, I need to contact the technician on my contract, Casey, the one who went to Orrick's that day, and set up a reason for me to see Tackman again.

Orrick said I have to take care of the client by any means necessary, so maybe outrageous lengths won't be questioned.

I find Casey's extension in the database and call him, reaching the voicemail. "Hello, Casey, this is Ms. Locke's assistant, Josephine. Regarding the Tackman contract, I'd like to set up a follow-up appointment to our installation for this afternoon at the client's residence. I want to make sure he's satisfied with the set-up, angles, and please bring extra cameras in case there are additions we need to make. If you could call me back with a time, I'll meet you then. Thanks, Casey."

After I hang up, I dig deep in the database, but my heart races thinking about where the gun could be at Tackman's.

How could I be so stupid to touch it, hold it?

I didn't care then, and the fact I do now scares me more than anything.

I've tapped into this side of myself, the survival mode, and it's never failed me before.

I've also never come up against murderers and black-mailers.

Wherever that gun is, I have to find it for my plan to work.

CHAPTER NINETEEN

JUST BUSINESS

I park behind the black Locke Industries van, and Casey the technician hops out of the driver's side to greet me in the middle of the driveway. He squints into the midafternoon sunlight, using his hand to shield the sun from his eyes.

"Ma'am." He nods. "The client said they'd only be here until five."

I lead him toward the door and knock on it. "Will that give you enough time?"

"Should."

No one comes, so I knock again, and the door swings open as Danes takes a step back and looks from Casey, to me, back to Casey. "Come on in," he says in the cheeriest tone I've heard him use. "Or did you want to take a look outside first?"

"Already did, sir," Casey says.

"Wait here." Danes walks with swagger to the study and knocks. "Tech's here."

No mention of me. Maybe I'm a surprise.

Tackman slides the metal door open and smiles at Casey, "Hello, thanks for coming."

"No problem, sir. We want to make sure everything's in great shape for ya."

Tackman presses his lips together and turns to me. "Thanks for being here."

"Of course. May we come in?"

He leads us into his study, and I sit in the same chair as last time, memories of our intense moment flooding back as the men sit. I can almost feel his finger grazing mine.

"What we'd like to focus on are the angles, sir." Casey's voice pulls my focus back to the task at hand. "Do you find you're getting full coverage, or are there any angles we haven't covered?"

"I can tell there are no blind spots." Tackman shoots me a smile. "Isn't that right?"

I press my lips together and nod once.

"Great," Casey smiles. "Are there any other cameras we can install for you today? I'm fully equipped to hook them up to your monitoring system. As many as you want."

So enthusiastic. Everyone's in a good mood today. Is it the sunshine or something else?

Tackman eyes him and turns to me. "Actually, there's one I'd like uninstalled."

"Are you sure about that, sir?" Casey asks.

"Yes," he says, still staring at me.

"Of course." I turn to Casey. "You can do that, right?"

"Yes. Which one?"

"Danes will show you. I've got a call to make, but once you set that up," he turns to me, "that'll be all."

Casey nods. "Yes, sure. Is the picture clear enough for you, sir?"

Tackman nods, still staring at me. "It's proved helpful already."

He saw me, seeing the body.

The way they shuffled around, carrying the weight across the foyer. The way the bloody arm fell out of the tarp...

Casey stands, and I refocus on Tackman.

"I've got a business call. Will you be fine on your own? Danes is waiting for you out front."

I nod and follow Casey to the foyer.

Blood must have dripped on these floors. Blood from the bullet of the gun with my prints on it. I have to find it.

I close the study door behind me and nod to Casey. "I'll meet you by the van once you're finished. Have to use the washroom."

"Sounds good." He steps out the door.

I wait in the foyer for Danes to come back in and insist I stay within his view. For Carver's footsteps to slap down the hallway and surprise me. For Tackman to come out of the office and want a word with me.

But he didn't, and he won't. His lack of interest in me is surprising, but I can't think about it a moment longer.

I rush past the hallway to the billiard room and check the drawer the gun initially came from. No gun. No brown bag. Carver brought it out of the room... Where did he take it?

I walk down the other hallway to the bathroom and check in the toilet tank, where I've seen people in movies hide guns and drugs. Nothing.

Would it be so simple that it's in the room full of guns? A room that's locked. That makes sense.

He waved a keycard in front of the wall. I need that card. I need to get closer to Tackman to get it.

I walk back to his study, and before I knock on the door, I hear his muffled voice, full of anger, "It doesn't matter what you want. You know why I'm doing this... Cami, stop."

I keep quiet and wait.

"You don't get to be angry. I stepped up." He shouts, getting closer to the door. "How should I know where he is? I don't care about that. I care about you!"

I take a step back and bump into something. I turn around and Carver stands behind me.

"I, uh, I guess he's on a call," I sputter.

Carver grins. "Back so soon? Want to play another game?" I sneer at him but hold my tongue. "Listen, sucks we had to do that, but I think it's for your own good."

I scoff. "How's that?"

"Now you know you can't get anything by us."

The study door opens, and Tackman stalks out. He notices us and barely slows down, walking into the kitchen.

"Mr. Tackman," I call, "when you have a minute—"

"Not today," he calls back. "I'll text you a better time. Carver, I'm heading out."

Carver follows him, and I stand awkwardly in the foyer. He walks back, crunching on a red apple, and Carver follows him to the door. Maybe this is my chance to be alone in here, in his study, but Carver waves me out.

"Don't forget your purse again," he says as I walk to the door and shoot him a look.

Tackman jogs down the driveway, hops in the red Camaro and reverses, kicking up dust around his spinning tires. He revs his engine, speeding away.

Danes and Casey walk around the side of the house by the garage. "All finished," Casey calls to me and shakes hands with Danes before they part ways.

Carver extends his hand to me. "Thanks for comin' out." I stare at his hand and back up at him as he laughs and lets it fall. "Ah, worth a try."

Carver follows Danes back into the house, and I walk with Casey to my car. "Everything went well," he said.

"Did you find it odd that he wanted to uninstall a camera?" I fold my hands over my chest. "Which one did you take out?"

"The one that overlooks the back pool, and no, not really strange. From what I've seen, our clients are very particular about their requests."

"You were at Mr. Locke's residence the day I waved you through for the installation with Ms. Locke. Didn't know if you'd remember me."

Recognition washes over his face—and something else.

He scratches his head. "Uh, yeah, right."

"You've been Ms. Locke's head technician for the residential sector for almost ten years."

"Has it been that long?" he asks and walks toward his van. I follow him. "Well, I love working for her. She keeps the hours coming." He swings his bag into the passenger side of his truck. "Will that be all?"

He wants to leave. Was it bringing up Cathrine that made him uneasy? Or something about that day of the installation at Orrick's home?

"Thanks for coming out, Casey. It's nice to officially meet you." When I shake his hand, a smile returns to his face. "Can I count on you should any more work be needed here?"

"Of course." He raises a hand. "Have a good day."

"You too."

I walk back to my car as he gets in the van.

I have to check out the work order for that installation at Orrick Locke's.

CHAPTER TWENTY

RIVALS

After a long day of work, taking small breaks of time to search through Cathrine's client files for any sign of scandal, I lost track of time. It's four, and I promised Maggie I'd watch Andy while she goes to her meeting before dinner. I pack up my things, toss my coffee cups in the garbage, and walk down the hallway toward the elevator.

"You're leaving earlier than usual." Cathrine steps out of the elevator.

"I've got a personal commitment, if that's alright? I came in an hour early to make up for the time."

"Yes, fine, but we need to talk before you go." I walk with her, through the glass door to Fern's desk. "We have a client meeting tomorrow morning."

"I'll be ready."

"And, Fern, could you call Mathison and see if we can do a meeting for the afternoon? I need to discuss the residential sector with him. Josephine, you'll be coming to take notes."

Fern nods, and we walk to Cathrine's office. She rests her briefcase on the satin chair by her bookcase and pours herself a clear drink from the cart. She swirls it in the glass as she looks out over the cityscape and sighs.

"I've spoken to Casey. He told me about your appointment with the client yesterday." She glances at me and I nod. "I must have taught you well, because it seems like you anticipated the needs of your client and catered to them with a follow-up." She turns to me and takes a sip of her drink from her crystal glass.

"Yes, Ms. Locke."

She purses her lips, and her gaze falls somewhere past me. "I was once your age, working here, right alongside Orrick's father, Lawrence. I did a lot of learning. *Hard lessons.*" She sighs, takes a sip from her glass and rubs her fingers across her neck as she swallows. "What I'm saying is, I'm not oblivious to the obstacles you face. You can be a hard worker, ever loyal, and still get the short end of the stick. You can still get held back."

I nod. I should leave to be back home on time, but this is my chance to get a little closer.

"May I ask your advice?"

"Is there an issue?" She squints at me.

"No, nothing like that. You've accomplished so much in your career, but you started from a place, like me, where you had to learn the business. I could only hope to one day own part of a share in the company, to have achieved so much." Her lips twitch as she absorbs my words. A smile? "What's been the key to your success?"

She releases a huff of air and walks behind the desk. "You don't get to where I am without an excellent work ethic; even if others might believe nepotism had a part in my success, I assure you, I earned this all on my own. I should have more. It should have been more," she whispers and takes a sip of her drink. "Being related to Lawrence Locke got me through the door, but it was my hard work—loyalty—that got me where I am today. I see that in you, Josephine. Your work ethic is unmatched by any of the other assistants." The comment almost flatters me, but I remember what Tackman said the other night. I was chosen because I'm in a desperate position. Because I don't make waves. Because they saw I'd do whatever it took to succeed. "I see so much potential in you." She sips her drink and sets the glass on the desk, sitting in her chair behind it.

"I appreciate that."

"I called your client yesterday, after you and Casey had been there. I wanted to know if the issue had been resolved."

"What did he say?"

"He said he was satisfied," she says gently.

Just satisfied?

I guess that's what happens when he has my fingerprints on a murder weapon. He has what he needs from me now, my trust, and he has no other use for me. Couldn't care if I was around or not. He's made that clear.

She taps her palm against the desk twice. "You know what? I'm going to contact Orrick and let him know you've appeased the client."

I raise my brows. "That would be great."

"Mhmm." She uses the desk to pull her chair close to it.

"He needn't worry about you, or my judge of character, any longer."

That's it. She lost trust in me, so Orrick lost trust in her. She still has to fight for his respect, even after coming up with his father. Being like a right-hand woman to Lawrence, if the rumblings are true. She's not used to having to appease someone who isn't already fond of her. Maybe that's where the noticeable friction comes from with them.

"Thank you, Ms. Locke."

"You keep working like you do, keep proving your loyalty to the company, and a new potential client will be sent your way soon."

"Thank you." I nod and leave the office, walking back to my desk and opening the residential sector database once more. I search the job order for Orrick Locke's home installation and open the file.

Extra security cameras on the exterior of the building.

An upgrade to the monitoring system software.

That's it. Nothing unusual.

Why would Cathrine herself have to be there, and what other reason did she have for wanting me to announce Orrick's arrival? Was she doing something sneaky? Was Casey involved? Was that why he wanted to shut it down when I brought it up?

I have to figure out how to approach it with him—but if he's Cathrine's most trusted technician, the one helping her—he'd never tell me, would he?

Maybe if he thought I already knew… but then I risk it getting back to Cathrine.

I look at the time. Quarter after four.

By the time I get back home to the apartment, Maggie's waiting with her purse by the door, and she looks nicer than usual.

"Sorry." I slide past her, giving her a double take. Something's different. "Are you wearing makeup? My makeup?"

"Yeah, I didn't think you'd mind me borrowing it."

"And that's my skirt."

"*Mom's* skirt." And it fits her better than it fits me. "See you."

"Back in an hour?" I ask as my phone vibrates.

I check it. A message from an unknown number. Tackman. *Come by at six.*

He remembered me.

But I can't. I can't bail on her when she has a meeting… but she looks more like she's going on a date.

No. Her health comes first. That's what all this is for. I can give her the benefit of the doubt.

"You remind me of my last parole officer," Maggie says with a smirk. "Yeah, in an hour. Bye, Andy!"

"Where are you going?" he calls from the couch, deep into his video game.

I text Tackman back. *Seven?*

"I told you, I have a meeting, but I'll be back soon."

If he wasn't in the middle of a game, he'd put up more of a protest, but he doesn't say anything, still focusing on the screen.

If Tackman says six, what will I do? Say no? Will he take that for an answer? He'll have to.

"Bye," she says, taking the chance to leave while Andy's preoccupied.

"Bye," I echo absentmindedly as another text message comes in, and she shuts the door behind her.

Six or nothing, he says.

My first urge is to stop Maggie.

I need to find that gun, and I need to get close to him for the keycard to the room and find a way to get in. If I go down for a murder I didn't commit, I won't be able to help Maggie and Andy at all.

I grab the door handle, but the way Maggie looked sitting at the kitchen table with the full bottle of whiskey in front of her... I stop. I can't put her through that. She needs support.

I tap the unknown number and press the phone to my ear as I walk to my bedroom and close the door behind me.

"What's so important that you can't come and see me?" The warmth returns to his tone that was missing yesterday before he left. Probably to see that Cami woman.

He wants the truth from me. He wants to trust me.

"My sister has to go to a meeting, and I have to watch my nephew." Just saying it aloud to someone feels odd, like a betrayal of my sister's trust, but he already knows my situation—understands it because of his brother, to a degree, I'd guess. "There's no one else who can."

"A meeting." It's not a question, so I don't answer. "Seven. Don't be late."

He ends the call, and I breathe a sigh of relief as I return to the living room with Andy, a surge of energy buzzing through me.

"Will you play with me?" Andy asks.

"I have time for one game, and then I need to make dinner." He smiles and taps the couch beside him. "How about classic Mario Kart?"

"Yeah!" He hands me a controller and sets up the game.

I want to ask him what he'd like to have for dinner and make whatever his heart desires, but groceries are getting low, always low, and all we have is soup, bread, baked beans, and condiments.

"Would you like beans and toast or soup and bread?"

"Umm, will you cut it in windows?"

He loves the simplest things, like cutting the toast into four squares he calls windows and eating each bean one at a time. It's what Tackman said he liked about me. That I enjoy the simple things in life. Maybe Andy gets that from me.

I smile and rub his hard-gelled hair until it comes loose a bit. He pushes me away, still smiling. "What? Who are you trying to impress?"

"No one," he groans.

"Why do you always do your hair?" I ask as the game starts. He's done it up with gel since he started school. "Did your mom teach you how?"

He nods.

"That's nice."

"Yeah, and she'd get too—too sick to do it sometimes, so I learned how to do it."

"You did." He'd learned how to do so many things for himself and was more capable than most teenagers around the house, all out of necessity.

"If I do it, she doesn't have to, and she can sleep and feel better."

"You were doing it so she didn't have to?"

He nods, and as we race our cars down the virtual track, my heart breaks for him.

So many things he did for himself that he's still doing, all to relieve the pressure on Maggie. He probably thinks if he doesn't take care of things himself, she'll get over-whelmed again. That she'll relapse and get sick, and he'll have to do it for himself anyway.

We have a lot in common, but I don't want those burdens on him. He's just a kid.

How much pain can I take away for him and how much will always remain, like scars, reminding him of his struggles with his mom?

"Do you want her to do your hair for you again? Would you like that?"

"No, she doesn't know how I like it anymore."

"Maybe you could teach her."

Although he doesn't respond, I know he's considering it. He's thoughtful about everything suggested to him, whether he likes it or not.

You're afraid to test the waters to see if you can trust her again.

Me too, buddy.

After dinner, Maggie comes back in and pours the rest of the beans in a bowl on their own from the saucepan on the stove. Andy sits with her while she eats, and I get ready to go to Tackman's. I brush my teeth, re-curl my hair, and add a little extra lipstick, a light pink I haven't worn since I was a teen, before I head for the door. "I'll be late," I call.

"Do you have a date?" Maggie asks.

191

"No. Business meeting with a client." And it's true, but to some extent, I put as much effort into preparing for him as I would a date.

I used to put my best foot forward and represent the company well—to be taken seriously.

Now, it's to play the part of a willing manager, eager to cater to her client's requests, capable of keeping his secrets.

When I pull up in his driveway, his red Camaro is the only one there. The house is dark, not a hint of light, and a whisper in my ears tells me something's wrong.

CHAPTER TWENTY-ONE

KEY CARD

I walk up the driveway, my heels clicking against the pavement the only sound in the darkness besides the rustling tree leaves in the wind, like a gentle spray of rain. I take a deep breath, easing my nerves away. I need to play this calm and cool like he does.

Did he forget I was coming? I check my cell phone. It's the right time. I'm five minutes early.

I knock on the door and wait, peeking in the windows as a flashback of the man in the tarp consumes me. I knock again and step back, checking my phone once again.

No messages from him. Should I call him?

I hit the unknown number I still haven't saved under his name, and I hear a light trill of a phone somewhere outside.

A muffled click precedes the sound of breathing by my ear. "Come around back." He ends the call, and I walk backward.

The backyard? What's he doing out there?

I round the side of the house, passing the slender floor-to-ceiling glass window at the end of the hallway to the bathroom, and as the pool comes into view, I remember Casey's words.

He wanted the camera on the pool uninstalled.

Each step forward I take is heavy; my feet are heavy, and my legs shake as the soft glow of gas lanterns illuminates the glass wall of the home by the kitchen. Tackman sits at the small table for two outside with a drink in front of him and one across from him with a pink lipstick stain on it.

Cami.

His face is sullen, and he wipes his hands over it as I approach, my heels clicking against the patio.

Is this a trick, or is it just him? Even if it is, don't let your guard down. Get the key card, get the gun.

He picks up his drink and takes a sip as I stop a few feet away, and as he sets it down, it slips from his hand, clunking against the table. He makes a hissing sound and shakes his head, staring up at me.

Is he drunk?

"What do you want?" he asks.

"I need to speak with you. May I?" I gesture to the white block seat beside him, and he nods. As we both look out over the pool, I take a deep breath. "After what happened the other night, I know you've got power over me. This whole thing seemed beyond my control, but what you said. That everything I need, I already have? It might be true."

"Oh yeah," he scoffs and leans back in his chair, taking me in. "How's that?"

"Maybe you were right. Maybe my morals are getting in the way, but there are certain things I can't—won't accept. You have control over me, reassurance you can trust me, but I want to be able to trust you."

He cranes his neck back. "You do?"

I push my hair over my shoulder, revealing my neck as he stares at me. "I want to know no one else is going to die."

He licks his lips and picks his glass up again. "I'd like that." He takes another sip, his lips lingering on the glass.

"Promise me."

He swallows hard and looks at me. "Is that what you came here for? That what you want?"

"Yes."

"Well damn, Josie. You sure grew a pair." *Josie.* No one ever calls me that. He leans back, gripping the glass with his fingers and spreading his legs apart a bit, revealing something white in his pocket next to me. It has to be the card. He shrugs, shaking his head. "It's not the nature of the business."

"The nature of my business is keeping you secure, but it's not in my nature to let people die."

He purses his lips and nods, pointing at me and squinting one eye. "That's right. I know that about you."

"You have your terms, and I have mine. Do we have a deal?"

He smacks his lips. "While you're working for me, you have my word."

I need a distraction. He's in a weakened state, and I need something to avert his attention while I go for the card.

"I see there's someone's drink here," I say. "But if you don't mind, I'll have what you're having—in my own glass."

He lets out a huff of laughter. "Didn't think you drank."

"I've seen a lot lately, nothing I can speak on, but I could use one. May I?"

I grab the bottle of tequila sitting in front of him, pop the cork, and take a swig. He smiles and watches, eyes open wide, as I take the lime wedge off his glass and bite into it, easing the unfamiliar burn from my tongue with the acidity.

"Josie, Josie." He smirks, and I smile too. I like the way he says it.

Is this what he wants? A drinking partner? Someone to keep him company now that Cami is gone? I take another swig from the bottle and hold it in my lap. "This is mine now," I whisper with a smirk.

He flashes a sexy smile at me, and I almost feel bad about what I'm about to do.

"So," I say, "you had company before me."

He waves me off. "Don't wanna talk about that."

"No? What do you want to talk about?"

We sit in silence, staring out at the pool and those wavy bright lines along the sides, against the back trees.

"Your sister had a meeting tonight?" He doesn't look at me, and instead, tips the rest of his tequila into his mouth and holds out his glass to me for more.

I hope she was at a meeting...

I pour the tequila into his glass. "I don't want to talk about that." I fill it past the halfway mark and take a sip of my own.

"Are you two close?"

"Yes and no. Sometimes we were; sometimes I tried so hard to be like her or relate to her, and she liked that. Most of the time, we fought like crazy. By the time we were adults, we didn't get to develop our relationship because of the drugs. What about your brother?"

"Very close. He was my younger brother." The way he says it, it means something more to him.

I nod. "My sister's older." It means something more to me too.

She was supposed to look out for me...

"I was supposed to protect him," he whispers. "That's what older brothers do." He takes a sip of his drink.

"I wouldn't know." I take a quick swig of my own, and it bites back the emptiness. The pain of not having anyone to protect me is overpowered by the alcohol for seconds.

"You live together now. You must be sorta close."

"Nope." And I can't. I won't. I'm always so close to losing her, and it hurts too much to let her in.

I take another swig, only remembering I have to drive after I swallow.

I think I've lulled him into a false sense of security well enough. It's almost time.

"You're angry with her." He leans in toward me. "You're soaked in it like I'm soaked in tequila right now."

I am, but I hate the thought of it.

"You keep being angry, you're going to have regrets." He takes another sip.

I shake my head and dangle the bottle over the side of my leg between us, swaying it back and forth, staring out at the pool. "I'm reminded every day about what she's done when I look at my nephew. How she's hurt us. All the time she was high. The times she O.D'd. The money I've spent, the bills I have, the debt I'm in. Of course I'm soaked in anger. I'm drowning. I can't see straight." Tears pool in my eyes, and he leans in closer. Close enough to reach for the card. As uncomfortable as it makes me, talking to him, it's working. He's distracted.

"Is she clean now?"

"For now," I mutter. "It's never for long."

"Then she's alive right now, and you're living with her, but you're not *living* with her. You have her, right now, clean and sober, and you have a chance to rebuild. To be with each other, just to *be*. I'd kill for that right now. I'd do anything."

I shake my head, tears spilling down my cheeks. "You don't understand what it's like…"

"I do. My brother O.D'd too. He stole from me. He promised me so many times it'd get better. That he'd be better. I was angry with him, but I also wanted to believe him, and we had our moments. Not enough, never enough, but those are what I hang on to. Those are all that matter." He reaches over through the short distance between us and rubs the edge of my hand holding the tequila bottle, down to my baby finger, and it's the perfect time to drop it, but I won't interrupt this moment—the way his skin feels on mine.

As he reaches the tip and lets his hand fall away, with tears in my eyes, I lean in, as if I'm going in for a kiss, and pull the card from his pocket at the same time I drop the bottle. It smashes against the patio, and I pull back, eyes wide open, and he stares at the ground between us as I shove the keycard in my pocket without him noticing.

"I'm so sorry," I choke out, wiping my cheeks.

He shakes his head, and I don't know if he's angry or not, but he stands and side-steps toward the house. "Don't move. I'll get that."

I stand up. "I got some on myself. Could I use the washroom to clean up?" I sniffle and follow him into the house. "I know where it is."

I walk down the hall and through the foyer, down the next hall, lean against the wall, and cover my face with my hands. The thought of Maggie relapsing. Dying. Without us ever making amends.

I have my sister, and I won't let her close. Do I have her at all?

I stifle my cries as I hear the glass door slide over again.

He's gone outside. This is my chance. Pull it together.

I clear my throat, wipe my face with my fingers, and creep back into the hallway. Through the window, I see him crouching by the broken glass with a dish towel in his hand, his back to me.

It has to be now.

I flash the keycard in front of the door, and it clicks. I take one last look outside and slip into the room.

CHAPTER TWENTY-TWO

WHITE ROOM

A man sits before me in the middle of the room where the table used to be, tied to a chair. The walls are bare. I take it all in as the door shuts behind me and turn around, reaching for the handle to get out.

"Mmm," he groans and tries to talk.

I whip around and press my finger to my mouth. If I open the door, and he's loud, I'll be caught.

The hostage stares back at me, rope in his mouth and his warm brown eyes wide. This is where he keeps the other hostage now. Maybe the other one tried to get out, and that's why they killed him. Maybe they moved this one here to stop him getting anywhere.

"Please be quiet," I whisper, "okay?"

He shakes his head and moans again.

I don't have much time.

I take a step toward him. "I can help you, but you have to be quiet so I can go."

He makes no sound, but his eyes are filled with fear.

The hostage who died—who was he to this man? Why are they here in the first place?

"If I take your gag out, you'll be quiet?"

He nods and I take it out. He gasps for breath, looking up at me desperately.

"Why are you here?" I whisper.

"They tricked us," he hisses, and I lean in to listen. "My brothers and me. They're bad men. You have to help me and my brother. He let one of us go, and he's keeping me and my brother—"

"Shh!" I creep back to the door and open it.

Tackman's still outside picking up glass. I have the urge to leave, but guilt keeps me in the room. I know what happened to his brother. His brother was murdered, and he could be next. I can't trust Tackman and his promises. I can't let another man die.

"I want to help you," I say.

"Oh, please! You have to tell somebody I'm here. Alexander Crass and Christopher Crass. I have a family, my wife—my children—I have to see them again."

"I'm going to do anything I can to get you out. If I do, you have to promise me something."

"Anything."

"You come to the police with me, and you tell them who did this to you."

More fear fills his eyes, and he doesn't speak.

"I have to go; you have to promise me."

"Yes," he hisses, "yes. You have to be careful. You're our only hope. My brother, have you seen him?"

In a tarp.

I swallow and shake my head.

"Please, miss."

I nod and put the gag back in his mouth, smelling a putrid sweat on him until I take steps back to the door. I peek out, and Tackman's not outside. He's nowhere in sight.

I glance back at the hostage, Alexander, and slip out the door. I walk back to the kitchen, outside and drop the key card in the bushes beside my chair before I sit.

Hopefully Tackman doesn't find it. He must have a spare once he realizes it's missing. When the time is right, I can use it. I need proof against Cathrine to make sure she doesn't come after me, and this is the proof I'll need to put Tackman and his men away.

He comes out the sliding door with a quizzical look. "Where were you?"

"I went to my car for…" No, he won't buy that. "I was going to leave."

He frowns.

"I never open up like that to anyone," I pick at my fingernails with my hands in my lap, "and I got scared."

He considers this, staring down at me, then reaches out for me. I let him, but he simply moves me to the side. "Don't step near the glass. I can't see it all. I'll have to clean it in the morning."

I nod and stand up, stepping aside as he walks toward the pool, and I follow him. He sits on one of the chaise lounge chairs, and I sit on the one opposite him. "We've been here before."

I nod. Despite having been grabbed and the gun action the day the hostage got loose, Tackman has a way of calming me.

Making me feel like while he's in control, and when he's around, I won't get hurt.

Maybe that's why I'm attracted to him, besides his good looks, he's a protector, or he wants to be. He tried to protect his brother, but he couldn't. He gets exactly how I feel about Maggie. Helpless.

The sadness in his eyes lingers as he stares out at the pool.

"It wasn't your fault," I whisper. "Your brother. You wanted to protect him, but we can't."

The words hit me as I say them. I know it, and yet I can't accept it.

"I didn't know how back then," he mutters, wiping his fingers over his lips.

"You're right. I have a chance with her, and I'm too scared to take it. I'm so scared to lose her, I can't appreciate that I have her." I let out a whooshing breath and rub at my tender bottom lids.

He stands, walks across the patio and takes a seat beside me, facing the pool with his back turned to me slightly. His woody cologne is heavier tonight. Because he was meeting Cami?

Maybe. But Cami came and left, and I'm the one here, sharing things with him—things I've never shared with anyone because he's felt the same. Feeling the warmth from his body close to me. Letting him see me cry.

"You ever learn something that could have changed everything if you'd just known it sooner?" he asks.

"I just did," I sway toward him enough for my arm to brush against his back, "tonight, with you."

He leans back against me, close—too close.

I stand, putting distance between us as quickly as I can. "I should go."

I'm close enough with the enemy now. Anything more is... What is it?

He turns to me, stares up at me, and his eyes ask me not to go.

It's dangerous. That's what it is.

Anything more is dangerous.

"Thank you for seeing me," I say. "And sorry about the bottle."

He shakes his head without a word, and I turn away slowly, then walk around the side of the house.

There's a hostage in the white room, and I was cozying up to the man holding him there.

The man who murdered the hostage's brother, or ordered it, or consented to it.

The only thing getting me up and out of there was that fact.

Danger.

But it's what brought me closer to him tonight in the first place. Danger of a different kind—intimate —vulnerable.

Confused, my chest fluttering, I drive home with all the windows down and the breeze flying through my hair, eager to talk to Maggie—really talk to her—and open myself up to the hurt for the chance to share something beautiful. For the chance to put aside anger, hope, fear, and the future, and be present with her and Andy.

The only things that matter.

CHAPTER TWENTY-THREE

BREAK

After work, I picked up a tub of ice cream from the grocery store. I figured Andy could use a treat, and Maggie and I could sit down and eat some on our own while we talk. I'll tell her how much I want to rebuild our relationship, and how proud I am that she's on the right track, because like Tackman said, I have that chance.

I won't let it slip by.

All day at work, I tried to devise a plan to approach Casey about what he might have on Cathrine, but I'm out of my depth. What could make a loyal employee of ten years want to betray their employer?

The only person I can think of who might have some knowledge is gone to Vancouver, but there is one person she put me in contact with before she left. I'll pay Billy a visit tonight after dinner and hope that he's at work.

I get in, and Maggie's wearing one of our mom's only dresses, a pink and blue floral print. She looks more like mom than ever, and it brings up emotions I've stuffed down with the anger and pain I've felt.

Mom wore that dress during good times, mostly. Family events. Holidays. We still had some of those before they passed, but I never think about them because I'm too angry at them for leaving us.

Maggie hasn't left—not yet. Not this time.

"You look nice," I tell her, and she smiles, the last of the golden sunlight kissing her cheek as she pulls on oven mitts. "You made dinner?"

"I baked some cookies for you guys."

"Chocolate chip!" Andy calls from their room.

"Well," I pull the ice cream from my bag. "Maybe we can make ice cream sandwiches tonight!"

"Yes!" Andy runs into the kitchen chanting "yes" over and over.

"Well, you guys can, because I need to go out for a while."

"Mom," Andy groans.

"Hey, you'll still have your treat with Jo."

He stomps back into the living room and buries his head in the couch for dramatic effect.

"Where are you going?" I ask.

She avoids eye contact as she pulls the tray of cookies from the oven. "I have a date."

"You do?" Don't get angry. Don't get judgmental. She's doing okay; she's healthy; she can make her own decisions. "Well, what time will you be back?"

"I don't know. Does it matter?"

I put the ice cream in the freezer. "I have to go out tonight."

"Oh, well, do you think you could cancel?"

"Why wouldn't you have asked me to watch Andy instead of assuming I can?"

"It was a last-minute thing." She pushes her curled hair from her face and takes off the mitts. "I didn't think you'd mind. You love hanging out with Andy."

"Of course I do." I take a step closer and lower my voice. "I also love when you don't just assume I'll do something for you and actually ask first."

I'm not proud of the edge to my tone, but going out for me is a means of actual escape, and this date might be something like that for her too.

"Okay," she sighs, "well, this is important to me, so can we compromise, and I'll be home when you need me to?"

I rub my brow, considering it, and she rolls her eyes. "What?"

"You expect me to just stay all locked up in here and not have my own life."

I shake my head. "I just expect you to ask me when you need my help instead of just expect you'll get it." This is getting so far off track, but I can't keep getting used like this so she doesn't have to take any responsibility for her life. This isn't a conversation to have right now, when I wanted us to get closer. This will rip us apart if I let it. "Listen, I need to leave by ten."

She frowns. "What are you doing at ten?"

"None of your business."

"So, you get to know mine, but I don't get to know what's going on with you? I've been worried about you. You've been stressed lately, and I know the bills are bad, and you have a lot on your shoulders, but you can talk to me about it. I hate when you shut me out." She leans against the counter and sighs. "You always shut me out."

"I wanted us to talk tonight. I want to be more open with you about things."

She raises her brow but refuses to look at me. She doesn't believe it.

"I want you to be happy, Maggie. I want you to feel like you can talk to me, and I want to be able to talk to you. Go on your date, be back by ten, and we'll talk tomorrow night?"

"Fine," she whispers, rounding the counter and disappearing into their room.

———

I PULL through the drive-through of the Yellow Dip, and the same young girl is in the window, handing me my order of chicken nuggets. Maggie can re-heat them tomorrow for Andy.

"Is Billy here?"

She shakes her head. "He doesn't work here anymore."

My heart sinks. "What? Since when?"

But I already know. Since Katie brought me here. He doesn't want to be found by Locke Industries—or us.

"About a week ago," she says. "You know him?"

I need to get his information. If it was less than a week ago when we saw him, he'll still have a paycheck coming.

"Yeah, he said he was coming to get his paycheck stub and that we'd hang out after. Can I pick it up for him?"

"We mailed it out to him." She leans out from the window, checking out the long line of cars behind me.

"Well, if you have anything else here of his, could I get it to take to him? Save him a trip back here."

Anything might help, even if it doesn't have his address on it.

"Calvin," she calls over her shoulder, "you got anything of Billy's back there?"

"Huh?" a man shouts.

"Could you please pull over into that spot, ma'am?" she asks, pointing to the lot. "If there's anything, Calvin'll bring it to ya."

"Thank you." I pull out of the line and into the spot, hoping he comes out with something.

A young man jogs out and stops at my window, his hands empty. "You the lady who's picking up Billy's things?"

I nod.

"Only thing he left was a t-shirt cause it gets hot in the back sometimes, but our manager threw it out. She didn't think Billy would be back for it."

"Ah, okay."

"Yeah," he rubs at his neck, "she's a real bitch. It was his favourite shirt. He shouldn'ta left it. I think he knew he wasn't coming back."

"You were here that night?"

"No, but Billy's my friend, well, work friend, and we game online together every night."

"Oh, yeah, us too! Man, it's been a while. What's his online name again?"

He chuckles. "Nighthawk38. His corny ass thought it was cool when he first told me."

I smile. "What do you guys play?"

209

"World of Wanderers."

"Nice. Any others?"

"Nah, just that one. I gotta get back in." He shuffles away, breaking into a jog as he nears the front door.

Thank you, Calvin.

CHAPTER TWENTY-FOUR

NIGHTHAWK38

When I get home, Maggie and Andy are in bed, and I plug in the new headset I just bought and key in my new, prepaid credit card for online gaming. I used the last of my paycheck from the week on the headset and card on the way home, and now the video game, hoping we can scrape by on nothing until the next pay at double the amount to make up for it.

Maybe I can return the headset after this.

I log onto the game and navigate to the friend's icon at the top and tap it. Then I enter Nighthawk38 into the blank field, but before I tap "ok," I stop.

I'm under an anonymous username right now. I need to change it to something he'll accept the request from.

Katie? No, it could be any Katie.

Maybe if I use her last name.

But even then, he left the Yellow Dip because she approached him there.

Calvin. He's the one he wants to play with.

Maybe he'll think Calvin updated his system or changed his username.

It's my best bet.

He thought Nighthawk38 was corny, and Billy knew it, so his name would be something simple, maybe?

Calvin2.0.

I change my username and then tap the friend's icon, type in his username, and click "ok."

If they play every night, he should accept it soon, and I need to be here when he does so I don't lose the chance. I cross my legs and lean forward, trying to get comfortable.

A notification comes up.

Nighthawk38 friend request accepted. Connect now.

I click the button, and he's already typing something.

Nighthawk38: New name, who dis?

Do I pretend I'm Calvin? No. I'll lose his trust. It has to be smart. Something he won't shut down. He seemed to have an affinity for Katie, that they used to be close, or he wouldn't have spoken to us at all. He tried to warn me.

Calvin2.0: *It's Katie's friend from the parking lot. It's happening to me. I need your help.*

I wait, but no bubbles pop up. I could have already lost him. I need his help, but what does he need? Safety? I can't promise him that.

Calvin 2.0: *Do you want revenge?*

Nighthawk38: *No one can win at their game.*

It's as if he knows I'm trying to blackmail them. Maybe he did too. Maybe he tried to report them to the police, and it didn't work. But revenge got him talking. He wants it.

Calvin 2.0: *I don't want to turn them in. I want to turn them on each other.*

I didn't realize it until I typed it, but it's my way out.

Something is going on between Cathrine and Orrick, and if I can use it to threaten her that I'll take the information to Orrick, if it's big enough, she'll make sure I can leave unscathed to protect herself.

Nighthawk38: *How?*

Now he's interested.

Calvin 2.0: *I need something on Casey.*

Nighhawk38: *Where we met. Across the street. Go now. Nighthawk38 has logged off.*

I FIND Billy in a dark alleyway, and he whistles to get my attention. I hesitate before following him into the darkness, stopping beneath a fire escape.

"You realize this could go horribly wrong," he says in his high-pitched voice.

"I'm ready to do whatever is necessary to get out. I can't stand by when people are murdered, drugs are sold, and my whole life is threatened. I'm already in danger. I need to get out."

"Okay, okay." He checks both ends of the alley before speaking again. "I'm telling you this, and I'm leaving. Like Katie."

"So, you know she went to Vancouver?"

He looks at me dead in the eyes. "She didn't go to Vancouver. She told them that, but she's in hiding."

It makes sense. How and why John would have

213

suddenly proposed, and she'd decide to move *that day* has eluded me. "She wanted to help you. She risked a lot leaving that note."

It wasn't enough, but maybe that doesn't matter. Maybe she really did her best for me.

"How do you know? Are you in touch? Is she okay?"

"Can't talk about it." He glances over her shoulder. "Don't have much time."

"What do you know?"

"I know you have access to something I could never figure out. Why Orrick Locke's father, Lawrence, left his son the company when it should have gone equally to all board members, including his son."

"How do I figure that out, and how does it help me?"

"Cathrine's been furious since Orrick took ownership of the company because his dad was the head of the snake, but Cathrine was the neck. She'd turn it however she wanted it to go. Now she's without that power, and she wants it back."

"How does this help me? It's Cathrine I want information on."

"You could blackmail Cathrine, *or* you could offer her information she'd never get any other way."

Help Cathrine gain even more power? She could be worse than Orrick himself for all I know.

"What information?"

"I was Mathison's assistant, and there were rumblings when I first started that Cathrine was blindsided when Orrick became the CEO. A lot of people said it didn't make sense, why she would think the son Lawrence adored wouldn't have the family business passed down to him, and it kind of got forgotten—by everyone but Cathrine, except..." He looks both ways again. "Mathison was surprised too. He was sure the ownership shares were supposed to be divided equally between Orrick and Cathrine, with Orrick as the official CEO, but Cathrine guiding Orrick with all her years of experience. I think she had a side deal with Mathison when she still thought she'd be equal owner, that if he voted with her on any issues the board needed to accept or pass on, she'd give him more power. That's how sure she was she'd be getting it. When she didn't, she never spoke to Lawrence again, and he passed away a few years later."

"But it's all just a rumor."

"Mathison seemed to think Orrick forged the signatures on a new document that gave him all the power, angry that his father would think he'd need the help of Cathrine. That because no one ever confronted or questioned Lawrence on his decision; he never knew what Orrick had done to hold the most power."

"So, the only proof would be in finding the old document. The original way Lawrence had intended it to be..."

"And using it as leverage on Cathrine to get out."

"What about getting even? I thought that's why you were in?"

He shakes his head. "There's no getting even with this company. It's never been done before, and you're not in the position to do it now. Buy yourself a way out and get far away from here. It's the only way."

"Why didn't you or Katie do this?"

He shakes his head. "Katie never had access to

anything like that, and I was like you—clearance for the board members only—not Orrick's documents."

"So how am I supposed to find it if you couldn't?"

"I had no reason to. Giving Cathrine more power made no sense to me, and it was just a rumor. I was already ruined. You can gain clearance to his documents with his assistant's password."

I frown. "How am I supposed to get that, and why would he keep a copy of the original? That's ridiculous."

"He wouldn't have. Lawrence would. His files are only accessible at that highest clearance level, and if they're anywhere, it would have gone by the legal department. Even if they later received the final copy from Orrick, the original would be in their system."

"But what if Orrick found them and deleted them? Covered his tracks?"

"They couldn't be permanently deleted from the system. It was created with a backup where they keep all the clients' files. Videos."

"So, they keep everything…" All the times Cathrine promised the client they didn't before they signed the contract. Why am I surprised? They have footage from Tackman's, then. My stomach drops, knowing I lied to him.

"Everything."

"Okay, but to get the password… I barely know his assistant. I can't get close enough to her."

"It's not hers you need, whoever she is. It's his old assistant."

"Tom something or other?"

"Lawrence's *original assistant* has access. It's the reason you're in the best position to retrieve the information."

"Who's that?"

"Fern Bishop."

My breath catches in my throat. The proof to give Cathrine the power she needs could have been under her nose the whole time?

"Wouldn't she have checked?"

"Nothing's guaranteed here. I'm giving you your best chance, because after tonight, I'm gone, and you're on your own."

I've always been on my own. But this time, that doesn't feel true.

They've been helping me the best they could—the best I've let them.

"Thank you," I tell him.

He nods and sidesteps down the alley the other way, leaving me in the dark, with a small light of hope within.

CHAPTER TWENTY-FIVE

FERN

W hen I said goodbye to Maggie and Andy this morning, I told my sister we'd talk when I got home, and through the whole day I dreaded being honest with her.

Will she relapse? Will the honesty be too much to take? Will she blame things on me? Can I really put my anger aside? Can I trust her? Has she changed?

Five in the afternoon rolls around, and I stay at my desk, filing. I've been waiting for the right moment to get into the waiting room, to use Fern's computer, but she almost never leaves it alone. Only when she's going over things with Cathrine every night at five.

She's usually with her for the time it takes to finish a drink, but she's been quicker and slower, depending on the day. I know by five o'clock, they'll both be in that room, which is perfect.

I walk down the hallway, past the women's bathroom, into the men's, and check that no one's there before locking it behind me. I grab a roll of toilet paper and toss it in the garbage bin. I grab another straight from the roll in the stall and use one of Cathrine's lighters I swiped to set it on fire. I toss it in the bin with the other and grab it, stepping up on the toilet seat.

The bin grows ever warmer in my hands, and I raise it high above my head, surrounding the fire detector. The flames burn bright, and my hands feel like they're touching a mug of boiling water as the fire alarm goes off.

I've got less than thirty seconds now.

I toss the remnants of the toilet paper rolls into the toilet bowl and flush them down. No trace of the start of a real fire will be found here. I'm going for a system issue. I rinse the bin out and put it back, unlocking the room and filing out of the men's washroom toward the stairs into the small crowds where everyone's whispering on their way to the stairwell, the designated exit during fire drills.

No one seems to notice me, as usual, and it's the first time it's paid off.

I stand by my desk and peer down the hallway as Cathrine exits the office with her briefcase in hand, and Fern, with her purse tucked under her arm, follows behind her, toward the stairwell.

"I don't have time for a fire," Cathrine says, her protests fading down the hallway as Fern pushes her through, and I stride down the hallway and slip in through the glass door before it closes.

The camera from the hallway might have seen me come in, but with no cameras in the waiting room or office, I'll just need a cover for why I came in here in case the video needs to be checked.

To check on you, Cathrine. Make sure you got out

okay. And then I saw the picture of the cats on your desk, Fern, and I had to grab it.

I sit on Fern's warm seat behind the computer screen and set her framed cat picture in my lap. The screen asks for a password as I shake the mouse.

She logged out before she left.

Panic sets in, vibrating through my body into shakes.

I've underestimated her ability to protect the company's assets.

At least the video footage outside in the hallway will corroborate my story.

I stand from behind the desk, push the button to open the glass door and walk toward it on shaky legs as Cathrine strides back in.

"Josephine?" She cranes her neck back, stopping a few feet shy of Fern's desk. "What are you doing in here?"

"I came to make sure you both were out, and I saw this picture," I hold up the frame, "and you know how much Fern loves them. It's an original. I wanted to make sure it didn't get destroyed."

She frowns at me, like she's considering whether to believe me, but I can't give her the chance to doubt.

"Ms. Locke, why are *you* back in here? We need to go." I usher her back toward the door. "See, this is why I came in. I knew even a fire couldn't pry you away from your work."

She walks out the door, and it closes behind us as we walk down the hallway. "You know just as well as I do, this is a drill. There's no fire. There's never been a fire here. And everyone should have this work ethic. Come hell or fire or whatever, everyone should be working until it's a real threat."

I enter the stairwell with her, mumbling something about being cautious as Fern climbs back up the steps.

"Where did you go?" she asks Cathrine and frowns at me.

"I was trying to get my purse. My cigarettes are in there, and if we're outside, I might as well use the smoke break."

"And you?" Fern asks me.

I hand her the picture frame, and she stares at it blankly before a tiny grin greets her lips. She doesn't look back at me, but instead turns around, and we descend the stairs together, clickety clack, all the way down until we're outside.

"Cathrine!" Mathison calls to her, and she parts ways from us.

"You know what this Saturday is, don't you?" Fern looks up at me.

"The fiftieth anniversary party." That came up fast.

The big celebration everyone's been looking forward to. I don't do well at social gatherings, but it was even a big deal to me before everything happened. Orrick and Iris Locke will host the party at their home on Saturday, and everyone from the company is invited.

She nods. "I've given this company fifty years of my life." She rests her hand on her hip and tucks the picture frame back in her purse. "It might be time for me to exit gracefully, but..."

"But?"

"I can't bear to leave Cathrine this way."

"What way?"

"So far from her dreams." And the key to reaching those dreams of hers could be on your computer. I wish I could tell her so she could get it for me, but then I'd have no leverage. "A lot has changed for women since I started here, and a lot has stayed the same, but I haven't." She presses her lips together and nods. "I think I'm done."

"Wow," I huff.

"That's between you and me. I won't be telling anyone until I'm good and ready to give my two weeks' notice, but, mind you, it'll come sooner than later. I think after the party, I'll tell Cathrine. It's time for me to enjoy what's left of my life with the only ones who truly love me." She gives me a smirk. "My cats." As she walks off in Cathrine's direction before I can say anything, I still haven't figured her out, but more importantly, I don't know she knows what I was doing up there either.

Before the party. I have to get the information from Fern's computer in two days.

I'll have to find the gun in two days too.

Everything has to be cleared up for my escape. Everything including what's left of my life with the only ones who truly love *me*.

CHAPTER TWENTY-SIX

SO CLOSE

I f things are going to be different this time with Maggie, we have to do something different. I'm only in control of myself, my thoughts, my behaviours. I repeat that in my head as I walk down the hallway to my apartment.

I have to bring back the part of me that can be vulnerable with her again. Something we haven't had since we were children.

I open the door, and all is still. Kitchen. Couch empty.

"Hellooo?"

No answer.

I set my purse on the kitchen table and saunter to the bedroom. On the way, I poke my head into the bathroom. Bedroom empty too. I parked right beside her car.

Could they be out for a walk? Somewhere else in the building?

Laundry. It's laundry day.

Despite my nervous energy surrounding the talk, now that she isn't here when I'm ready, I just want to get it over with. I walk back to the front door, checking to make sure there's no note on the table, and grab my key from my purse, locking the door behind me. I turn left toward the elevator and the laundry room on our floor.

A door opens behind me, and Don steps out of his apartment with his pup on a leash. I nod hello as jittery nerves envelop me, and I can't make it to the laundry room fast enough. I leave them behind at the elevator and step into the laundry room, where a few machines clunk and whoosh, echoing through the empty room.

I walk back out, and Don glances at me as the elevator door grumbles open.

"You haven't seen my sister and nephew, have you?"

"Yeah," he says, "the last time I took Sandy out, they were leaving with a man."

"A man?" Maggie's date. She's introduced him to Andy already? Even as a friend, that's so careless. What is she thinking?

"Yeah, tall fella."

The breath deflates from my lungs. "Tall?" I choke out. Something doesn't sit right.

Carver? No.

"Was he blond? Shaggy haircut?"

He nods, stepping into the elevator.

How?

"Did she get in a black truck with him?"

"Oh, I can't say. I was coming up as they were making their way down."

"Did they look distressed? Scared?"

He shrugs as the elevator door closes over, and I race back to my apartment, unlock the door and rush to the table, grabbing my phone. I dial Maggie's number, and it goes straight to voicemail.

I could be wrong. It could be someone else. But all the hairs on my arms are up.

They know. They know I went into the room and saw the hostage. I break into cold sweats, clutching my cell phone, my heart in my throat.

Tackman threatened this. He said if I didn't mind my business and keep his secrets, he knew where I lived, with my family.

My phone vibrates in my hand.

Tackman's number, still unassigned to a name in my phone. I answer, pressing it to my ear, my heart thudding fast and heavy.

"I'm texting you an address," he says in a cold, removed tone. "Meet me there."

"My family," I blurt out. I could be wrong. I want to be wrong. I can't give myself up. If he didn't know, he'd have no reason to hurt them.

"They're with me."

"Why?" I blurt out, covering my mouth with my hand.

I have to think first before I speak. These are killers.

"Meet me at the address. Right now. Come alone."

"Please," I whisper, but he's already hung up.

I grab my purse and run out the door without locking it behind me, take six flights of stairs two by two, and practically stumble out the door. I get in my car and add the address to the GPS on my phone.

It's a building I don't recognize in the rough side of New Gilford. A bad part of town. Is the building shut down? Did he take them to an abandoned building?

I wish I'd found the gun by now. That I had any other way of protecting myself.

They'll kill a man, but would they hurt a woman? A child?

The broken glass with pink lipstick in the kitchen flashes through my memory as I drive out of the lot in the direction my GPS points me.

The bloody, tattooed arm from beneath the tarp.

How does Tackman know what I've done?

His key card. He knew it was missing, and he did something. He checked and found out somehow.

After almost half an hour of driving, I turn onto the street, guided by my GPS, and pass a large field with a rundown playground full of children playing on it, and I tear up.

Andy. He's got to be so scared. He doesn't deserve this.

I've done this to him. He's in danger because of me.

I pass the park and pull into the lot of the brick building down the road with no sign out front, but a red Camaro by the backlot. I park and jump out of the car with my keys in hand, scanning the lot for anyone.

The front door to the building by the road opens, and Tackman steps out in dark jeans and a black t-shirt, staring at me. The doors close behind him, and he stops, waiting for me. I can barely breathe as I rush across the lot, stopping just out of arm's reach.

I should have let someone know where I am—but I have no one.

Maggie and Andy. They're all I have. I can't let anything happen to them.

"Where are they?" I blurt out, tears clouding my vision as I turn from him to the building.

"Walk with me." He strides in front of the building on the dirty boulevard by the street I just drove in from.

Is he going to push me in front of a car? Will Danes or Carver drive by and abduct me?

I walk behind him slowly, my heart thudding in my ears, scanning the area for cars as we approach the corner of the building. He turns the corner and walks around to the other side of the building lined with a few dumpsters and stops in front of a metal door.

The distant laughter of children in the park could fade as we walk through that door, and the screams of my sister and nephew could replace them—unless they've been gagged like Alexander in the white room.

I picture them like that, stopping several feet away from Tackman.

He faces me, his calm demeanor taunting me.

"Where are they?" I can't conceal the edge to my voice anymore.

"I did some thinking after last night." He shoves his hands in his jean pockets. "After you opened up to me."

I look past him at the metal door.

Once we go inside the building, I might not come out alive.

Over my shoulder, all the women watch their children from benches and picnic tables. The urge to scream for help overcomes me.

"Don't," he says, and I turn back to his intense gaze. He's read my mind, and if I'm not careful, he'll hypnotize me into letting my guard down like he has before. "Listen to me carefully. You opened up to me, and I know that was difficult for you. It was for me too. Being vulnerable has certain drawbacks, doesn't it?"

I stare up at him, tears sliding down my cheeks.

"Don't move," he says in a soft, low tone, his gravely timbre warm once more. " Just stay with me...but turn around."

I inhale a deep, shuddering breath and turn around, muffling my cries with my hand over my mouth, pressing my fingers against my lips. What's going to happen to me?

He steps up behind me, and I feel the warm shield of his body as he extends his arm by my side and points over my shoulder at the park.

I follow his finger and see my sister first, laughing and talking with a few other women by an old, rundown picnic table. Then I hear it. Andy's laughter. He's one of the children running across the field with a kite in his hands.

They're safe. Happy.

My chest heaves as I turn back to him and sputter, "I don't understand."

"I know you're struggling—that your sister is struggling—so I wanted to bring her to a group I work closely with. Recovering addicts who are mothers, mothers of addicts here and gone, supporting each other. It's a weekly meeting."

I shake my head, and he stops. "What?" Is this really why he called me here? "Why didn't you tell me about it? Why would you scare me?" This doesn't feel right. "No, they wouldn't have just gone with Carver."

"Speak of the devil," Tackman says, and Carver walks

from the broken chain-link fence around the field by the road toward us.

He was watching them, my sister and Andy. He waves to Maggie, and she waves back with a smile.

As he gets closer, an anger burns from within.

She wouldn't go somewhere with a stranger. Not even if they said they knew me.

Carver is the new man she's dating.

They've set this whole thing up, and Maggie has no idea who this man is because I've been lying to her. Because I haven't listened to her.

"How could you?" I shout as Carver reaches us, glancing at Tackman before stopping before me. "You're pretending to like her?" I spit. "Set it up so she thinks you met by chance, but really, you were spying on me? Keeping tabs on me. Getting closer to her to *use her*." And hurt me.

Carver shakes his head, but Tackman holds his hand up. "Carver already knew your sister."

"What? How?" The world is spinning before me, feeling like it's about to close in.

"Maggie came into my life on New Year's Day." Carver's chest heaves.

I hate how he says her name. She's *my sister*. "She's not your pawn!"

How? How could they know each other? What do they have in common, living almost an hour away?

Drugs. She O.D'd for the last time around New Years.

"Were you her dealer?" I hiss, my whole body shaking, searching for any small movement in his face as confirmation. That stupid thing he does, fussing with his hair when he's nervous or guilty.

Tackman steps between us. "I didn't know she was your sister until Cathrine assigned you to the contract and I did a background check."

I hold up my hand to him and turn to Carver. "Were you her dealer?"

If he says yes, I'll attack him right here for what he did to her.

If he says no, how can I believe him?

"I wasn't her dealer," Carver huffs, already tired of defending himself, but we've just gotten started.

I shake my head in disbelief, and Tackman steps between us again, blocking my view of Carver.

"What is this?" I shout, stepping back so I can see them both. "Why are you doing this? How *dare you* use my sister when I've done nothing—" My words get stuck in my throat, and I heave, trying to catch my breath as tears burn my cheeks. "Haven't you done enough? Don't you already have enough on me?"

Carver shakes his head. "We aren't using your sister. You are. You use her as a crutch, an excuse for why you don't have what you want in life—"

"Enough." Tackman turns to him. "Carver, you can go. Wait for them and take them back home."

"No." I step toward him, but Carver's already walking toward the field again and doesn't turn back. I turn to Tackman. "*I'm* taking them home."

Tackman runs his fingers over his beard, and his chest heaves as he stares down at me. "I brought you here because I wanted to help you. Not scare you."

"How does he know her?" I shift my weight from foot to foot, my toes digging further into the tips of my heels, but I feel no pain—or all of it—and it doesn't matter. "Tell me right now."

"The last time your sister O.D.'d, he's the one who brought her to the hospital."

I scoff. "What?"

"Her on-again, off-again boyfriend, baby daddy, whatever he is, he left her, and Carver came across her while we were doing our rounds and took her to the hospital."

"Rounds?" I scoff, trying to keep all the new information at bay because the timelines are lining up, and it's all possible, but it still doesn't make sense. I can't accept that it was a coincidence. Not with these men.

"We bring warm clothes to the homeless and less fortunate in the winter, and that's when he found her."

I give him a dirty look. "You're drug and arms dealers, murderers, and you want me to believe you do charity work during the day?"

He shakes his head and rubs his hands over his chin. "I'm not a good guy. I do what I can for my community. And you can believe what you want."

"What's the point in helping your community if you hurt them too?"

"I protect them."

"From what?"

"Sometimes each other. Sometimes from outsiders, gangs, new dealers wanting to claim this as their territory. Sometimes from themselves. After my brother passed away, I wanted to do something that honours him. I want to protect my community in a way I could never help him.

That's why I started that group with my mother, for my mother, after Nico died." He nods to the park, and I turn, watching Andy show Maggie something on his kite.

I turn back to him, and his eyes are glossy with tears.

Nico. His brother.

So, what, Tackman's this bad guy who has a heart? He's a killer with a conscience? He can threaten people, hold them hostage in his house, have them killed, and then run a community group? Hand out warm clothes to the homeless? Rescue women who've overdosed?

"And now," he takes a step closer to me, "I want to help *you*."

The wood and citrus fragrance washes over me, and I remember our night by the pool. The tequila. How we opened up to each other.

And the man in the white room, tied up, scared for his life.

Tackman decides who he wants to hurt and who he wants to help.

Who he wants to release the true, primal wolf in him to, and who he can be a sweet puppy for.

"Why me?" I spit. Why am I both of those kinds of people to him?

He just stares down at me, his eyes searching mine.

"Leave my sister and nephew alone." I turn back to the park.

"Josie." The way he says my name, like he knows me well, like he's desperate for me, makes me want to step back, into his arms.

"What?" I ask with my back still to him.

"Your debt to the rehab facility has been paid."

232

My jaw goes slack, and I twist around, staring at him, wide-eyed. "Is this a joke? Are you playing games with me again?"

He shakes his head. "You can check. It's all paid off."

I believe him, but, "Why?"

"Because I can." He lifts his chin, and the golden light of the sunset screens his skin a golden brown.

Standing there like a hero, like I asked for a handout, when he's a cold-blooded killer.

"I told you from the start," I clench my jaw, "I don't want your money."

"Well, it's done." He shrugs and smiles at me with his eyes.

The anger boils inside me for the debt I wasn't able to handle on my own. For the way they've inserted themselves into my life, my business. For the way he pretends to care, but really, he's buying my silence. Why? He has the gun with my prints.

He's half the cause of all my troubles. He's the bad guy.

And if he's not—I don't know who he is at all—and that scares me.

I need to know.

"Who killed that man?" My chin quivers as the breeze sweeps my hair across my face. From beneath it, I watch him press his lips together and stare past me, to the park.

I push the hair from my face, and he's staring at me, his eyes finding mine and burning through me. "Who killed that man in your house?" I raise my voice, and he grabs my arms, tucking them into his chest, still looking past me.

I weep in his arms, so scared of the answer, but I need

to know. There's a chance it wasn't him. There's a chance I could believe in him. Trust him. "Who killed the man in the tarp—"

"I did," he says, his voice soft, his face hard.

I push away from him and step back, shocked at his admittance.

He's no safe place.

He's a wolf in wolves' clothing, and I've been looking for a sheep like an idiot since that night at the pool.

"Your good deeds can't save you," I mutter as I walk past him and march away, back to my car, and as soon as I jump in and slam the door behind me, I burst into tears.

He paid that debt, I know it, and the relief washes over me in heavy waves of guilt, and shame, and disbelief.

It's not my burden anymore. But I didn't pay for it.

The debt collectors will stop calling. But because of a killer with ulterior motives.

And the realization of Carver's words washes over me.

Who am I, if not a martyr? Who am I now without that burden of debt, twisting me into the person I've become? The woman I can barely stand to be.

Carver saved Maggie? Because of *him,* I have a chance with her? How is this possible? And they knew about that connection. They've known since the beginning.

What would they have done if I'd told the police about the drugs and guns?

About the body.

I can't trust them, but the swirling emotions inside me are a nameless confusion, a battle within myself to understand and accept what's happened.

And what do I do now?

CHAPTER TWENTY-SEVEN

WHAT YOU DESERVE

When Andy bursts through the door, I stand from the kitchen table. He runs into my arms for a big hug and smiles up at me. "I flew a kite today!"

"That's great." I rub his back before he lets me go and grabs a drink from the fridge.

"Sorry I'm a bit late. I went to a meeting."

I nod.

"No really, I did." She pushes her curly hair from her face.

"I believe you." I smile and nod again as she studies my face.

I've decided I won't tell her what I know. That I can't tell her anything that's been going on, but we can talk about us. I don't want secrets between us and people, dangerous people, weaseling their way between us, into our family's life. She needs to feel like she can be open with me, and I have to do the same.

Thinking something could have happened to them today pushed me over the edge.

She sets her purse down, and I approach her with open arms, hugging her. She hugs me back and lets out a gentle laugh.

"We haven't done this since... I don't know when," she whispers.

I pull away with an awkward grin. "And I'm sorry for that."

"Andy," she turns to him, "would you go work on your kite in our room until dinner?"

"I'm making a kite!" he says, waiting for my reaction.

"Awesome, Andy. You learned how to make a kite?"

"Nope. I'm teaching myself." He wanders back toward their room.

"I'll help later," Maggie calls.

After he disappears into the room, we sit opposite each other at the round kitchen table. My nerves are shot from the afternoon, and the calm of being debt-free has already changed the way I live.

No debt collectors calling. No worries about my next paycheck being swallowed whole by a debt payment.

And a future, unburdened by the past, that I can't even picture yet—that I don't want to picture without having Maggie to dream it up with me—right there within reach.

"So," she says, her finger tracing the knots in the wood of the tabletop. "You wanted to talk."

"I wanted to apologize."

She frowns but lets me continue.

"Since you've been back, better, I've been very controlling. Judgmental."

"Angry," she says, and I nod. "And you have every right to be."

I sigh. "But I don't want to be."

She folds her hands on the table in front of her with a small smile. "I want to build back your trust. It's very… difficult with a past like mine."

"I want to understand you better, take the time to listen."

"I'd appreciate that." Tears pool in her eyes, and she lets out a self-soothing, whooshing breath. "I really think this time's different."

"Why?"

She runs her fingers through her hair and cocks her head to the side, taking a deep breath. "Last time, I came the closest to death. Before, I was only thinking of myself and my pain, but after, in the hospital, I thought about Andy. What would have happened… if…" She wipes her eyes and clears her throat. "I don't want that for him. I haven't always been good for him, and when I see the pain I've caused him, the bad things that seem to stick, it hurts like hell, but next time… I don't think I'll make it." She sniffles and releases a loud sigh, holding her face in her hands.

I stand, rounding the table, and sit beside her, grabbing her hand. "I want to be more open and honest with you, and I want to let you know that's part of the reason I am the way I am with you. It's like I'm protecting myself from disappointment—devastation."

"I get that," she says in a shaky voice, "but I need you, Joey." She breaks down, and I hug her, rubbing her shoulders as she weeps gently into my neck. "I can't thank you enough for what you're doing for us. You're the best person I know. Besides Andy."

We both laugh a bit, and I nod, but everything I've done this last week would prove the opposite. The things I've let happen, been forced to do or chose to do. I want an end to it, and if I do this right, I'll be free. We'll all be free.

"Do you trust me?" I pull away, searching her face.

She nods. "More than anyone, *ever*."

"Okay, then I'm going to tell you a few things, and you can't ask me about them. Not yet." She nods. "I need you to pack a bag for Andy, and for you." She frowns. "And I need you to be ready to leave here if I text or call you, or if I don't come home one night."

"What?" Her expression changes to fear. "Leave?"

"I'll meet you at dad's old hunting cabin, alright? I don't know what condition it's in, but we'll go from there—"

"Jo, are you in trouble?"

"I might be leaving my job, and if I do, we can't stay here anymore. That's all I can tell you for now."

"But I can get a job."

I nod. "You can. I believe in that now, and I'm sorry I held you back, but we'll do it somewhere else, okay? You trust me, right?"

"Yes," she whispers, her head bobbing a little as she rocks herself back and forth in her seat. "You're really scaring me, Jo."

"I want to be able to tell you things, so I need you to handle them as best you can until I can tell you more. There's one other thing, and it's good news."

"Okay," she whispers, leaning back, as if preparing herself for another shock.

I stare into her eyes, selfishly wanting her reaction when she digests my words. To see the burden lift from her face. "The debt's been paid."

She frowns. "The rehab debt?"

"It's paid in full, and you can't ask me how, not right now, but it's something we don't have to worry about anymore." You don't have to worry about.

I knew the price of rehab. I don't know the price that accompanies having the debt paid off for me.

She shakes her head. "I'm so confused." But her eyes light up, a little sparkle in the last of the setting sun.

If I could just understand Tackman's intentions, I'd know if this was the greatest good deed I've been given or a debt that looms over me even worse than the creditors calling me all the time, than Cathrine's threats, or than my own shame and guilt for what I've gotten myself into.

He doesn't have to call, or write, or anything for me to know I owe him.

The threat is there, no matter what.

"Joey, you're out of debt?" she asks with a laugh, like it's just sinking in, or she's somehow put her curiosity aside to live in the moment. "This is wild."

"I know." I smile, taking her hand in mine and squeezing it tightly. "Just trust me, and in a few days, I'll tell you everything. I promise."

And I will. No more secrets between us.

Tomorrow, I'll try again for the password. My last chance before the party.

And then, I'll go for the gun.

CHAPTER TWENTY-EIGHT

FLASH DRIVE

A s I ride the elevator up to the seventh floor, I absorb the fact that this morning is the first I haven't been called by the debt collectors. The remaining weight I carry is this tray with four coffees, an empty flash drive, and the gun with my fingerprints at Tackman's, waiting to ruin me if I step out of line.

I step off the elevator and turn down the dark hall as Orrick strides toward me, giving me a charming smile that grows as recognition flashes before his eyes.

"Josephine." He nods his head slightly as he passes me and steps into the elevator. "We'll see you at the party, yes?"

If all goes according to plan with Fern's password, I won't be able to free myself before then, but it could be the last time I have to see any of these people.

I give him a polite smile and nod as he presses a button. "Wouldn't miss it for the world."

"That's what I like to hear," he says as the door closes over.

I take a deep breath and keep walking as Fern catches my attention, waving me over from her desk behind the glass door. I stop in front of it and wait. She stares at me, like she's forgotten to push the button, completely oblivious.

I stare down at the handle, my hands full, and shake my head, but she keeps staring. No—glaring.

An air pocket rises in my throat.

I can't enter without her buzzing me in, and she knows that. She knows that about yesterday.

She stands up, walks to the glass door slowly and holds up the framed photo of her cats. "How did you do it?" she mouths.

I try to fix my face with a confused expression, but she knows I know I'm caught. "You must have just left, and I caught the door at the right time."

She walks back to her desk and focuses on her work as if nothing happened, but letting me know she has confirmed her suspicion.

I need to sort this out with her. I need to make sure she doesn't talk to Cathrine about this. What was I thinking? I wasn't. I'm too stressed out.

I stand there with the coffees like an awkward fool, but she doesn't look up. A pit forms in my stomach—an aching, heavy pit. I've been caught. She still doesn't know my motive for going in, but she knows I took the opportunity when they'd just left.

She knows I must have seen them leave, even if I wasn't the one who planned it. I have to come up with another excuse, a reason I was in there that she'll believe, fast. Today's the last day I can use her password to get the proof of Cathrine's equity in the company—a document that may not even be there anymore. If I can't get in through the system, is there another way? Would the proof be anywhere else? Would anyone else know besides Orrick? No. And he won't confess it to me.

Fern's password is the only way.

Okay, why was I in there? Why would I have gone in if it wasn't to check and make sure they'd evacuated?

Maybe it has to be something bad. Maybe I have to reveal something that makes me look bad and hope she doesn't tell Cathrine. I can't. I can't take that chance. But it's misdirection, and it's all I have left.

What would be in that room or Cathrine's office that I'd want? What would Fern believe I'd want access to that she might not tell Cathrine about?

My own file.

The records of my employment and the notes they have on me. She'll believe I know I'm in over my head—she knew it even before I did on the day I was given the client opportunity. She'll believe I'm desperate to know where I stand with the company.

This has to seem natural, real, and who I was last week would have done it. Would have cared where I stood. I have to channel her.

Fern glances over at me. "Please," I mouth.

She pushes the button, and I walk in, setting the tray of coffees on her desk beside her pictures, as usual, and she stares up at me from behind her thick-framed glasses.

"Can we talk?" I ask. She continues to stare at me, unflinching. "I need to explain myself, for yesterday—"

"You need to take Cathrine's coffees to her." She turns

away, back to her computer. She doesn't want to listen. I have to make her.

"I started the fire," I say in a low voice, just loud enough for her to hear, and her gaze shifts toward me slowly, eerily. "I did it on purpose to get in here. To get on your computer." She raises her brow, her expression stoic. "That day, when I got the opportunity to have my own client, I didn't know what I was getting myself into. I've disappointed Cathrine, and I've caused some issues."

"You have." Not a question. She knows. Maybe she knows everything.

"All I want is to advance in this company." She raises her brow, purses her lips, and turns to the computer. She doesn't believe me. I don't believe me. "It's just business— you've taught me that—I know that now, and the only thing I care about is redeeming myself."

I shake my head, staring off past her at the far wall with the door in the middle to Cathrine's office.

Everything I've been put through flashes before my eyes—and it began there. "I've done things. Unspeakable things," I mutter under my breath. "Not just because I have no one to talk to, but I'm not allowed to discuss them with anyone. I thought I was being given a chance to prove myself. That people were finally seeing what I've fought so hard to prove. That I've earned all the opportunities I've ever been given in life, and that I'll earn my place in each position I'm promoted to, and earn the respect of everyone here. I thought I could do that. I was wrong."

You can't earn these people's respect. They'll give it when it suits them, profits them, and take it away just as soon as it doesn't. As soon as I do something they don't approve of.

I was fighting to be seen, known, successful, worthy, and now all I want is my life back so I can live it the way I'm supposed to. The way I was always supposed to, with my family.

"I was all wrong, and now I'm scared there's no way—" No way out. I turn to Fern as tears drip down my chin, and her face has softened. I wipe my chin and take a deep breath, shaking my head. Not out. Up. "No way to redeem myself. I'm scared of what Cathrine thinks of me. That everything I dreamed of accomplishing here will never come true."

But not as scared as I am of the person I became when I still wanted that same dream, despite what I'd seen and done.

"I wanted to see my file, the records on me, to see if I even have a chance. If I have a hope of digging my way out from beneath all this."

Fern's face hardens again, and she squints back to the computer, pursing her lips. It doesn't matter to her. Whether she believes me or not—she couldn't care less about my hopes and dreams, or my fears. She'd know best what I'm afraid of, having been with the company for fifty years. An assistant to Lawrence Locke—the man who created a place where the wealthy can feel safe— protected. Now an assistant to Cathrine Locke—the woman I wanted to be like.

Fern knows this insidious company better than anyone here, I'll bet. What has *she done*? What has *she seen*?

Staring down at the small woman behind the computer screen, I feel sorry for her.

Did she still think it was worth it when she realized what this company really was? Was she ever scared like me? Did she share Lawrence's vision from the beginning? And now she's finally ready to leave, and with her goes my own hopes of leaving.

I turn toward the door, my last hope. "Thank you for all you've done to guide me. I'm sorry I wasn't enough."

And maybe I'm not for this company, but it doesn't matter anymore.

I take a step toward the door.

"Josephine." I turn to her. "Come here."

I step back in front of her, and she flicks her finger around the desk with a tight-lipped, forceful expression. Frowning, I walk around the desk as her fingers tap the keys and she tilts her head to the side. Come closer. I stand beside her, and she gestures to the screen. I bend down slightly to read it, my name sitting at the top.

Employee file 2035: Josephine Oliver
Click here for employee contact information.
Click here for payroll information.
Click here for history of employment.
Click here for employee review information.

Fern clicks the last button, and Cathrine's notes come up. She scrolls from the top where only a few sentences were written beside each year I'd been with the company to the bottom, this year's notes.

She stands and grabs two of the coffees from the tray.

"I'll be in with Cathrine for a moment." She walks toward the office and leaves me stunned, behind the desk, in front of the file I'd have done anything to get my hands on. The answers to why I was chosen for the position. Why I was chosen for the client. What they really think of me.

She tucks one coffee between her arm and her blouse and grabs the doorknob, then turns over her shoulder to face me with a sparkle in her eye. "I think you have a bright future at this company, Josephine. If you can get out of your own way and learn to mind your business. Have a little faith in Cathrine, hmm?"

As she disappears, I turn back to the screen, the words of all Cathrine's personal thoughts and opinions in front of me, and without wasting a second, I minimize the page and click on the database on the home screen of the computer.

The interface for the system opens on the screen and asks for a password.

No. No, this can't be happening. Not another password.

I have to try. What could it be? I turn to her frame. Her family. The only thing that truly matters to her. I type in her cats' names, each on their own, and all nine variations of the three of them together, but it doesn't work.

Her family...

I type CathrineLocke

Please reenter the correct password. 3 more attempts and you'll be locked out of the system.

I type LawrenceLocke

Please reenter the correct password. 2 more attempts and you'll be locked out of the system.

I might never get it.

My palms sweat as I rub my cold hands together.

I have to try. I scan her pictures for something I miss, and my eyes land on the two coffee cups left behind.

I type caramelmachiatto.

Please reenter the correct password. 1 more attempt and you'll be locked out of the system.

A new red asterisk sits beside the open field for the password.

I turn to the keyboard, and a little dot above the caps lock key is turned on. I hit it and type caramelmachiatto again.

The screen opens up, and a huge list of folders appears. Billy said it would be in a legal file…

I cast nervous glances at the door as I scroll through the folders to the "L" and click on Locke Industries Legal Department, scrolling through the list of names and reaching Lawrence Locke. I click on it and scroll down to Transfer of Assets and Ownership and open the file as the door to Cathrine's office opens.

Fern steps out, walking backwards, still talking to Cathrine, her hand hanging on the doorknob.

I scan the file and at the bottom, under the division of assets and shares section, it's written plain as day.

Ownership shares to be divided equally between Founder's son, Orrick Locke, and Founder's cousin, Cathrine Locke.

I scroll all the way down, glancing at Fern as she takes another step back, and find Lawrence's signature at the bottom.

I don't have time for my flash drive or even to take a picture. Fern closes the door and her eyes meet mine.

No way to prove this.

But I know it now. I know where it exists, and she doesn't.

I exit out of the first box as Fern walks over to me, heels clicking against the floor, tick tock, time's up.

I exit out of the interface and maximize my file as she rounds the desk and smiles down at me while I tap the caps lock key discreetly.

"Do you feel better now?" she asks with the hint of a smile.

I release a deep, dark breath and smile up at her through the tears in my eyes and nod. "Much."

CHAPTER TWENTY-NINE

CELEBRATION

S itting in my car, phone in hand, I type a message to the unknown contact in my phone.

It's Tackman's number, but I can't assign his name to it any more than I can assign a name to who he is in my life.

Private Benefactor. Drug and Arms Dealer. Volunteer. Murderer.

Client—for now.

He said it multiple times, and Danes shared the sentiment with me personally.

He needs someone he can trust, and I think he trusts me now.

Can I come over tonight? I send the message and stare up at the gates on Cordelia Lane.

It has to be tonight.

If Cathrine believes me, if I buy my freedom at this party, Tackman won't be my client anymore. He won't be anything to me, not even my captor, as long as I can get the gun.

Then I'm taking Maggie and Andy away from here, and we'll all get to start fresh with each other.

We'll have to leave fast, tonight, but we can do it. We'll pack light, sell Maggie's car to help with first and last month's rent where we end up, and we'll live off my last paycheck until we can get other jobs.

Where will we work?

Who will I be?

A businesswoman—no. A free woman—yes.

That's all that matters.

I drive up to the gate and press the button. "Josephine Oliver for the celebration."

After a moment's pause, the gates open, and I drive through, stopping in front of a valet several feet from the house. I hand him my keys, drape my purse over my shoulder, and step through their grand, open entryway where everyone is dressed up in fancy dresses and suits.

I chose the pink and blue dress of my mother's, and although I'm underdressed for the party, I blend in well enough. That's all I've ever been doing, anyway.

I pass through a few groups of people in the foyer, some I recognize, and a man approaches me with a tray filled with champagne flutes.

"No thank you," I say, and they move on to the next guest.

I search the crowd for Cathrine. Has she arrived yet? Scanning the beautiful modern, formal living room, I take a few steps toward it, and two men in suits part, revealing a young woman with dark hair I recognize.

Olivia.

She's standing near the doorway with a glass of champagne in her hand, dressed in a purple, calf-length dress.

I gravitate toward the familiar and friendly face among the crowd and stop in front of her.

"Hello." I crack an awkward smile, hoping she'll remember me. "Nice to see you again, Liv."

She seems distant, and it takes a moment for a smile to form on her lips as she recognizes me. "Oh, wow. Hey, Jo. I...I wasn't expecting to see you." Her gaze darts across the room, even as she's speaking. "How have you been?"

My smile disappears at the question, and I clutch at the sides of my flowy dress, staring at the ground. I don't want to lie to her, but I couldn't possibly begin to explain. She lives with them, though. Maybe she'll understand that I need to be vague.

"I've had...a lot going on since we last saw each other." I sigh and turn to face the rest of the room, stepping back beside Liv. "Quite the party, isn't it? How've you been?"

Olivia smirks wryly. "Oh, yes, Mr. and Mrs. Locke spared no expense. It sounds like our luck did little for either of us, then. I've been dealing with *a lot* too," so she *does* understand, "but today will be better." She shrugs one shoulder. "Who doesn't love a party? Hopefully it's a good day for the both of us."

Could it be, though? Only if I get my freedom. I turn to her, and we exchange a knowing glance before looking back out at the party.

"Hopefully. Liv, have you seen Ms. Locke?" I turn to her, remembering her confusion the first time we met, and laugh a little. "Cathrine, that is."

"She was in the kitchen earlier," Olivia's gaze bounces

around the room, "but...I don't remember seeing her in the last few minutes, I'm sorry." She lets out a light laugh. "At least she let you in the gate this time, right?"

I purse my lips, hiding a little smile, still scanning the crowd. "Figures. This time—I'd rather be *anywhere else*." I wring my hands together, full of nervous energy, and shake my head.

I'm in the lion's den now, but weeks ago, I'd have been proud to be part of the pride.

Pride cometh before the fall.

Olivia's expression turns sad, and she takes a sip from her glass. "I know, trust me. Things look different from outside the gate, don't they? I hope you get out, too, Jo, for what it's worth."

It's worth a lot. More than she could ever know.

"Thanks, Liv. I better go find Cathrine now." We turn to each other and exchange a knowing glance one more time.

"Goodbye, Jo. I won't wish you luck this time, but I hope you find what you're looking for here. Take care of yourself." She drains the last of her glass, the sadness disappearing from her eyes, as if refueled with liquid courage.

My chest heaves as I give her a nod with a warm smile, wondering what she might need that courage for.

"Bye, Liv." I stride back into the foyer, wasting no time, scanning the halls for signs of the kitchen. I turn over my shoulder, where I stood with Liv, and she's gone.

"Josephine, there you are," Cathrine says.

I turn toward her voice as she walks out of a room, a deep red, floor-length, formal gown hugging her curves, arm in arm with Mathison. His tall, solid frame looks dapper in his expensive navy suit.

Cathrine turns to him and taps her arm with her other hand. "Will you excuse us, please? I'll see you on stage shortly for the speeches."

He nods, raises his champagne flute to us both and disappears through the now crowded foyer.

"I need to go to the washroom," she says, raising her voice over the hum of chatter, "I need to make sure I look presentable for the photos. Follow me." She walks through the crowd, her dress swaying behind her, and I rush to keep up, my feet aching in my mother's heels.

"While I'm in there, could you get me a flute of champagne and a sandwich triangle, please?" I stop in front of the stairs, and grab the railing, catching her attention. "I *need* to eat something before I go up for the speech."

"I need to speak with you for a moment."

"Yes, after. Please find Fern for me as well. She wanted to talk to me about something too. I want her right by my side on stage."

"Ms. Locke, I need to speak with you *now*. Privately." My heart races as I press her to take me seriously.

Why would she start now if she never has?

She frowns, her hand still resting on the railing. "I haven't got the time."

"You'll want to hear this." I stare at her, not letting her go with my gaze.

She smacks her red lips together. "Fine, in here."

She leads me into a smaller room off the foyer and closes the door behind us. It's full of books, wall to wall, and a desk in the middle before a fireplace.

"This is very poor timing, Josephine," she huffs, smoothing her dress.

I fold my hands together behind my back. "I've come across some information that would be of interest to you."

"Well, come on then, out with it."

"I'm not sure I can tell you until I have certain—assurances." She frowns and shakes her head as I continue, "If I give you this life-changing information, I want you to be part of a big change in my life. I want you to let me go."

She cranes her neck back and rests her hands on her hips. "What on earth are you talking about?"

"You want power within this company, and I want my freedom, Cathrine." It's the first time saying her first name to her face fills me with joy. There are no places to be put anymore. No respect to be earned. Just two people, making a business deal. Hopefully my last. "I want you to let me leave Locke Industries, and I want your assurance that you and anyone from the company who'd mean me harm will leave me alone."

"It's gotten to you," she sneers at me. "Despite my better judgment, I gave you opportunities, but the responsibility has gotten to you. I chose you because you've worked harder than anyone for me, besides Fern. I chose you because you're easy to mold. Most of all, I chose you because you've seen the ugliness of this world, yet you continued to live in it. Your parents dying of overdoses. Your sister, almost doing the same. You have such a heavy burden on you, Josephine, and what I've offered you is a way out, but you're rejecting it like a slap in my face?"

"Cathrine, I don't give a damn why you chose me, and

I don't need you anymore. You need me. You need what I know."

She shakes her head, her silver and white locks bouncing on her shoulders as she struts back toward the door. "You've made a grave error, Josephine. I was crystal clear with you about what would happen if you stepped out of line. If you crossed me."

"Never cross a Locke, right?" She stops and turns on her heel. "I remember. Seems like you should have taken your own advice."

"What is that supposed to mean?" Her eyes twitch, but her blood red lips remain tightly pressed together as she waits for my response.

And I make her wait. I need her to want this just as much as I want my freedom.

"I have the knowledge you need to regain power at Locke Industries—"

"You've got no such thing." She squints at me and takes a step closer. "You haven't come anywhere close to power in your life. If you had it, why would you be giving it to me?"

"Because I don't need it. I want my freedom. I want to buy my freedom. That's the cost for my information."

She shakes her head. "You have nothing I want or need." She jabs her finger in my direction, "And you'll regret this."

"You'll regret not hearing me out, unless of course, you don't want to take over Locke Industries."

Her hand with her pointed finger falls to her side, and she looks over her shoulder to the door, then back at me. "Don't waste my time."

"What if I could prove that you're an equal share owner of Locke Industries, in partnership with Orrick Locke?"

Her gaze falls to my left, down toward the floor as she shakes her head.

"It's true. I have the proof, and I'll give it to you for my freedom."

Her chest heaves as she takes a few steps toward me, closing the distance between us. "And how did you come upon this information?"

"Doesn't matter."

"Well, it's not true. As much as I wish it were, as hard as I worked to earn my position and the respect of Lawrence, he betrayed me. The chauvinist gave his son the job, and I remained right where I was. He died, knowing it, at peace with his decision, and that was that. I learned the hard way: you never cross a Locke. It *can't* be true."

"For a woman who wants power so badly, it's funny how you're so sure you couldn't have it."

"What is this *proof*?" she chortles with the last word.

"I couldn't tell you unless you accept my offer, contingent upon my freedom and you receiving the information to claim your rightful place in the company."

"And if I accepted this offer, how would you know I wouldn't just ruin you afterwards?"

"I want a video recording of you right now, with a witness, declaring that any statements made against my character and time as an employee at Locke Industries, regarding any damning or illegal activities, is categorically false."

"Fine," she says, quickly. "If you can prove it. Fine."

"I want you to relieve me of my position." She nods. Let's tack on extra then. Hazard pays. "Pay me the bonus I *should have gotten* for my first client, and then leave me the hell alone. *Then*, you'll get your proof."

Standing in my mother's old dress, across from Cathrine Locke and her dress worth thousands, I've never felt richer. More powerful.

She takes another step closer, within arm's reach. "I want to see it now."

"There's only one person who can give it to you. Do you want to ruin me, or do you want to finally take your rightful place in the company? It's your business, Cathrine. Isn't it time you mind your own?"

She stares me down, her chest heaving and her face red. "Who? Who's the witness?"

"Mathison."

"What? Why?"

"Because aside from Fern, he'll be the first person you tell about this, so he might as well know now. I know about the little side deal you had with him."

Her eyes open wide. "How would you know that?"

I can't help but smile as she loses her power over me. "Time's ticking. You're to go on any minute now. Do we have a deal?"

"Find Mathison," she blurts out and turns away from me, leaning against the shelf by the wall.

"Find him yourself." I stand my ground in the heels pinching my toes harder by the second.

Her hand flinches, like she's going to slap me until she clenches her fist. She storms out of the room instead and I grab my phone to set up the video camera. An unopened text from an unknown number awaits me.

Tackman.

Tonight. Nine.

Good.

My chest tightens as I fumble with the phone, trying to set up the frame of the video on a shelf by the desk as Cathrine comes back with Mathison, who looks more confused than I've ever seen him.

She takes a seat in front of the phone, I press play, and she begins her statement. With each sentence, I grow more eager to have it finished, and wrought with worry that the recording won't be enough. They're two of a kind; they could still decide to come after me together, but I don't have many of their secrets. I'm not a big threat to them. Just to my one and only client, and I bet

Cathrine doesn't care much about him anyway.

She finishes, and I stop the recording, checking to make sure I got it all as she rejoins Mathison's side.

"In preparation for his retirement," I tuck my phone in my purse, "Lawrence Locke originally had a contract drawn up to divide ownership in the company. He chose to leave equal shares to both you and Orrick, naming Orrick the acting CEO, and yourself his advisor. He signed the papers and transferred them to the legal department, but Orrick created a document of his own, one where he received the lion's share of the ownership and made sure you were left with only power equal to the board. He forged his father's signature and submitted the document on his behalf."

"How is this possible?" Mathison asks. "If Lawrence

really wanted what you claim he did, and saw Cathrine didn't get it, how could he have stood by? Not fixed it? That's what I've never understood."

"Lawrence Locke never knew a new copy existed. I don't know what he thought, but if I had to guess, I'd say, from his perspective, after he left you half the company and you stopped communicating with him, he thought you were an ungrateful bitch and was glad he made his son acting CEO."

"How is that possible?" Cathrine whispers in a hiss, turning to Mathison.

"In a family that's as sinister and secretive as yours," I say, "I'm sure there's a lot you don't know about each other."

Her eyes open wider, and Mathison turns to her, brow raised, waiting for her reaction.

I've rendered Cathrine Locke speechless.

Speaking of…

"The speech is beginning," I turn to the door, "and this is the last you'll see of me. If you come after me again, you'll find out what else I know about you—like what was really going on that day at Orrick's, with your *special* installation job with Casey. And, no, it wasn't Casey who told me. Think bigger."

She cocks her head to the side, her jaw and fists clenched tight as she stares daggers into me.

Whatever they really did that day of the installation, the fact that she thinks I know it is enough to show her I'm serious.

Enough for me to know it was sinister.

"Goodbye, Cathrine." I clutch my purse strap on my

shoulder as someone on the stage out there taps the microphone, then I stride out of the room and through the foyer. My heels click against the concrete front drive on the way to the valet.

The click-clacking of the businesswoman I no longer am in shoes I never fit into. I take them off and pinch them together as I scurry down the path to the parking lot.

"Almost free," I whisper to myself. "One down. One to go."

CHAPTER THIRTY

LIZARD

"We'll leave tonight," I whisper in a hushed tone as Maggie peeks out from behind my bedroom door at Andy playing his video games.

Rain splatters against the window beside my bed as I take off our mother's dress and pull on a pair of tight, dark jeans. Since leaving the party, I've agonized over Tackman and whether I should even bother with the gun and hostage anymore. Did his payment of my debt soften me to him, or do I not have it in me to go there again? To put myself in danger. To say goodbye.

Maggie sits on the bed as I pull a black tank top over my head, crossing her legs and picking at her fingers. "I was starting to like it here."

"You were?"

"Just starting to get into the groove of things again. Meeting new people..."

I pull my hair out from beneath my black V-neck shirt, catching the sad look in her eyes. "Your new friend?"

She nods and sighs. "He's not really new." I wait for her to continue. "He's the one who found me and brought me in the last time I overdosed when Brad pretty much abandoned me. He came to the hospital after to make sure I was okay, and we've been in touch since."

"Even through rehab?"

"No," she shakes her head, "but he did take me to this really nice support group of mothers. He took Andy and I there the other day."

"Have you gotten close with him?"

"Only in an unspoken way. He rescued me. He's seen me at my absolute worst..." She stares down into her lap, thinking about the same man who trapped me in Tackman's home. Our perceptions aside, I can't deny he saved her. That because of him, I've had this new chance with her, and Andy has his mom back. "But no. We haven't gotten to know each other that well yet—haven't had the time."

"Do you resent me for making us move?"

She twists a curl between her fingers. "No way. You and Andy are the most important to me. Bobby and I, maybe we'll keep in touch, maybe we won't, but I'll never forget what he did for me."

Bobby. I guess that's his real first name.

If this goes badly, I'll have to tell her about him, so she knows never to talk to him again. So she knows who he really is, what he really does, and what he's done to me. But if I don't have to hurt her, I won't.

This could go okay. I could find the gun, get out, and maybe Tackman will forget me.

If that Cami woman comes around, it should be easy

enough. He shouted into the phone that night that he cares about her. She gets declarations. His attention. His protection.

Maggie stands, and I squeeze her hand. "I appreciate you trusting me. When I leave, don't open the door for anyone, not even your friend Bobby, and if I'm not back by midnight, or you haven't heard from me, go to the cabin."

She nods. "I got it. And Jo," her chest heaves as she looks at me with a little apprehension, "it won't always be like this."

"Like what?"

"You protecting me. I want to be there for you too, however you need."

I nod. "I know."

We walk out of the bedroom, down the hall, and stop in the living room, watching Andy play.

"I'll tell him after you leave," Maggie whispers.

"Can we tell him as a family?"

She smiles and nods, and we sit on either side of him on the couch.

"Hey, buddy," I say, "we've got some exciting news."

A smile pops up on his face, and he rests the controller in his lap, turning to me. I look at Maggie with a smile, and she smiles too.

"We're taking a trip," Maggie says.

"No way! Where?" He turns to her, and she beams down at him.

"A place we used to go when we were about your age. Maybe a little younger."

Right before our parents died.

"Cooool," he says. "When?"

"Tonight!" Maggie laughs and tickles his armpits. "We have to pack."

"Okay!" he shouts and stands, turning to me. "Are you coming, too?"

It breaks my heart that making the decision to go back to Tackman's means I can't promise him I'll be back.

I want to so bad, but he's had to deal with the pain of too many broken promises, and a lump forms in my throat so I can't even speak.

"She's going to try," Maggie says. "We're going to have so much fun. A fresh start."

"Can I bring my lizard?" he asks.

"You can." Maggie smiles and leans back on the couch. "If you're good, and you promise to take care of it, a *real lizard* could even be in your future."

"No way!" he shouts and runs to his room, bringing back his lizard that transforms into a car. "Can I bring my glow in the dark shoes?"

"Sure," she says and turns to me as I stand.

"I've gotta go out for a bit, so be good for your mom." I open my arms, and he stares up at me holding the lizard. "Can I have a hug?"

He smiles and rushes to me, his weight slamming against me as his scrawny arms squeeze me tight. Tears pool in my eyes, and I have to choke down the emotion rising from my chest.

What if something goes wrong tonight? What if they catch me looking for the gun? What if I can't get the nerve to help the hostage get out, and I leave, knowing I left someone there to die? What if they catch me helping him?

The worries swarm, bees in my brain, until Andy releases me from his grip, and I squeeze him tighter, pulling my focus back to the present moment, to the little guy whose life matters more than mine. Whom I'll protect at any cost.

I have to settle my business so we can get a fresh start without looking over our shoulder.

"Bye, Joey." He sprints to the couch again and leans back against the cushion with his mom, handing her a controller.

I grab my purse and the small package I picked up on the way home from work after shopping for my own clothes for the first time in years. Cathrine came through with the client bonus she owed me, and I sent her the information on retrieving her proof.

I don't love the idea of using money from Locke Industries, but it's a decision I don't have the luxury of making based on my morals, and I don't want to, either. I deserve this payday.

I walk through the door and wave to them, holding it open. "Love you guys." Choking back tears, I smile, and they smile back.

"Love you," they call before I close the door behind me.

If I can get through this, I'll never get caught up in anything like this again.

I promise.

As I leave the apartment and walk down the hall in my brand-new black boots and faux leather jacket, thunder booms above me, shaking the nerves within me until I'm a human rattle.

Just focus on the plan.

Go to Tackman.
Give him his gift.
Get the gun.
Get out.

CHAPTER THIRTY-ONE

THE GIFT

The pattering against my windshield slows to a gentle stop, and a heavy fog settles in. As I exit the highway into Copperfield County, I squint as I approach the first traffic sign and see it shining green at three car lengths behind the crosswalk line. I can't do more than forty miles per hour as I travel down the familiar roads, past the wheat fields I can no longer see as trees appear in my headlights on the side of the road, passing just as quickly.

Turning down the dirt road I almost missed the first time I came, I lick my lips and squeeze the wheel tight, passing the tree line. Tackman's house glows through the fog, most of the lights on, shining through the glass windows, guiding my way up the drive.

Clouds roll across the waning moon behind Tackman's home, rising from the back forests, and I park beside the red Camaro and a black truck. His home, his whole property, is enshrouded in the same thick fog.

I grab the box and my purse, step out of the car, and

hesitate before shutting the door. The front door opens, and Tackman steps out in jeans and a black button-down dress shirt.

I remember him standing there on the day we met. How he said at the end of our first meeting that he didn't think I could handle the job, not after I ran from the white room. That I was too green, and he was right, in a way.

Signing that contract, I didn't know who he really was —still don't—but I knew I was putting aside my morals and taking a risk to get ahead. Never again.

I walk up the driveway, purse over my neck, across my chest, and he lifts his chin as I stare up at his solid frame, backlit by the foyer light.

"Hey, Josie," he says in a warm whisper, and I'm almost under his spell again.

That's how I know this should work.

"Thanks for seeing me." I hold the box in front of me with both hands. "May I come in?"

He presses his lips together, hiding a small grin, and leads me into the house, shutting the door behind us.

"Is that for me?" he asks, pointing to the box.

I nod, but keep it held against my stomach. I look him in the eye. "I want to apologize," I say, and he raises his brow slightly as his chest heaves, but he keeps eye contact. "I was caught off guard by everything the last time I saw you. I was afraid for my family, and I'm still—I don't like what's going on with Carver and my sister. I'm protective of her."

"But no one's protecting you." He crosses his arms. "That's what you said the other night." He presses his lips together and glances away. "I don't know if you remember…"

"I remember. Thank you for what you did for me. Paying off the debt." I frown, unable to hide my discomfort, and maybe I don't have to. "I don't accept help easily."

He laughs a little and runs his hand over his beard. "But you didn't have a choice this time."

"And that's part of why I got so upset. I don't like handouts. I don't like owing people things."

"Who does? I never said you owed me anything. In fact, I'm sorry if I led you to believe I expected something from you. That wasn't a business transaction. That was personal."

The hum of tension between us lingers until I hold out the box.

He takes it, and his hands drop a little. "Heavy."

I smile, ready to deliver my next line.

He opens it and lifts a bottle of tequila out, the same kind I dropped and shattered. "Oh, you didn't have to do that."

"Just like you didn't have to help me." I say with a genuine smile. "Funny now that you're in my position, only imagine that bottle was almost twenty-thousand dollars."

His chest heaves again as he studies the bottle and then me.

"Do you think we could," I take a step closer to him, "pick up where we left off the other night?"

The only way to get near the keycard and grab it.

He cracks a smile as his eyes light up. "I think we could manage that."

He leads me from the foyer, past the study—the gun could be in there—past the door to the white room—the hostage—down the hallway to the kitchen.

He grabs two lowball glasses, and I walk ahead, opening the sliding door for him. A breeze sweeps my hair across my face, and I pull it away as he sets the glasses on the patio table and pops open the tequila bottle. Fog lingers around the trees in the backyard, and the pool light glows eerily before us. No squiggly little distinct lines of light—just a soft haze of jade green.

He pours two shots worth into both of our glasses and grabs them, holding one out to me. I take it, and we raise them a little higher before taking sips to hide our grins.

I can't deny the way he makes me feel any more than I can keep letting it happen.

Stay in control. You can only control your own actions.

"Have a seat."

I take the white block closest to the bushes and pull the hair out of my face as he sits next to me.

"I'm not used to seeing you like this." He looks me over, taking his time, smiling.

"Not dressed up?"

He smiles. "More Josie than *Josephine*. It suits you."

I laugh a little, my cheeks flushing, and take a small sip of my drink, eager to tamp out the tension between us or slow it down somehow. Work. Something about work.

"So," I say, a little too loudly, "why did you uninstall the camera above the pool?"

He swirls the tequila around in his glass while looking straight at me with a smirk. "I like to swim naked, and while there's *some people* I wouldn't mind watching me, it's not an open invitation."

"Ah." I take another sip without meaning to, desperate for something to hide my smile.

Focus on the plan. On the keycard and the gun.

"Have you eaten yet?" I ask.

"No, are you hungry?"

I smile and nod, and he leans forward.

"I have some chips and salsa."

"That would be perfect. Thank you."

He gets up, taking his drink with him, and steps into the house. With the glass wall, it's easy for him to see me when his back isn't facing me. He'll have to go in the fridge to get the salsa if it's not a new jar. That'll be my chance. Hopefully the fog can conceal some of my action.

He turns his back and opens the fridge. I lean back, spotting the white amongst the greenery and grab the card, tucking it into my purse.

"Phone's for you." The new voice makes me jump.

Danes.

He sees me through the glass and nods hello to me, holding his phone up for Tackman.

"I'll call them back." Tackman shoots me a quick smoldering glance.

"It's Cami. She says it's important."

Tackman continues pouring salsa into a bowl.

"Boss?" Danes asks.

"I'll call her back," Tackman says, enunciating each word.

Danes sighs and walks back down the hallway to wherever he was before.

Danes is here too, and once I go inside, I risk running into him. There's so much at stake here, staying for a gun, for a man I don't know.

Tackman steps back out with two bowls and sets them on the table. I better eat them, since I asked for it. I dip a chip into the salsa and cover my mouth as I take a bite and a little juice runs over my lip. I lick it off and crunch on the salty, tangy snack, the aroma of lime filling my nose. "It's the perfect snack with tequila."

I look back at him, and he's watching me. I swallow and wave him off. "You can stop staring at me now."

His smile fades as he stares into my eyes. "Can I?"

My chest flutters as I lean back, away from the chips, away from him.

I can't let this go on any longer. I can't keep forgetting who he is and what he's done.

What a threat he is to me and my family.

He takes a sip of his drink and leans forward. "I haven't always made the right decisions when it comes to you. I'm sorry if I've made you... afraid of me. Or angry."

I'm afraid of myself with you, for so many reasons.

He reaches behind his back and pulls out a handgun.

My chest tightens, and I freeze as he stares down at it. "I shouldn't have had you anywhere near this." He shakes his head and sets it on the table. "I'm sorry."

I look from the gun to him, back to the gun. "That's the one with my..."

"Not anymore. I wiped it, but in case you don't believe me, I want you to take it."

"What?" I cock my head to the side and study him. Is this a test?

"Actually, I think it's better if you take it. You'll have something to protect yourself with, if you ever need to, until you find someone, and you let them protect you."

I reach out for the gun slowly. The gun with *his* prints on it now.

"The safety's on. If you're not comfortable with it, you can get rid of it, but I want you to trust me. I want you to have the option."

I feel the weight of it.

"It's loaded, and if you ever need ammunition—just anything—you can come to me."

"Why?" I let my question slip out before I can filter it. "What about the police? You said you have friends. That they'd believe you. Why are you giving this back to me?"

He takes a sip from his drink and puts the glass down, leaning closer to me. "Because I trust you. And I want you to trust me. The police will never have a reason to connect you to anything. You can trust me, Josie."

I ache from a place within me that wishes any part of what we feel for each other could be real, but it's based off fear, lies, and a business transaction gone bad. This is the stuff of nightmares.

And I have to end it. I have to get away. I have the gun. I can go now. And I have to go.

I can't risk my life for a stranger when my family needs me, and I need them.

"Thank you," I whisper, tucking the gun in my purse, the bulk of the weight in my lap and some resistance across the strap on my neck.

He pinches his bottom lip with his fingers as he stares at me, and I look away.

I can't get caught up again, not in his life, and not in his eyes.

He stands and walks past the seating area to the pool and rubs the back of his neck until he stops at the edge.

Now. Now I should tell him I have to go.

I stand and walk toward the pool, stopping a few feet away, just out of arm's reach.

"I should be going," I say, already feeling guilty it sounds like I got the gun back and that was all I cared about.

He doesn't turn around, and I can't move.

I don't want him to let me go so easily, but I can't stay either. I walk up beside him, standing at the edge of the pool, and look over at him and his face glowing from the pool as he stares out into the woods. The natural smell of pine and cedar fills the air, not his cologne, but nature, overpowering even the chlorine.

"Am I going to see you again?" he asks without looking at me.

I study him, wondering what he means. Does he know I'm leaving?

"Cathrine told me she'll be my contact until further notice. That you're leaving the company."

No point in lying now. "I am."

"And you weren't going to tell me." He crosses his arms over his chest, making his shirt tight over his muscles. "I get it. After everything, I do, but I don't want it to end this way." His dark eyes light up. "You did it. You did what was right for you."

"I did. I am."

He smiles and lets his arms drop to his sides, losing the

barrier between us. "I like Josie better than Josephine," he says in a low voice, "do you?" He reaches his hand out, his finger caressing the side of my hand, sliding down my baby finger.

Before it falls, I wrap my finger around his. "Yes."

He takes a step closer until his cologne drowns out my other senses as he entwines his fingers with mine, holding my hand. "I want to get to know Josie."

"I—" I whisper, staring into his eyes as he leans in toward me and his lips crush into mine.

The bristle of his mustache barely tickles my lip as his lips part mine, tequila-infused, and he runs his hand over my neck, his fingers through my hair.

"Boss," Danes calls. We both turn in his direction, and I pull my hand away as he steps through the sliding door, finally noticing us and stopping. "She's blowing up your phone, man."

Tackman lets out a huff of breath. "Fine." His shoulder presses against mine, and in a lower voice says, "I'll be right back." He leaves my side, striding over to Danes.

This is my chance. My escape.

"I should go," I call to him.

He stops and turns back to me. "This won't take long. Stay. Please."

I fold my hands in front of me and nod, following him. "I have to use the washroom."

He nods, and we walk through the kitchen, Danes following him into the study, and they close the door behind them.

I stop in the foyer by the door, press my back against

the wall and touch my lips where the sensation of his kiss lingers.

What am I doing?

I push myself off the wall and stare down the hall at the door to the white room, where the hostage sits, the remaining one, hoping every second I'm coming back for him.

I take a step toward the hallway and tuck my finger into my purse, feeling the smooth plastic of the keycard.

Just me and him. No cameras. I'll tell him to run out the back, stay close to the pool, away from the cameras, and out the woods there. To run and never come back, and I could do the same.

I take another step toward the door and can hear Tackman's muffled voice in the study.

He trusts me. He wants me to trust him. I can get away without any issue and be there for my family without looking over our shoulders.

"And I told you no," his voice rises at the end.

Did he and Cami have a thing, and now they're not together?

"And stop calling Danes! You don't know that! You don't know how hard it's been for me..."

Did he break up with her... for me?

It looked like she broke up with him the day the glass shattered in the kitchen. He ran after her, but she's been coming after him ever since with all the phone calls.

She won't let him go.

"She hung up on me," Tackman says, and I turn around, facing the kitchen sliding door, ready to start walking.

"Maybe that's better," Danes says, "and thanks for telling her to stop. It's getting too much, you know? She's harassing me."

"It's not going to stop," Tackman says. "Not until it's done."

"And when will that be? When are we finally done with them?"

A long pause hangs in the air.

"Tonight," Tackman says. "We'll take them out tonight."

Take them out?

A phone rings in the study. "It's her again," Danes says.

"Don't answer." Tackman's voice gets quieter, further away.

"You want me to do it?" Danes asks. "You got the gun?"

"No. I started all this. I kept them here. I'm done with him. She needs to stop asking about him, and this is the only way. I'll finish it myself."

Finish it… the hostage.

He's going to kill the hostage.

CHAPTER THIRTY-TWO

THE HOSTAGE

S he needs to stop asking about him?

Cami knows about the hostage too.

I step away from the sliding metal study door and turn to the hidden white one.

I have the key. I can set him free, but if I get caught, it's over for me.

Can I walk away knowing I left a man to die here? Is that what Cami's been so upset about?

Does she know Tackman better than me, so well she knows what he's capable of? Does she see him for the wolf he is, and has she been trying to free the hostage all along?

A bad business dealing is how he described it to me, but what justifies this? What justifies their murders?

I can't get the picture of Alexander's brother's arm out of my mind, and if I leave now, I'll never forget Alexander, begging me for help, to see his family again.

I step up to the door and flash the card in front of it. It clicks open, and I step inside, shoving the card in my purse. The smell hits me, fear and sweat, overpowering.

Alexander's still tied to the chair and gagged. I take the gag off his mouth and pick at the knots. "You'll turn left, go straight out the sliding door, stay close to the pool, and disappear in the woods."

"Thank you," he huffs. "I'm so weak. I don't know if I can get far."

I finish untying one side of him as he works toward the other. If they come in right now, we're both dead.

"You have to run. You'll have to run; there's no other choice."

He works with me to untie one leg, and I leave him to do the rest as I turn back to the door.

"Thank you," he wheezes. "Bless you."

"This is it, your only shot." I peek through the door, and a light shines from the study onto the tile foyer floor. They've left the study. Where are they? I close the door again and turn back to Alexander.

"I won't make it. I'm so weak."

I dig through my purse and find my keys. I need my car, but he might need it more.

"You can use my car," I tell him. As he struggles to stand using the back of the chair, I hold out the keys. "Small black car out front. I'll—I'll say you took them from me."

"My brother," he wheezes, standing on his own and taking the key. "Do you know where Christopher is?"

"I don't think he's here. You have to go now."

"I can't leave my brother." He frowns and rubs his eyes. "I can't."

"You're going to get caught." I turn back to the door.

Tackman and Danes are arguing about something,

walking out into the foyer from the sitting room. I shut the door and take a step back. "They're out there now. We'll have to do this differently. You'll have to pretend I'm your hostage to get out. We'll just get to the car, and then you go on your own, okay?"

"I won't leave my brother."

He's gripping the keys tight. "Your brother," my voice shakes, "he might not have made it."

Fear sears through his eyes. No anger. Rage.

"You have to get out, or they'll do the same to you," I hiss. "You understand the plan?"

He nods and grabs my arm. "I don't have a weapon."

The gun.

No. I can't. He could hurt them—hurt Tackman.

I don't want anybody hurt.

I dig through my purse, and my metal nail file shines in the overhead light. I grab it and present it to him.

"This will have to work," I tell him, and he pulls me close in front of him and presses it against my neck. "Not too hard."

He eases up and limps to the door with me. "Open it," he whispers. "Let's do this."

I open the door, and he pushes me through, hobbling toward the front door. I can't see Tackman and Danes anywhere. We might have a shot at escaping.

"What the hell?" Danes shouts from the kitchen.

The man swivels around, holding me between him and Danes as Danes barrels down the hallway, reaching for something in his back pocket with Tackman behind him.

"Stop, or I'll stab her neck," he says, shouting in my ear.

"Please," I whimper, more to them than him, but they don't need to know that.

Danes slows down as Tackman pushes past him into the foyer where he stops, his eyes open wide, taking in the scene.

We're several steps from the door, and I keep backing up into him toward it. Danes pulls his gun, and the man pushes the pointed end of the metal nail file into my neck too hard. He's doing whatever he must do to get out, like a caged animal.

"Ahh," I yell, "stop!"

"Stop!" Tackman shouts at Danes.

"Drop your weapon," Alexander says, and Danes shakes his head, only stopping as he squints at me.

Something warm trickles down my neck. He made me bleed.

"Where's my brother?" he shouts. "Go get my brother."

Tackman and Danes turn to each other and stare back at him, still wide-eyed. When they tell him, he's going to hurt me again.

"Please stop," I whisper to him. "You're hurting me."

"Get his brother," Tackman shouts. "Get him now."

It's a trick. A way to stall.

Danes slides past us, down the hallway the man's brother originally came from. Maybe where they both originally were.

"Josie, you're going to be okay." Tackman finally seems to relax and regain the control he's always had over a room. "Just relax."

I whistle out a quick breath and repeat, nodding.

"I told you you'd never get away with this," Alexander

tells him. "When Ari finds out about this, about what you did to us..." He laughs. "You better still have the guns and coke, or he'll kill you and every person you love."

"I don't think so." Tackman widens his gait. "In fact, there's not a worry in my mind about it."

"You're crazy, Tackman."

A shadow creeps along the floor from the hallway, and the man I saw try to escape walks out, Danes following, holding his hands by the rope behind his back, his arm of black and white tattoos clear in the light of the foyer.

"Chris," Alexander shouts.

"Awwll," his brother lets out a muffled shout.

How? How is he still alive? Wasn't he dead in that tarp? Yes.

Tackman admitted he killed him.

"Untie him," Alexander says.

Danes shakes his head. "You let her go, and *then* you can have him."

There's not a cut on the other man that I can see. There was so much blood on his arms. On his black and white tattoos. This makes no sense.

Unless it was another man—one with similar tattoos.

"I call the shots here." Alexander jabs the nail file into my cut.

I shriek in pain and fear.

How far will he go?

"This is my house." Tackman jabs his finger into his puffed-out chest. "And as guests, you'll go by my rules. We'll do a tradeoff."

He shakes his head behind me. "No trade off. You've got guns. We don't. You give me my brother, and I let her live." He scoffs. "If you don't have Ari's drugs and guns, he'll just come back and kill her anyway."

Tackman took someone else's stuff?

Why? Who's Ari?

"You're going to let her go." Tackman glares at him. "And then you're going to go crawl back into whatever hole you came from, and I'll never see your face again. I'm giving you the chance to leave with your brother. Give her over, and you can go. I won't offer it again."

"Now why would we be scared of you? You never met Ari?"

"Sure I have." Tackman lifts his bottom lip, and a glimmer shines from his eyes. "I killed him."

The man behind me goes still, and the other brother shouts from behind his gag.

Is Ari the man who left in a tarp? Their boss?

"You couldn't," Alexander spits.

"You want to threaten me with a man who's a drug-dealing prick, wife-beating coward, ghost long gone? How could I be afraid of a dead man? *How about* you'll come back yourself to get revenge on me? Wanna try that one on for size?"

Alexander pulls me toward the door, and I take a step back with him as Tackman's lip twitches.

"Didn't think so. Let her go, and we'll send you on your way with your brother."

He saws at the cut on my neck, and I scream in pain, scratching my nails into his arms as hot tears pour from my eyes. The searing pain burns through me.

What have I done?

"Let him go!" Tackman shouts and turns to Danes.

I stifle my cries as Tackman and Danes shout "yes" and "no" back and forth at each other.

Why did I set him free? Why didn't Tackman tell me they weren't his drugs and guns? But he did. I didn't believe him. Why did he let me think it was the hostage who died?

This is my fault. I brought this on myself.

Danes pushes Christopher toward us, his hands still tied, mouth still gagged.

"Untie him," Alexander huffs in my ear, his hot breath on my cut, burning it again.

Every small movement burns as I reach out for his brothers' hands and untie the rope.

"You have him." Danes steps forward. "Let her go."

Christopher steps past us and mutters to Alexander, "Get their gun." He opens the door behind us, and I remember the gun in my purse again.

"Give me your guns," Alexander says. "Your guns and we let her go and leave."

"No way," Danes says, but Tackman nods. "They'll kill us."

Tackman stares Alexander down. "I don't have one on me, but Danes is going to give you his gun now." He shoots Danes a piercing stare, and his eyes dart from me back to him.

From my neck back to him.

It's bad. The pain has kept my mind off the constant trickle of blood.

Danes grabs his gun from the floor and turns it around, holding the barrel as he extends his arm toward

Alexander. Christopher steps back in, sliding by us, and reaches for the gun.

"No," I whisper.

They could shoot both Tackman and Danes dead. Then me.

"It's okay." Tackman catches my eye and glances at my purse and back.

I need to get him the gun. My fingers fumble on the top flap of my purse, shaking from adrenaline and exhaustion as the blood drains from my neck.

Christopher takes a step toward Danes again as my fingers find the cold metal of the gun, and Alexander pokes the file into a fresh patch of my skin until I cry out. "Don't try anything," he sneers.

"Okay," Danes whispers, and I realize he was talking to him.

Danes takes a step closer to Christopher, and I can't tell if he's watching me pull the gun from my purse, but Tackman is. He keeps his eyes on mine and gives a little nod.

I take it out and toss it to him. He catches it, and I exhale as jagged metal slices into my neck.

CHAPTER THIRTY-THREE

HEAR NO EVIL

I release an anguished scream as Tackman clicks the safety off and Danes twirls the gun in his hand around against his palm and pulls the trigger right beside me.

The burst of noise and pain overcomes me, the sounds vibrating internally as the echo from the gunshot rings in my ears and a throbbing pain surges through my body. I reach for my neck and fall forward, opening my eyes in sheer panic as Tackman steps forward and catches me with one arm, then squeezes the trigger of the gun in his other hand.

A muffled thump follows, and he pulls me tight as I wrap my arms around him and push my neck against his arm until I feel my blood soaking into his shirt as I cry into his chest from the pain and terror.

Tackman's saying something. Talking to me?

I can only hear through muffled vibrations, and I pull away, looking up at him.

"...here," he says, grabbing my hand and pressing it against my neck. "Keep it here."

I press both hands against my neck as he lets me go, brushing past me, and I spin around. Christopher is slumped against the open door, his eyes open and blood running from the bullet wound in the middle of his head. Danes stands over Alexander, who's lying on the floor, clutching his chest and wheezing.

Tackman walks over to Alexander, stopping a step away, and both men stare down at him. He lifts his arm, aims his gun at Alexander, and shoots him. I squeeze my eyes shut too late, the image of his head bouncing against the floor stuck in my mind.

The pain edges back into focus, and so do their voices.

"Call Carver," Tackman says, "...clean up."

Danes nods and steps toward the door.

"No," I scream and reach out, "stop!"

When they both turn to me, I press both hands against my neck again. "The video camera outside," I say, my own voice unfamiliar. "It covers the front door."

Tackman nods to Danes. "Drag him in by his feet. Don't let the cameras see you." He turns back to me as a cell phone rings. My cell phone.

"Will security be on their way?" he asks me.

"That's probably them calling." I point to my purse behind him, by Alexander's knee. "I'm still the contact on the file. Cathrine hasn't had time to change it. Grab it for me."

"We should take her to the hospital." Danes stares at my neck as his Adam's apple bobs in his throat.

Tackman ignores my cell phone and walks over to me,

287

gliding his finger across my jaw and tipping it back ever so lightly. I take my hands off my wound, exposing it to him, offering myself to the wolf. He studies my neck as I close my eyes.

I don't want to know how bad it is. I don't want to see him frightened ever again like he was when he was coming down that hallway behind Danes when Alexander had me.

I caused all of this, and he doesn't even know.

Something soft presses into my neck, and I open my eyes as Tackman tucks his dress shirt in a ball against it.

"You're going to be okay." He presses his shirt against me as my cell phone rings again. "I'm so sorry, Josie," he whispers in my ear.

I shake my head, tears in my eyes, and whisper, "My phone. I have to stop them from coming."

He steps back and turns around, picking up my purse as Danes presses his cell phone to his ear.

"Carver," he says, "get here now... Yeah, the brothers." He walks into the sitting room. "Yeah, we need a clean-up."

Tackman hands me my purse and turns back around, evaluating the bodies as I grab my phone and answer it.

"Josephine Oliver," I say with such control, I scare myself.

Tackman and Danes protected me. I'll protect them.

"This is Locke Industries dispatch. We're contacting the case manager of the Tackman residence. We've got a potential security breach—"

"False alarm." I clear my throat and wince. "No need to dispatch security."

"Are you sure, Ms. Oliver? We always advise a visit from our security team, and the client usually appreciates when we go that extra mile. Even for a false alarm."

Tackman turns around, left with just his tank top as I press his dress shirt against my neck, a comfort through the pain, and gives me a nod.

He's everything I thought he was, all at once, good and bad, killer and hero.

A wolf through and through, but he wants to be *my wolf*.

I nod back. "I'm sure. No cause for concern. I've confirmed with the client."

"Okay, Ms. Oliver. Have yourself a good night."

I end the call and my neck throbs as I scroll through seven missed texts, all from Maggie.

We're leaving now.

Be careful.

I wish you could tell me what's going on.

We're stopping for gas, and I'm worried about you. If you could just call me, please?

Jo?

We need you.

We're here. CALL ME.

"I have to call my sister," I whisper. "She's worried about me."

Tackman nods and joins Danes in the sitting room as I tap Maggie's name and clear my throat, wincing as it rings in my ear.

"Jo," she hisses. "What's happening? Tell me you're on your way."

"I'm glad you got there safe," I say in a whisper, hoping

it'll help hide the pain in my voice. "Everything's going to be okay. I'll be joining you guys, but not for another day or two, okay?"

"What's going on?"

"I promise, I'll tell you." Tackman walks back into the room, stops before the puddle of blood on the floor, and catches my eye. "I'm safe now. We're really going to be okay."

"Just come as soon as you can."

"I will," I whisper as Tackman joins my side. "I have to go. Just a day or two. I promise."

I end the call, toss the phone back in my purse and let it drop to the floor where I feel like I might go as my legs wobble and my energy escapes me. Danes' voice is soft in the background somewhere, still on the phone.

"I should have been honest with you." Tackman wraps his hands over my arms. "I'm sorry."

"No." I shake my head, the guilt stopping me from enjoying this moment. "I wouldn't have understood. I still don't. The man in the tarp?"

"Cami's husband," he says. "He was a drug dealer from New Gilford, Ari, and he was moving drugs into Copperfield County. I intercepted a load and took them too." He tilts his head to the side, behind him. I peer over his shoulder at them, but Tackman moves in my line of vision and waits until I'm looking him in the eye to continue.

"Ari came looking for them, like I knew he would. I told him if he stays out of Copperfield County, he could have them back, but I was keeping his stash. That wasn't going to work for him, so I had the cameras installed, and he came the day you came to apologize. We saw him coming, and I was ready for him. That night, that's who you saw in the tarp."

Protector of Copperfield and the people here. He had a choice, but nothing could have protected more people than the decision he made.

I shake my head. "They have the same tattoos?"

"A lot of them. They're a gang."

"How does Cami factor into this?"

"She was my brother's girlfriend, became like part of the family, and she met Ari through him. After Nico died, she got together with Ari, got married, and I came to find out he abused her the whole time. She's an addict too, and she doesn't want help. She doesn't understand, but when Ari went missing, she knew I was part of it somehow."

"You didn't tell her."

He shakes his head. "She won't understand. She still wouldn't think that man deserved to be buried in the dirt. All she needed to know was that he wasn't going to come back and hurt her anymore. When someone finds their bodies, she'll know, and she knows I'll be here for her if she needs me."

I nod, my gaze falling to his chest. I wouldn't have either.

"Do you know that now?" he asks me.

I stare up into his eyes.

He risked their lives for me and saved me. I can't lie to him about why this happened, but it'll hurt him so bad.

"What?" he whispers with a little smile and frowns. "You're going to be okay. I'm taking you to the hospital myself right now."

I lick my lips and swallow, the pain in my neck biting,

threatening me if I tell him, expose myself, I'll risk everything.

But when I told Maggie I was safe, I meant it. I feel it with him.

"I let him go." I stare into his eyes. "It was a mistake. I thought he needed help."

He frowns and leans back, letting his hands drop from my arms as Danes walks back into the foyer and a car's tires squeak to a stop outside.

"It's Carver," Danes says. "Be right back."

I keep staring into Tackman's eyes, but understanding seems to flash across his gaze as he processes my confession.

"I heard you with Danes in the study. I heard you say you were going to kill him."

Tackman runs his fingers through his beard, his eyes turning dark. I press my back against the cold wall behind me as he leans down, his nose almost touching mine.

"I know." He holds something white beside our faces.

I turn, my neck throbbing, and come face to face with the white keycard. I turn back to him with confusion.

"It was in your purse," he says, his hot breath on my face.

Fear fills me as I realize he grabbed my purse for me, for the phone, and must have found it in there.

He knows I betrayed him.

"Now what?" I press his shirt into my wound, volume edging back into my voice to accompany my fear. "What are you going to do?"

He wraps his arm around my side and heaves me up, leaving me breathless as he wraps his other arm under my legs, hooking it behind my knees. I wrap one arm around his neck, keeping the other with his shirt pressed against my neck. He carries me through the foyer, out the front door, and into the fog where Danes and Carver stand by one of the black trucks.

"She okay?" Carver nods to me.

"Better than okay." Tackman carries me down the driveway, past them. "You know where to leave them."

"We got this, Boss," Danes says, and they walk back up to the house together.

Tackman stops at his red Camaro and eases me down by the passenger side door. I catch my footing, and he keeps one arm around me, staring down into my eyes, drinking me in.

"Do you forgive me because I told the truth?" I stare up at him, searching his eyes for my answer, but I can't read him.

"Who says I forgive you?" A hint of a smile emerges beneath his mustache. "It was a *big* mistake."

"It *was* a big mistake," I whisper and nod. "Who says I'm sorry?"

His eyes light up, and he leans down toward me, holding me tighter. I close my eyes, and as our lips meet, the hum of danger lingering between us melts into one.

THE
LOCKE
INDUSTRIES
NOVELS

**Don't miss the rest of
the LOCKE INDUSTRIES series!**

If you enjoyed *The Assistant's Secret* and are dying to learn more about the insidious Locke Industries, I'm thrilled to tell you about *The Nanny's Secret* by Kiersten Modglin. For your reading pleasure, we have ensured the books in this series can be read in any order or as standalone stories.

Get your copy of *The Nanny's Secret* on Amazon or Kindle Unlimited today:
https://amzn.to/2KMeWzN

Happy reading!

READY TO DISCUSS LOCKE INDUSTRIES WITH ITS CREATORS AND OTHER FANS?

We're so thrilled you enjoyed this installment of LOCKE INDUSTRIES. If you have read the entire series, THE NANNY'S SECRET and THE ASSISTANT'S SECRET, we'd love to invite you to the exclusive and highly secretive Spoiler Group.

The only rules?
1. You must read both books before entering
2. You must be ready to have fun with Emerald, Kiersten, and other LOCKE INDUSTRIES fans!

Enter if you dare:
www.facebook.com/groups/lockeindustriesspoilers/

DON'T MISS EMERALD O'BRIEN'S NEXT RELEASE!

Emerald would love to offer you a free ebook along with updates on her new releases.
Subscribe to her newsletter now:
http://www.emeraldobrien.com/your-free-ebook

ACKNOWLEDGMENTS

To my co-writer, beta reader, collaborator, and friend, Kiersten Modglin, thank you for igniting the spark that started the fire for this series. The exciting idea of creating this world together brought my focus back to writing for the first time since the pandemic began. I'm grateful for your friendship and this supportive, motivational, challenging, and beautiful experience together.

Thank you to my formatter and cover designer, Tadpole Designs, for the exceptional visual components of this novel. To Krista at Mountains Wanted Publishing, I am grateful for your professional editing services and the extra support you've given me through these years.

Thank you to my colleagues in the book community for your support, encouragement, and sharing your knowledge with me. I'm proud to call you my friends.

For the continued support of my family and friends, I am forever grateful, and I love you all. Each and every person in my life who has supported me and my writing career hold a special place in my heart.

Thank you to my true-blue readers, newsletter subscribers, and my reader group on Facebook for sticking with me and for your company on this journey.

DON'T MISS THESE SUSPENSEFUL
AND UNPREDICTABLE READS BY
EMERALD O'BRIEN

The Knox and Sheppard Mysteries
The Girls Across the Bay (Book One)
Wrong Angle (Book One Point Five)
The Secrets They Keep (Book Two)
The Lies You Told (Book Three)
The One Who Watches (Book Four)

The Avery Hart Trilogy
Lies Come True (Book One)
Bare Your Bones (Book Two)
Every Last Mark (Book Three)
The Complete Avery Hart Trilogy

Standalones
What She Found
Closer
All the Dark Corners

To view the complete list of books and purchase links, please visit: http://www.emeraldobrien.com/books

ABOUT THE AUTHOR

Emerald O'Brien was born and raised just east of Toronto, Ontario. She graduated from her Television Broadcasting and Communications Media program at Mohawk College in Hamilton, Ontario.

As the author of unpredictable stories packed with suspense, Emerald enjoys connecting with her readers who are passionate about joining characters as they solve mysteries and take exciting adventures between the pages of great books.

When she is not reading or writing, Emerald can be found with family and friends. Watching movies while cuddling with her two beagles is one of her favourite ways to spend an evening at home.

To find out more, visit Emerald on her website: http://emeraldobrien.com

If you enjoyed Emerald's work, please share your experience by leaving a review where you purchased the story.

Subscribe to her newsletter for a free ebook, exclusive content, and information about current and upcoming works: http://www.emeraldobrien.com/your-free-ebook/

Printed in Great Britain
by Amazon

82038631R00181